# FALLEN PREY

USA TODAY BESTSELLING AUTHOR
# JEN STEVENS

# CONTENTS

# C O N T E N T
# W A R N I N G S

This book is intended for a mature audience only. Anyone who considers themselves as a sensitive reader should review the list of content warnings below prior to starting this book.

Stalking & Hunting, Dubious Consent, Mention of Mental Health Hospitalization, Mention of Suicide Attempt, Depiction of an Abusive Relationship (Physical, Emotional, Verbal), Drug & Alcohol Addictions, Drug Abuse, Needles, Overdose, On-page Death & Murder, Blood & Gore Depictions (Flaying, Drowning, Knife Violence, Torture, Mutilation), Physical Assault, Gun Violence, Cult Mentality, Hazing, Profanity, Sexually Explicit Scenes, Grief & Loss Depictions, Sexism, Mention of Childhood Neglect, Mention of Poverty, Fire

Please read at your own risk.
xoxo, Jen

# MULTIVERSE
## (MUL · TI · VERSE)

a theoretical reality that includes a possibly infinite
number of parallel universes.

*For my angel*

# PROLOGUE

*The Lamb*

A CERAMIC PLATE flies past my face before it collides with the wall behind me, scattering into a thousand pieces on the floor. My heart stills in my chest as I turn to see the dent it left in the wall.

That could have been my face.

He had *aimed* for it.

"Next time, I won't miss," Gabe promises in a deep snarl, as if hitting the wall was on purpose.

I want to tell him to fuck off and run out the front door, but my lungs have constricted so tightly, I can hardly draw a breath. The plan was to pack a bag and quietly leave while he was at work. To escape this hell hole before he caught on and never look back

I've been putting cash aside for months in anticipation of it. Nothing noticeable. Just a few fives and ones skimmed off the top of my tips each night. I'd pick up random gift cards for restaurants and grocery stores each time I got gas or snacks, discretely adding to the tab so he wouldn't notice them coming out of our shared account.

Last week, he almost found it all.

I kept it shoved deep inside my pants drawer on the bottom of my dresser. Gabe never does laundry—not mine or even his own. There should have been no chance he'd be rummaging through my dresser.

Except, my mom started staying with us a couple weeks ago. I was against the idea completely. Not because I don't love her. In fact, it's quite the opposite. As a newly recovering addict who could relapse at any moment, I knew being around someone like Gabe would trigger her.

My mom has never pretended to be perfect. She raised us and got us through by the skin of her teeth, but once we were old enough to fend for ourselves, she took her leave from our lives.

Ever the proverbial party girl, she's always been running from her own demons that haunted her growing up. Whiskey was her drink of choice—at all hours of the day— until mine and Halen's father got her hooked on harder drugs. It's been a roller coaster of benders, rehab, sobriety, recovery, and relapses. No one can force her to stop, as much as we'd love to. The choice to quit has to come from within.

Naturally, this past relapse caused her to lose another job and get evicted from another home. Halen and Kennedy decided they couldn't go through the cycle anymore, so she came knocking on my door.

The problem is, I don't even plan on staying here. I'm hardly scraping enough money together to get myself out and bringing her along with me will take twice the time to prepare. I don't want to know what could happen when I leave and Gabe takes it out on her. So, I said no.

The next day, she came back while I was gone and asked Gabe. He said yes, and she had her things moved into the basement that night.

How could that lead to Gabe going through my drawers, you ask? Well, Mother Dearest was cold one night and didn't have any sweat pants because all of her belongings were spread across the front lawn of her old house. Gabe, ever the perfect host and landlord, offered her some of mine.

"They'll probably be two sizes too big now that Jovie's been eating at the bar, but you can make them fit," I heard him say as he came down the hall.

I was lying in the bed, reading a book when he walked right in and opened the drawer. I've never moved faster in my life.

"I'll get them," I rushed out, shoving him to the side.

I could tell he knew something was up, so the next day, I grabbed the wad of cash and opened up my own private savings account. The stack of gift cards was hidden in my trunk, beneath my spare tire.

In the two weeks that followed, Gabe's attitude toward me grew more persistent, his fuse shorter. He and my mother were getting along swimmingly. I'd come home from work late at night to find her curled up on the couch with him or to discover that they went out to dinner and drinks together. It should have bothered me. He's *my* boyfriend, and she's never respected boundaries.

But it didn't. Not at all.

The only reason I've stayed this long with Gabe is purely out of survival. My mother knew exactly what she was getting into when she came knocking on our door. Gabe has never been good at being sober.

I was days away from leaving. I had somehow saved over two thousand dollars to get on my feet. I planned to fill my tank and drive as far as it would take me, then figure it out from there.

Until the bank sent a statement for the account in the mail. One that my mother grabbed from the mailbox that evening. One that Gabe opened, thinking it was to our joint account.

He waited for me to get off a long shift at the bar that night before giving any indication that he knew. Those hours of him sitting in fury only led to a bigger explosion.

"I can't believe you thought you could fucking *steal* from me," he seethed, grabbing another plate from the dish rack.

*I didn't steal from you*, I want to say back.

That was my own hard-earned money. Money he was never meant to see.

Instead, I drop my gaze into my lap and shake my head, holding back the sob that wants to escape. He can't see me cry. He'll only view it as a weakness, and Gabe preys on weak women.

"What was your plan?" He slurs, his tone rushed and hostile. "Were you going to sneak off into the night and leave me fucking high and dry after I just helped out your mother?"

*Helped out my mother.* I didn't ask him to take her in, and if my instincts are correct, she's been "helping" him a lot more than they want me to know.

"ANSWER ME," his voice booms, and I can't help the shudder that rakes through me at the deafening sound.

"I was going to surprise you," I lie, lifting my eyes to look at him in his reddened face and make it more believable. "I was planning a trip for our anniversary as a surprise."

*That's good. Our anniversary is in three months. This could work.*

His expression softens the smallest amount.

"Our anniversary…" he drawls, rolling the idea around in his head. Testing it's validity.

"Yes," I insist.

*Our anniversary that you forgot about. Feel guilty about that.*

"Where?" He's testing me. Checking for holes in my weak excuse.

"A cruise," I quickly blurt out.

I've never wanted to go on a cruise. I'm too afraid of being stranded in open waters. But Gabe has. He's wanted to go on a cruise since we met.

"To the Caribbean," I add, pushing my brows up into my hairline for a more dramatic effect. He has to feel like he's leading this. Like he's in control and I'm just submitting.

"I'm supposed to believe you opened a whole ass bank account to hide a small vacation from me?" He asks doubtfully, and I can sense his anger creeping back in.

"I couldn't pay with cash, Gabe," I say condescendingly. "And you'd see the payment come out of our checking. Plus, I needed a place to put our play money for the trip."

Crossing my arms over my chest, I take a page out of his book and spin it back on him. "I'm offended you think I'd be doing anything so sinister. I just wanted to make it a special trip where you didn't have to worry about money for once."

Dropping the plate onto the counter, Gabe crosses the kitchen and drops to his knees before me, shoving himself between my legs. The shattered fragments of the plate he already threw crunch beneath him, a dark reminder of how quickly he can flip.

"I'm sorry, baby. I thought you were going to leave. Please, please, *please…* forgive me," he begs, laying his head onto my stomach as his arms tighten around my hips.

I scowl down at the back of his head, brushing my fingers through his thick hair, pressing his scalp a little harder than necessary.

"Of course I forgive you, baby," I coo quietly.

My heart beats finally regulate as my body realizes the danger was averted. *For now.*

But my relief is short-lived as the realization that the light at the end of this tunnel has quickly died out. I'm trapped. Now more than ever.

# 1

*The Lamb*


I WAKE WITH A SUDDEN JOLT, eyes snapping open to the white-tiled ceiling above. My hand moves to wipe away the sweat-soaked hair that's stuck to my face, but there's a web of wires and tubes sprawled around me, holding it down. Each one is measuring, injecting, or reporting my every move. Halen is fast asleep on the small couch beside my bed. She hasn't left this room since the night I was admitted, too afraid of any sudden change that might happen. This past week and a half has been a roller coaster ride that both of us are ready to get off of.

The black night sky is a beautiful mural outside the uncovered window above her. The only light source is the cool white hallway lights peeking in from the cracked door.

He was in my dreams again.

The masked man who always whisks in to save me just a moment too late. I never get a good look at his features. All I can see is that he's dressed in black from head to toe, with a black mask covering the bottom half of his face and his entire neck. Silky, dark hair sits atop his head in messy waves —hair that I can practically feel between my fingers. I know it's just a dream. Some small thing my mind has latched onto in this traumatic mess. But when it's happening, it all feels so real. So significant.

That pure, palpable agony radiating off of him each time he reaches out before Gabe can inject me with that fatal dose, just to have our fingers only brush, and then we're completely heaved apart. Just before I fall back into an endless abyss, I startle awake.

My memory of everything that happened that night after I stepped into the shower is fuzzy. From the ambulance ride to the emergency room to the first two days they kept me hooked up to machines to ensure my organs wouldn't fail on me—it's all masked with thick fog that I still have to sort through.

It's lost time I'll never get back. A brief window that I spent teetering on the other side which will haunt me for the rest of my life.

There's a shadow cast in front of the door before my night nurse slips through the small crack, quietly shuffling into the room to do my hourly vital check. They claim I've made a miraculous recovery—one unlike anything they've seen before with the amount of drugs that were shoved into my system all at once. It's usually delivered with some sort of awkward grimace, as if they aren't sure whether I'll find that information elating or disappointing.

They all think I'm here because I failed at something. That I believe coming out of that short coma and having strong enough organs to sustain the type of stress and injury that was put on them is a bad thing. But they're dead wrong.

Words can't describe the level of gratitude I feel for my body—this thing that I've spent most of my life hating—and its capabilities. They'll never know how incredibly strong and empowering it feels to know that I've managed to fight through the worst time of my life and come out a brand new version of myself. One that will sure as hell ensure that every single person who got me here will pay for their sins against it.

When the nurse realizes I'm awake, she smiles down at me guiltily. "I'm sorry if I disturbed you. I just saw a spike in your heart rate so I had to come check you out," she whispers, eyes flicking over to Halen's sleeping form.

"I had a bad dream." In fact, it feels like I'm living in a bad dream now. Perhaps if I pinch myself hard enough, I'll wake up in my real bed and this will all be over.

Just as I reach my hand across my abdomen to squeeze my other forearm, the nurse grabs it up to check the IV taped to it.

I'll be happy to be home, away from all the suffocating observation happening at all times. Of course, that time won't be coming for a few months, thanks to Halen's over-protectiveness and need to control everything. Unless I can find a way to convince them it was all a misunderstanding.

"There was a note added in your file just a few minutes ago. Your team of doctors will be meeting today to come up with a discharge plan. Looks like you're leaving us soon."

She looks down at me with a hopeful smile, and when I don't respond, she takes it as disbelief and nods her head enthusiastically, as if to say, *believe it. It's really happening.*

It doesn't matter though. Even if they let me out of here tomorrow, Halen has arranged for me to go to a mental rehabilitation facility. Freedom is nonexistent at this point, and discharge is not worth celebrating. Not when I've been stripped of all my basic rights.

"We'll talk more about it later. Get some rest, and try not to have any more bad dreams."

With that, she turns in her heel and walks out, never looking back. I don't fall asleep again. Instead, I sit quietly on the bed while Halen snoozes and journal in my notebook, forcing myself to recall any detail I can from that night. To put together small clues from the weeks leading up to it that appeared out of place, so I can use them to plead my case later.

I know the biggest one that happened just over two weeks before he attacked me. When he found my escape fund. I thought I had convinced him with my quick lies, but he wasn't fooled. And the fact that he'd rather kill me than let me leave is a terrifying realization that I push away each time it comes.

The nurse was right. A few hours later, when the sun made its appearance and the hospital began waking up, my team of doctors filed into my room and informed me that I've been cleared to leave and will be discharged within the next twenty four hours.

And sent straight to Sunnybrook Recovery Center.

**2**

*The Wolf*

STARDUST CONSUMED my thoughts the entire ride home from the hospital and long into my first two weeks in my own bed.

I thought I had been alone in this odd, shifted reality. I assumed that when there appeared to be no evidence of her in my life *before* whatever happened to me, all hope was lost. But that wasn't true at all.

When Fate grabbed me by the throat and shoved me into this alternate universe, she made sure to send me into a spot on the timeline where Stardust hadn't even had my family's cabin—our starting point—in her radar. A time where she was still with her waste of oxygen ex-boyfriend, and her mother was still feeding off her like some sort of starved energy vampire.

Fate ensured that I would be here when those horrible, traumatic things happened, so that I could be the one to personally save her from it. And I'd already failed miserably.

"You're not supposed to be drinking with those pain

meds," Sienna chastises from the doorway of my office just as I pour myself two fingers of whiskey. Instead of answering, I grab a second glass and pour her some too, then lift it between us in a silent offering.

Her slender fingers hesitantly wrap around the glass, and I half expect them to go right through the solid material the same way they would have when she was just a ghost and I was just a broken shell. Somehow, I'd grown more used to her being dead than having her stand beside me, flesh and bone.

Before she can say another thing about it, I clink mine against hers in silent cheers, then down the contents. Sienna tips hers up to her lips and lets the expensive liquor slide down her throat, savoring it the way it's intended to be. She watches me like a hawk as I slump into my chair, releasing a long sigh.

"You look like shit," she comments, leaning her hip against the leather couch set against the wall before me.

"You're so good to me," I snark back, my voice rough from the long, sleepless night.

"What has you drinking alone at…" she lifts her arm to check the watch on her wrist, eyes widening as she realizes what time it is. "Five in the morning."

"I'm not drinking alone."

Rolling her eyes, she falls onto the couch in the same, exhausted way I had just done, and then lays back against the soft cushions. She's been staying with me for the past week since I was discharged from the hospital, and it's been equally torturous as it is helpful. I've somehow forgotten what a pest my sister could be, especially as a living, breathing being.

"What happened to you that night, Bash?" she asks in a barely audible voice.

It's not an odd question. Everyone wants to know how I

ended up dumped half-dead, miles away from home and sat alone in a hospital room for weeks before anyone realized it was me. Before I even woke up.

Several news stations have written stories on me, all of them hounding Eliza to schedule an exclusive interview or statement. They can't understand how a well-known billionaire managed to float under the radar for so long in some small-town hospital, or what kind of criminal things I was wrapped up in to get me there.

But I know that isn't the question Sienna is asking. Not really.

She realized almost immediately that I woke up in that room with a piece of myself missing. That there was more to the story than what everyone else was alluding to. She sensed it—whatever *it* was. But neither of us has dared to put words to the feeling we both have. Not until now.

"You wouldn't believe me if I told you," I say dismissively.

"Give me a chance to try. *Please.*" When I begin shaking my head, she sits forward and clasps her hands in front of her, a silent plea. "I almost lost you. Do you know how terrifying that was? We thought you were dead, Bash. Gone forever, without a body to even honor or mourn. And we're all so grateful to still have you here—*I'm* so fucking grateful.

"But you've been walking around like a ghost. You aren't acting like yourself, and I know that whatever happened must have been traumatic and life-altering, but it feels like…. God, it feels like you've got one foot here, and another one somewhere else."

How ironic is it that the woman I've spent the past year of my existence mourning—the woman whose ghost haunted me day in and day out for months—is now accusing me of the same thing? What kind of sick sense of humor does the universe have to use us as entertainment? Are we all just pawns in some odd little game?

I consider that for a moment, grabbing the empty glass back up and rolling it around in my hands to buy myself time before answering her. What can I even say that won't have her sending me off to the mental institution? Perhaps this is how Stardust felt. This is why she just rolled over and went with it all.

Her fear of losing her freedom outweighed he own self-preservation.

"Who was that woman in the hospital?" she asks, as if my drifting thoughts somehow encouraged her to bring her up.

My head whips in her direction, my face so hard, she winces.

After my outburst with Stardust in the hospital, the nurses pried me away from the trauma room door and sent me limping back to my mother and sister, who were each looking at me with their own horrified expressions. I'd never acted that way before. Never allowed my emotions to take over so powerfully and lose my composure in such a way that would both mortify and terrify them so thoroughly.

I stormed past them and out the front doors, not bothering with the discharge paperwork we had been waiting for, or the bag of possessions that Sienna had to quickly gather up. They didn't speak to me the entire ride home, both of them sharing worried glances in the front seat that they tried to mask with bland conversation.

Honestly, I was grateful they kept their mouths shut. There was no telling what I would have said if I'd been forced to put words to what happened when it was all so raw, or what I would have admitted. In true Lancaster fashion, they brushed it under the rug and moved on, silently hoping that my outburst was a one-time thing.

I've spent every moment since then pouring over the possibilities and mustering up a plan to get to her. But with

Sienna in my face, coddling me all hours of the day, it's been difficult to execute anything.

Sienna hasn't brought it up until now.

"You knew her, but I didn't recognize her. The doctors were saying she overdosed on multiple drugs. What have you gotten yourself caught up in, Bash?" The last part was nothing more than a whispered breath.

She's scared. Scared of who I've become, of what I might be withholding, of having all of it happen all over again. I know that none of this looks good for me. I can't explain anything to her when I'm not sure myself. I have to give her *something*, though. Anything to stop her from looking at me like I'm a complete stranger.

"I do know her. Or, at least, I did," I admit carefully. "But she isn't who you think, and you have no right to judge."

Sneering, I pin her down with my eyes to let her know there will be no more accusations or insults thrown in Stardust's direction.

"One day, you're going to have to explain how this all connects, Bash…" Her tone is soft, but the words still fill my stomach with dread.

I know she's right. This space that everyone has given me to recover will expire soon enough. My disappearance was too public for it to be swept under the rug and left a mystery, especially with my company on the brink of major expansion. People will want answers and assurances that it'll never happen again. That it was all just a fluke.

They'll feel entitled to it.

And as much as I wasn't to kick and thrash and tell them all to go to hell, my reputation and everything I've built depends on it. But when I finally tell my story, I'll be leaving Stardust out of it. She'll remain untouched. At least until I can sort through our new reality.

**3**

*The Lamb*

"THEY AREN'T GOING to let you bring that back to the room," my roommate, Ginny comments across from me as I stuff a dinner roll and a packet of butter into my pocket.

I was perfectly content eating alone before she slammed her tray down onto the table and plopped into the seat before me. Ginny is kind enough, but my irritation at my situation has bled into every aspect of Sunnybrook, and my roommate is no exception.

Something no one tells you: psychiatric hospitals are boring as hell.

Especially when you aren't supposed to be there in the first place.

I've spent hours vollying between group therapy and individual therapy to work on restructuring any suicidal thoughts I might have. And I've spent every moment of all those hours begging someone to just *hear* me. To believe that I *don't have suicidal thoughts.*

The sheer waste of space I take up here when there's potentially someone out there who truly needs these resources is enough to turn my stomach into goo.

I'm not like Ginny or any of the other people here, who seem to have one foot placed on the other side and are just waiting for another opportunity to fully jump in. Whose demons have convinced them that they don't belong here or they're not deserving of a full life. It's heartbreaking. I wish I could help each and every one of them.

But I have my own fight ahead of me, and that's part of the reason I find it annoying that Ginny is so tireless in her attempts to befriend me. I don't know if I'll be able to handle it if she succeeds one day.

"They won't know about it, will they?" I spit back at her bitterly, throwing in a pointed stare to round out my tough facade.

She lifts her hands in front of her, rearing her head back. "Hey, I'm no snitch."

We stand from our table and walk our trays over to the garbage, and I try not to notice that Ginny didn't even touch her dinner. She says an empty stomach makes the meds kick in faster. Why she would ever want them to kick in at all is beyond me. I refuse to take mine, but I've found her snooping around my bed for the pills I discard as soon as the nurse disappears multiple times now.

"So you really think they're going to let you out of here if you kick and scream long enough?" she asks when we're back in our room.

We're free to walk around as we please during waking hours—save for any therapy or counseling appointments we may have—but I spend most of my free time on my bed and Ginny seems to view me as her only source of entertainment for the night.

"I think that I don't belong here, and eventually they're going to catch on to that," I clarify.

Ginny releases a throaty laugh, as if to say, *yeah right.* She crosses her legs on her bed and hugs her pillow, resting her head on it. "Hey, if you do get out early and you need a job, me and my sister own a coffee shop. She's stuck running it by herself now."

I raise my brow, reading between the lines. She runs it alone because Ginny is in here. My tight expression softens as I realize what a generous offer she's making. Although, I hope it doesn't mean she plans to be here much longer than me.

My stomach drops at the possible alternative.

"Thanks. I'll probably need a job since I haven't shown up to my old one in a couple weeks," I sarcastically scoff, rolling my eyes as my irritation settles back in. This whole situation is ridiculous.

"For sure. Rosie tries to look tough on the outside, but she's all fluffy clouds on the inside, just like you." She winks at my scowl. "You can cover for me until they can heal me up here." Knocking on the side of her head, she sticks her tongue out at me. *Good.* At least she plans on making it out.

The relief that sweeps through my stomach sobers me. *I can't get attached, I can't get attached, I can't get attached.*

"It's called Old Soul Cafe. Just tell her I sent you and she better hire you or I'll break out of here and kick her ass," she adds when I don't respond, then grabs her sketch pad and leans back against the wall, tuning me out.

**4**

*The Wolf*

I THOUGHT my desire for Stardust was unquenchable *before*. Back when I could have her at any time I wished. When I took without asking and couldn't comprehend the full gravity of what it would be like to lose her. I had no idea then what kind of torture it would be for me to live through having her *exist* in a world alongside me, yet completely untouchable. To be so close and impossibly far away at the same time.

My restraint against her wears out after only three weeks. Sienna returned to school last week, and I've essentially been cleared to continue normally with my life.

So I hunt her down, the way any predator would do with their precious prey.

It's incredibly easy to find the facility she's in, which proves that she's far too accessible. Too vulnerable. My twisted mind takes that as enough justification for violating her privacy.

I'm free falling into this obsession all over again. Only this time, I don't have the cushion of grief or insanity to rationalize it. The monsters haven't shown themselves yet, and my irrational behavior is making it hard to differentiate myself from them anymore. So unhinged—disrespectful of her privacy and free will.

But I can't stop. Every time I try, I'm propelled back into that moment I walked into the cottage and found her bloodied body lying on the ground. Or the helpless expression the emergency room doctor wore as he explained that she was pronounced dead moments before.

I'd gone mad. And even though I'm not *there* anymore, I haven't been able to fully come back from it.

Her medical records are spread before me on my desk, out in the open for anyone to burst in and see that I'm not doing anything related to work. And Eliza *would* burst in here without warning. She's far more protective of me since my "accident." Unwilling to stray far from me for too long.

The first time she laid eyes on me the day after I was discharged, she punched me in the chest, and then pulled me into the longest, tightest hug I've ever experienced. It was far more of a heartwarming welcome than the one my own mother gave me, and only proved that our relationship runs much deeper than boss and assistant. She sees me as a son, and she was tortured over my disappearance, the same way she would have been if it happened to any of her kids.

She's been on edge, afraid like everyone else that she may blink and I'll no longer be standing before her.

The smile decorating my face from the thought of Eliza falls away when I come across the notes from one of Stardust's therapy sessions, where she explained in detail exactly what happened to her the night that brought her into the hospital.

I never knew the details. How he sprinkled a cocktail of

narcotics into her meals for weeks before that night. How he forced her to the ground, nearly killing her from the impact of her head hitting the tile—a variable he likely forgot to consider when he planned it all out.

Because he didn't want her dead. He wanted to build up a tolerance in her system that would allow her body to take such a high dose of drugs without failing her. It was a round-about, failproof way of stripping her credibility when she tried to insist that she didn't do this.

Or so he thought.

Session after session, day after day, Stardust insisted she wasn't suicidal. That she was a victim of her mother and Gabe's narcissism and need for control. And after every single session, her therapist noted that she didn't believe her. That her mind was foggy from the blow to her head and the coma she was in, therefore rendering it unreliable. That her sister agreed.

They've failed her. *We've* failed her.

But I refuse to fail anymore.

She needs someone behind her in this fight, and I can be that. I can advocate for her.

Before I second guess myself, I'm dialing the number to the facility and asking to speak to the person who handles donations. The woman on the line audibly gasps when I inform her of the amount—a number that would more than likely buy the entire facility if I chose. And when she asks me for a name to credit the donation to, I give her my own. I want them to remember me. To feel like they owe me. Money rules everything in this sick, deprived world. I just so happen to have an abundance of it.

And I'll be calling in my favor very soon.

5

*The Wolf*

I CAN'T THINK STRAIGHT ANYMORE. Every thought I have is centered around *her*. Work is just a mere distraction—an annoying inconvenience that pulls me away from the things I should be doing to get her back on solid ground.

No one notices that I've got one foot out the door at all times. Lancaster Tech is thriving, with or without me there to guide it. And it will be there for me to bury my head into when she's finally free and it's time to let her go.

"Hello, Mr. Lancaster," the office manager at Sunnybrook coos into the phone after the third ring.

Since I've offered them a donation large enough to demolish the entire building and start from scratch, they've grown quite fond of me. I'd like to assume they'll be putting the money into developing their recovery programs and adding beds to help more people, but the short conversations I've had with them have proven that's not likely to be the case.

Stardust deserves better. Hell, everyone in Styx deserves better than a half-assed recovery center.

"Can I speak to Dr. Forrest?" I ask in a curt, polite tone, refusing to even acknowledge the flirtatious lilt in her greeting.

"Sure, I'll check if she's available."

Dr. Sarah Forrest is Stardust's primary therapist and, according to the notes in her medical record, the only one who even slightly believes the truth.

She's also the only person in that hellhole who doesn't treat me like royalty—another tell that she realizes the money I've given them will never benefit her or the patients. She'll be the one to carry out my request to release Jovie from that hellhole.

"Mr. Lancaster, what can I do for you today?" She greets after a brief hold, her tone mug less friendly than the last girl.

"I'm checking for an update on our patient. Are we set to release her yet?"

There's a loud sigh, and then a chair squeaks as a door closes in the background.

"I told you," she mumbles into the line, dropping her voice an octave. "I cannot discuss my patient's care with non-authorized personnel."

"A simple yes or no is all I'm looking for, Sarah." I have access to more medical records than even she is authorized to see, but I leave the tidbit out.

"It's in the works. The family member with Power of Attorney has to sign off on her discharge."

"That only applies if she's incapacitated," I argue. Her sister has no right deciding what's best for her anymore, and the idea of her having more control over my little Stardust than I do pisses me off.

"I'm not going to explain the ins and outs of my job. All I

can tell you is that I'm working on it and she should be out in the next week or two."

"The second half of my donation relies on this…" I remind her, leaning into the role of the rich asshole she views me as.

It's true either way. If they don't let her out, their funding is pulled completely.

"I understand, Mr. Lancaster," she clips. "I'll call you when I have news. Goodbye."

With that, the line goes dead, and I'm forced to sit another day with my girl in that cesspool.

**6**

*The Lamb*

THEY'RE DISCHARGING me from Sunnybrook tomorrow.

I've been stuck here against my will for twenty-seven long, miserable days. Every second has felt like a fight to get my life back into my own hands, no thanks to Halen's newly found—albeit limited—power. The burden of proof that I'm in fact, of sound mind, has been a weight on my shoulders unlike anything I've ever experienced before.

It is way too easy to lose control of your own life. I absolutely refuse to find myself in a position like this again.

Thankfully, my therapist was not only sympathetic to my situation, but she was willing to actually listen to what I was saying and see the truth within my words after weeks of hearing them. Of course, it helped that Gabe and my mother's statements from that night were all over the place, hardly fitting into the story they were quickly trying to weave together.

Feeling like there was finally someone on my side made it

easier for me to open up to her, which led us to realizing that Gabe began abusing me long before I gathered my escape fund and he shoved those drugs into my veins. She helped me through the process of filing charges against him, and even went as far as obtaining the paperwork for me to get a restraining order.

Then, in our next private session two days later, she informed me that I'd be getting released as soon as possible.

"I'm not the only one who seems to know the truth," she explained vaguely, her face twisted in a confused grimace. "But I'm happy to see you have the chance to move forward regardless."

Ginny couldn't believe it when I told her. Despite my best attempts to keep her at arms length, she's weaseled her way into a friendship with me that she'll never be able to escape from. I can only hope she's willing to travel the long, winding path to recovery. Until then, I'll be sure to show my support in any way.

The only person who appears to be upset about my departure from Sunnybrook is Halen. When she realized that going to therapy was only helping my case, she turned her efforts in a different direction.

"Have you thought about going to church?" she asks me over the phone on the night I called to let her know I'd be getting discharged.

"Why would I ever do that?" I ask through a laugh, gripping the phone tighter.

Of all people, Halen is one of the people who has been rejected the most harshly by the church we used to go to as kids.

It was never about religion or forming a relationship with God for me. Church was a place we could go once a week and actually be seen and cared for by adults we thought we could trust. Every Sunday and Wednesday, Halen and I would walk up those steps and feel like we were a part of a community—a family. That was something we desperately craved when our mother was always gone on a bender and the rest of our family was nonexistent in our lives. It was great, until Halen and Kennedy went public as more than just best friends, and then the rude and condescending comments started to trickle in.

Within a matter of months, the people who claimed to love us like family proved how conditional that love really was. They showed us that, unless we were willing to live our lives by their nonsensical rules, we no longer deserved the basic respect owed to every human being. *To God's creations.*

Instead of welcoming us into their homes with open arms, they passed us in the grocery store as if we never met, whispering snide comments about how Halen and Kennedy's relationship was *unnatural* and how they should be with a *man* instead.

Beyond all of that, I had my own qualms pop up with this God they all love and fear so ferociously as I got older and more aware.

What kind of being made purely of love and light would give such an unfit mother like ours two children to look after? What kind of God would allow those children to starve and beg? What kind of God would allow that same mother to nearly kill her own child over a handful of drugs? To allow a man to use his power and force against the woman he claims to love and send her to the other side?

What kind of God creates a life so miserable and unbearable, full of dissension and strife?

I don't think I was sent here by God. I think I was sent here as a punishment to anyone who believes in him. As a reminder that there's far more sinister things in the world than the seven deadly sins.

"I just think you might need to get back to the basics," Halen's low voice interrupts my internal rant.

"I need to get out of here," I insist, the confrontation clear in my tone, discouraging her from arguing back. I won't be entertaining anymore talk of church or God.

There's a loud sigh through the line, and then I hear her footsteps drag through her hallway and into her room—probably out of Kennedy's earshot. "I just want you to have *something* besides me and Kennedy. I'm afraid we aren't equipped to give you all the support you need."

The admission hits me harder than I expect it to. It cracks through my bones and shatters my heart. She thinks she can't handle me—that I'm too much for her. My relationship with my sister has morphed from best friends and partners in crime to dysfunctionality and encumberment. I've been moved to the same tier as our mother—an obligation she has to deal with. I slump into my chair as the disappointment settles in and takes root, telling myself it's another thing to add to the list of what Gabe has stolen from me.

"I have to go," I croak, my voice breaking and giving me away.

"Wait, Jovie. I didn't mean to say-"

I hang up and pull myself to my feet, dragging myself down the hall and back to my room with a heavier weight than when I left it to make the call.

7

*The Lamb*

HALEN AND KENNEDY keep quiet as we walk through their modest, two bedroom condo toward the finished basement, where I'll be staying until I can get back on my feet. My fingers white-knuckle the small tote bag that contains everything I own as tension pulsates through me. Halen's lips have been stuck in a straight line since the moment I walked into the lobby of Sunnybrook this morning after being officially discharged, and I know it's only because she's keeping all her ugly and offensive thoughts to herself.

Kennedy stumbled through awkward small talk through the entire forty-five minute drive home, desperate to ensure there wasn't a single gap in conversation for Halen to try shoving her twisted logic down my throat—the same way she's been doing since the moment I was admitted to the facility against my will.

Our conversation from the other night has been effectively avoided and shoved away into the imaginary *never talk about it* box we usually designate for our mother. Ever since that night, we've been piling things into it and forcing it shut before anything breaks free. I know it's just a matter of time before something pops out.

Halen doesn't believe Gabe tried to kill me. She refuses to even acknowledge that our mother valued a bag of coke over her daughter's life, and she wholeheartedly thinks I should still be in Sunnybrook until the end of the supposed "treatment plan" that I was admitted into.

*She's our mother, Jovie. Regardless of how many mistakes she's made, you can't deny that fact.*

*He's taken care of you so well for years. I just find it hard to believe he'd try to* kill *you.*

Every word is delivered in a chastising tone with a saccharine smile to go along with. An attempt to gaslight me into believing the narrative she's fallen for so easily.

If I didn't already know that from our conversations in the past few weeks, I would have found out when my therapist warned me about her on my way out the door.

It's been an impossible feat, trying to convince the therapists and administrators at Sunnybrook to see that I'm *not* suicidal and had absolutely nothing to do with what happened to me that night. That on top of the pure exhaustion of being in that facility with energies that do nothing but suck me dry was enough to make me *truly* go mad

When my counselor slipped and told me that my sister was adamant that I had taken those drugs with the intention of never waking up, I completely flipped. I told Halen I would rather sleep in Roxana Park with the rest of the homeless in the middle of downtown Styx than stay with her if that's how she felt. Of course, Kennedy came to her rescue, ensuring me that she was just concerned and wanted what was best for me. That was a hard thing to believe when it felt like everything Halen decided was against my will—a will that should have never been taken from me in the first place.

When that didn't work, Kennedy visited me behind Halen's back one day and explained how difficult it's been for them since all of this happened. How my mother and Gabe have doubled down on their alibis and made Halen their number one target to convince her that I was lying, knowing she was given power of attorney over me.

They want control.

Over me. Over the situation. Over their tarnished reputations.

Control that was given to Halen by sheer luck, because despite all of Gabe's careful planning, he never anticipated that she would happen to be driving past the hospital on her way home from a late shift when they called with the news of what I had supposedly done. That she would be running into the emergency room ten minutes before he even bothered meandering in. Or that in their rush to save my life, the hospital needed someone to be my voice when I didn't have one, and it only made sense for it to be her—my next of kin.

And since his plan didn't work, Gabe had to move fast to recover. While I've been fighting to prove how badly I want to live, he and my mother have been doing damage control behind my back to ensure I came out looking like the crazy, suicidal flight risk they painted me as that night.

I didn't immediately give in to Kennedy's request to blindly believe that Halen would see the truth once I got out and lived with them. But in the spirit of honesty, Kennedy and Halen are the only ones I truly care about believing my truth.

Plus, Roxana Park is a dangerous and volatile place.

So after thinking it over and obsessing for a week straight —because there's nothing else to do in a mental hospital—I informed Halen and Kennedy that I'd still like to take them up on their offer, if it was still on the table. Two weeks later, I was found to be in good mental health and discharged.

I had no idea how difficult it would be to face Halen when she looks at me with such animosity. Such distrust. As if she has anything to be pissed about just because I managed to convince the professionals the truth.

Still, I bite my tongue and move along, knowing that I need to save my energy and fight for the people who truly wronged me. Halen's reactions stem from her unconditional love and support. She wants me there because she thinks it's what I need to get better. But just like Kennedy said, she requires time to see past the cloud of lies she's been fed. Lashing out on her won't help with that.

I had a moment in the hospital, prior to being transferred into Sunnybrook, where I considered not telling anyone what they did. A fleeting thought of how freeing it might be to let them say what they want and focus on keeping my peace in complete silence. How much easier it would be for everyone to see me as the suicidal girl instead of the one whose boyfriend plotted a long, extravagant story to gain more control over her, as if the abusive grip he already had me in wasn't enough.

The girl whose mother sold her out for drugs and a man.

And while that silence may have been easier for everyone else to endure, it would have been deafening for me.

Catastrophic to my own life—a life that I fought like hell to come back to.

So just as fast as the thought entered my mind, it was shoved right back out. I won't be shrinking myself down to make anyone else more comfortable. I refuse to deny myself any sort of closure or justice because of how hard the truth might be to swallow for them. I didn't make those horrific actions, and I certainly don't deserve to be treated as *less than* because someone might find it hard to look at me and see the tough shell that was cast when I was thrown into the flames and left to die alone.

No. I plan to take my truth and scream it from the top of the highest mountain. And if anyone has trouble swallowing it, I'll be sure to shove it down their throats to help them digest it.

There won't be any denying that Gabe and my mother are monsters lying beneath sheep's clothing. There won't be any doubt that I deserve a long, bountiful life, free of all the terrible and ugly things I've spent enduring for the first half of it.

I'm done living in this trap that was cast for me by weak, vicious people.

"I found a car for you to get around in. My friend agreed to take payments on it under the table. I paid the first three months so you can focus on getting a job," Kennedy rambles on, her eyes nervously skirting between Halen's hateful glare toward me and my weak attempts to look anywhere *but* my sister's direction.

"You didn't have to do that."

Kennedy shrugs. "It's not a big deal."

"I'll pay you back," I insist sheepishly, chancing a look over at Halen, who makes a face that says I will *absolutely* be paying them back.

But Kennedy waves off my offer. "Don't worry about it. You're family."

I can tell Halen wants to disagree, but her mouth goes even more rigid and tight, stopping the words from coming out. This is going to be another reason for her to resent me. Yet another thing that makes me look helpless and for me to earn her respect over.

*Why are you even here?* I want to ask her. If she's so hell-bent against this situation, why bother standing here with her sour face and unspoken retorts?

But like her, I bite my tongue. For now.

When the silence is too much to bear, Kennedy loudly claps her hands, then rubs them together. "We'll leave you alone to get settled in. I'm sure you're looking forward to some peace and quiet."

I nod, offering her a half-smile and they take that as their dismissal. Once they leave though, the sheer aloneness is uncomfortable. After weeks of hardly being able to wipe my ass without being monitored, and years of living with various roommates, this feels incredibly odd. Even with Kennedy and Halen's footsteps and hushed arguing above me. It doesn't take me long to settle in, given that my whole life fit into one small bag. Gabe has all my belongings— clothes, mementos, furnishings—in the home we shared a few miles away from here.

And with nothing else better to do, I end up passing out on the spare bed they moved down here for me, thinking about all the things I'm going to do tomorrow to get back on my feet.

Starting with applying to a job at the coffee shop Ginny and her sister own.

8

*The Wolf*

I'VE BEEN BACK at work long enough to prove to everyone that I'm alive and well and show our board that I'm no longer a risk, securing my position as CEO yet again. Our expansion has officially been completed after two months of delay, making Lancaster Tech the fastest growing tech startup in history. Of course, the novelty of such a huge accomplishment isn't quite as strong the second time around. I've been here before—lived this already—and it serves as yet another reminder that I may be a part of this world, but I am not entirely from here.

While everyone else at Lancaster Tech celebrated with an elegant dinner on my treat, I spent the evening in my parent's home, convincing my mother to sell me her Styx cabin so I could begin the first phase of my plan to get Stardust back.

I wanted to leave her alone. To let her settle back into her life and readjust. But I haven't been able to shake the idea that she's going through the same level of torture as me. That she's been thrown into this cursed reality with a full memory of the one before, and she's yearning for me the same way I've been yearning for her.

She recognized me in that hospital. I called out for her, and she responded with my name. She was wearing Sienna's locket, for fucks sake.

The moment I allowed myself to acknowledge that fact, the obsession with hunting her down and bringing her back to me bloomed. I've spent every waking hour finding a way to get her to come to me.

But there's still a small shred of a chance that she doesn't know me. That her memories have been stolen away again, and I'll be forced to earn back her trust. In that case, I'll need a backup plan. A way to get close to her without raising her suspicions.

What better way to do that than to take us back to our beginning? To offer her the cabin and bring her under my protective wing without her even realizing it.

I can manage to get through a few more months without her by my side if it means I get the lifetime we were owed before all the shit hit the fan.

My mother isn't making it easy, though.

"I just don't think this is the right time to be making any financial decisions, Sebastian," she tells me, her voice rising the same way it always did when I irritated her as a teenager.

Her patronizing attitude she masks as concern since we left the hospital has pissed me off beyond return. I've officially lost patience for anyone who questions me. They have no idea what I know or what I've seen.

"I'm perfectly well. If you haven't heard, I signed off on a deal that has tripled the size of my company just this afternoon. I can handle a small real estate deal."

Rolling her eyes—a trait Sienna has inherited whenever

they want to ignore logic to get their way—she busies herself with straightening up the dining table we're seated at.

"Since when are you interested in property management? Aren't you a little busy with your *new deal?*" She throws the words back in my face with a sneer.

"Who says I have to stick to one thing?"

"I just don't understand why it has to be this *one* property. You've made it clear you're well-off. You can afford any property in Styx. What if we decide we want to go back there?"

"You haven't stayed there in years and Sienna is nearly done with school. This is a great, low-risk opportunity to dip my toes in. I'm familiar with Styx because of Sienna. It's a quarter of the price I'd pay for a loft here. And I want to try it on something small before I make the full investment."

The excuses fly off my tongue in rapid-fire, a little too fast to make any of them believable. But I don't care. They're serving a purpose either way in showing her that I won't be dropping it. Not until she gives me what I want.

She's right: she doesn't get it. She never will. But it *has* to be the Crystal Cottage. It has to be the same place me and Stardust got our start.

"I need to talk to your father about it…" she lets her voice drift off as her eyes scan me in the same violating way they have been since the day she walked into my hospital room and realized something might be a little off with me.

She's excused it away—never one to confront things directly the way Sienna would—but I can tell it worries her. She senses the shift in me the way my sister does—the way only a woman truly could. She knows that her son disappeared one night and is terrified to face her biggest fear that he may have never returned. Not fully.

She'll give me the cottage. I know she will, even if my father tries to refuse.

She'll do it because bending to my will is easier than confronting her true fears. Because giving me what I want is better than fighting it out and forcing me to admit something she's not ready to hear: that I may be caught up in something beyond her wildest dreams. Something that could snatch me up and take me away from her again.

I can't decide if it makes her weak or smart. Either way, I'm grateful for it. That it provides one less roadblock between mine and Stardust's reunion.

Nodding, I stand up and clasp my hands together behind my back in a submissive show of false disappointment, letting her think she's won.

"Let me know what he says," I tell her, then start toward the door.

"Congratulations on your deal, Sebastian. We're more proud of you than you could ever know."

I don't turn back until I've reached the elevator that serves as their front door, and when I do, I see that pride shining clear across her features. Beside the guilt and fear and exhaustion—it's there. And for the first time since waking up in that hospital room, I'm experiencing something *new*. Something my past reality sorely lacked. Because regardless of how far beyond my wildest dreams my company shot, my mother was so caught up in her own grief over losing Sienna, she never even blinked an eye at my accomplishments.

To see her so happy… it's new. I'm not sure how to process it, so I refuse to let my emotions show until I can sort them out myself. Before she can see how it affects me, I offer a stiff nod and walk into the elevator, keeping my eyes glued to the ground until the doors slid shut.

*Proud of me.*

They wouldn't be too proud if they found out who I truly am or the horrible things I've done in the name of revenge.

Fate may have separated me from that reality, but it still lives inside of me. That insatiable need to take the lives of those who have wronged me and my family. To make them pay for what they did before—what I know they would do again if the opportunity presented itself. But I can't give in. I can't justify senselessly taking the lives of people for decisions they haven't made yet.

Instead, I'm going to focus on keeping the people I love close and preventing them from ever being touched by the monsters who live in the shadows of our sick and twisted social circle.

9

*The Lamb*

THE FIRST THING I do with my freedom is drive my car to the bank and check on my escape fund. Nothing ever came of mine and Gabe's cruise, and he seemed to drop the subject completely after feeling like a heel for his tantrum. I had countless hours to comb through the weeks leading up to his attempt to kill me, and him finding that account appears to be the catalyst that set everything into motion.

I've spent more nights than I'd like to admit wishing I had just abandoned my mom and taken the full wad of cash as soon as I was ready.

He never found out about the stack of gift cards. They're probably still tucked away safely in my trunk. The problem is that Gabe sold that car the moment I was sent to Sunny-brook in another fit. He had wanted Halen to send me home from the hospital, and when she didn't obey, he claimed he needed the money to pay the bills I was abandoning him with. At least, that's what Kennedy told me.

The car was probably worth less than the amount of money sitting in the back of it, but I can only hope it helps whoever bought it.

"The balance of that account is five dollars," the teller politely chirps.

My stomach flips, disappointment falling over me so heavy, my chest begins to feel tight. "How is that possible? I had thousands in there…"

I was relying on this money to get me out of Halen's.

The girl swings her head back to the computer, squinting her eyes as she clicks around. "Looks like there was a cash withdrawal three weeks ago."

"That can't be possible," I lay my hands on the counter, dropping my keys and wallet onto the surface. "I was in a mental hospital three weeks ago."

Her eyes go wide, and I tilt my head, daring her to say something. I'm so worked up, I don't even care about explaining that I shouldn't have been there. I just want my money.

She looks back to her system and clicks one more thing. "The receipt was signed, but it's illegible."

"Let me see."

Twisting the screen, there's a digital receipt pulled up with Gabe's scribbled signature. When my eyes go wide, she turns it back to face her.

"That is the man who I was going to use this money to leave," I explain slowly, despite the rush of fear flooding my chest. "He was not on the account or authorized to take anything from it."

He knew about the savings, but I made sure I was the only one on it. I even explained the situation to the woman who opened the account for me, earning the same sympathetic stare this teller is giving me now. She assured me that if he ever came in here looking for me, they would never mention this money existed.

This is the second time they've betrayed me now.

"And there's no way you were able to withdraw this money yourself?"

Shaking my head, I tell her I need to speak to a manager and she immediately takes me over to one. The woman apologizes profusely, explaining that once I can provide proof that I was in Sunnybrook, they'll conduct a thorough investigation and likely have my money back in the account once it's over.

I leave feeling even more defeated than I was when I left Sunnybrook. Without that money, it could take me months to get out on my own again.

With no other choice, I put the cafe Ginny told me about into my GPS and head out to beg for a job.

**10**

*The Wolf*

As EXPECTED, my father is the biggest obstacle in my plan. It takes a frustratingly long time convincing him to sell me the Crystal Cabin for no other reason than him being an opportunistic prick who can't resist a chance to hassle me. At least I can rest assured that he is the same toxic asshole he was in the last lifetime.

While he's kept his Order talk away from me since the accident, he seems to be viewing this as the perfect opportunity to leverage my participation. And because I have time working against me, I had to agree to some of it.

"Joining such a prestigious brotherhood is an opportunity that many men would kill for," he explains across the table, repeating the same words he's been spewing at me since the moment I turned sixteen and admitted I had no intention of following in his footsteps.

My mother rolls her eyes and scoffs, nervously catching my gaze to gauge how well I'm going to take his pushy talk.

After everything that happened the last time he tried to pressure me into this conversation, she has refused to take any chances and leave us alone for even a second, despite my father's rude attempts to dismiss her.

*"This is a conversation between two men. It's not for your ears,"* he had told her when he first brought it up.

Thankfully, my mother stood strong. She leaned back in her chair, casually sipping her drink to mask the jolt of pain I know she felt at his condescending words, and then waved her hand at him to tell him that he'd better keep talking, because she had no intention of leaving.

And because my father is a spineless pig, he looked to me for support. When I made it clear that I didn't agree with him, he continued on with his bullshit spiel.

"I'm well aware of what *men* do to get into the Order." My nose scrunches in disgust.

Of course, he can't take a hint, so he continues to push, bluntly spewing his stipulations. "I'll sign the papers if you join us for the Stargazing Ball next month. Just come and see what you're missing out on. There's an entire brotherhood waiting to welcome you with open arms."

His desperation is disgusting. The sheer embarrassment he must feel for the fact that his son is one of the only legacies that absolutely despises their organization is enough to make him lay down every shred of pride he has and practically beg me to reconsider. To leverage something as menial as a real estate deal only proves how deep his mortification runs.

Which begs the question: What are they threatening to make him feel this way? And how much time do I have to stop it?

"I've been to the Stargazing Ball countless times. I know what the Order is about." I've been to far more of their events than I'd like to ever admit. Enough for a lifetime.

But the Stardust Ball is one that is used to flaunt wealth before all of the elite. To rub elbows with some of the richest and most powerful people on the planet. Prominent Members fly in from across the country to attend with their families and assert their dominance over one another with silent raffles and outrageous donations. It's all done under the guise of a charity fundraiser to cure cancer.

They'll raise millions to find a cure, but not a single person will have done it for the cause. All of these charity galas are public pissing contests for the men and excuses for their wives to continue their caddy drama behind the scenes. It's a way for them to blatantly demonstrate their wealth to one another without looking like the righteous jackasses that they truly are.

"Then what's one more? If you want the cottage, this is how you'll get it."

He taps the paperwork I set between us on the table when I first entered three times, then leans back in his chair and crosses one leg over the other, resting his ankle on his knees. As if this is such a casual conversation, and not one where he's asking me to abandon all my morals for a piece of property that he finds useless either way.

"Fine," I concede, earning a surprised scowl from above my mother's martini glass.

"Sebastian, is it a good idea for you to be around all those people…" she begins to protest, but one look at her darling husband has her shrinking back into herself, her words trailing off and dying.

"It will be good for you," he tells us both confidently.

"Then, it's settled. I'll go to your little ball and you'll sign the offer my realtor sent to your email this evening."

"I'll look it over and let you know if I have any changes," he says with a superlicious lilt.

I want to grab the side of his head and slam it against this marble tabletop until the entire thing is stained with his blood. I want to finish what I started to do on the night he pulled a gun and killed me before I got the chance. The smooth feeling of my knife slicing into his skin is one that I dream of. Out of all the men I killed, his death was the only one that mattered, and I fucked it up so royally that I can't even see straight.

Instead of succumbing to my violent thoughts, I stand from my chair and start toward the elevators, not bothering with a formal goodbye.

"We'll see you at dinner this week, won't we?" My mother calls out to my back, her tone wobbly as she struggles to catch up to my long strides. Of course, my father stayed out on the patio.

"I'll be here," I assure her gently, pressing the button to go down.

We hold each other's gazes for a long, drawn-out moment before she closes the gap between us and wraps her arm around my neck, yanking me into a rare and tight hug.

"I'm sorry he trapped you like that. Please don't pull away from us." Her voice is a desperate plea full of terror and doubt.

She knows this will be what breaks us. She just has no idea how much it already has.

Instead of arguing or threatening, I tell her, "I'm not going anywhere."

The elevator opens up and she pulls away, swiping a stray tear from her eye. I nod my goodbye, too thrown off by her display of affection to say anything else, and then step onto the elevator.

I'D SELL my soul to get my girl out from beneath her

controlling sister's thumb, and I've done worse things in exchange for far less.

The following morning, once we confirmed again that I would attend their charity gala in a few weeks, he signed the papers and sent them to my realtor. Chantel had a contract drawn up that afternoon, and we closed on it this morning—just two weeks after I presented the idea to my mother.

**11**

*The Lamb*

OLD SOUL CAFE is an eclectic little gem buried on a side street in downtown Styx amongst a row of similar double story buildings. So small, you might miss it if you didn't know where to look. The white cinder block exterior and tinted windows make it feel slightly run down and urban, but the instant you open the front door, you're hit with the true magic of what Ginny and her sister built.

The ladder is standing before me, clad in a patchwork knitted cardigan, purple cargo pants, and curly hair in the brightest shade of pink I've ever seen piled on top of her head. She's stocking the utensil station at the end of the ordering counter, but turns to offer me her full attention the moment the bell rings above my head.

"Hey, I'll be with you in just a sec," she greets, quickening her pace.

I take a moment to fully absorb the space, immediately missing Ginny and her quirky personality. Everything my eyes land on reminds me of her in some way. Each wall is splashed with a different color—purple, blue, orange, and green. The yellow counter stretches all the way through the cafe, separating the workspace from the dining area. A hodgepodge of mismatched tables and chairs are scattered all around with bookcases lining the long wall across from the counter, below the tinted windows. There are three red doors in the back that I assume would be bathrooms and an office, and then a small kitchen space sits just outside of my eyesight.

A handful of straws fall onto the floor as Rosie goes to dump them into their designated caddy, and I rush over to help her pick them up.

Two people sit at different tables, working away on their laptops with headphones shoved into their ears and blind to what just happened.

"Thanks," she says, mumbling a string of curse words under her breath as she realizes all of these straws are now garbage, then tosses them into a black trash bag. The door opens and the bells ring again, signaling the arrival of three new customers.

"How can I help you?" She asks me once we get the straws cleaned up, rounding the counter to meet me by the ordering window.

"Actually, I'm a friend of Ginny's. She mentioned you may be looking for some help…"

My voice trails off as her expression tightens, her lips pursing and pushing to the side as her eyes roam over my body.

"You're from Sunnybrook?" She asks quietly, her tone suddenly hard.

Nodding slowly, I place my hand on the counter—a natural, knee jerk reaction to plead my case. "I am, but I didn't belong there, so I got out."

"You didn't *belong* there?" She eyes me disbelievingly.

"No, I'm not like those people in there..."

That was the wrong thing to say. Rosie's head rears back as if I've slapped her, her arms crossing over her chest as she moves her legs in a defensive stance. The three people behind us have quieted down their conversation, no doubt sensing the shift in her demeanor.

"My sister is one of *those people*. I thought you claimed you were her friend."

*Shit*. This isn't going well. I've managed to offend her and Ginny at the same time without even trying. I might as well just turn and leave now.

But do I? No. Instead, I dig myself deeper by trying to explain.

"No, I mean... I *am* Ginny's friend. Well, technically we were roommates, but you know what I mean. I don't think there's anything wrong with the patients in Sunnybrook. I just mean that I shouldn't have been sent there in the first place and... well, it's a long story." I've been rambling for an embarrassingly long time, and Rosie has made no move to stop me or assure me or kick me out. She's just standing there, staring at me like I have three heads with her arms still tightly crossed.

"I'll just go," I finally concede, hooking my thumb backward.

But just as I turn to leave, Rosie's arms untangle and she reaches behind her to grab one of the pink aprons hanging on one of the hooks drilled into the wall.

"I thought you said you wanted to help," she calls out to my back, holding up the apron for me.

"Yeah, I do. It just seemed like... I don't know." I reach out to take it from her hands, slowly tucking it into my chest as a broad smile breaks out across her face.

"I'll start training you now."

There's a weird, awkward moment where I'm frozen to one spot, staring at her with a goofy, disbelieving smile. When an uncomfortable amount of time passes, her eyes widen, brows raising up to her forehead—second guessing her decision. Before she can back out, I snap out of my reverie to step aside for her to take the other customer's order while I loop the apron around my neck.

Rosie whips up their drinks at record speed, buzzing behind the counter with comfort and familiarity, the same way I used to do at my previous waitressing job. A pang of homesickness for my old life hits me in the gut, taking me by complete surprise. As miserable as I was in my relationship with Gabe, drowning in bills and debt with jobs that paid less than a livable wage, it was comfortable and familiar. Two things I haven't felt since the night I stepped out of that shower and was tackled to the ground by Gabe.

I can't go back to that place anymore, though. Even if my old boss would take me back—which she won't—there's no telling what such a huge move backward would do to my mental state. I'm already barely holding on in Halen's basement like some kind of homeless squatter.

It's not until the three customers are walking out the front door that Rosie offers me her attention again, tilting her head toward the small break in the counter, gesturing for me to come behind it with her.

"The least thing Ginny could do is offer some help while she's away," she begins, emptying the espresso machine into the garbage. "I've had a help wanted ad posted for weeks and haven't gotten any bites on it, so you're the best option I've got. I suppose I can't be picky."

"Thanks… I think."

She winks at me, shoving the group filter back onto the machine.

I train with her for two hours before she sends me off

with a stack of paperwork to fill out and a menu with recipes to memorize. By the time I'm walking back out the front door and toward my car, a new sense of relief is sweeping through my body, because I did it. I still managed to snag a job, even as an ex-mental hospital patient.

The pay is incredible for a small coffee shop, the hours are great, and Rosie seems like someone whose personality only gets better the more you get to know her.

As I approach my car, my phone pings with the notification of an email alert I set up for any new rental listings in the area. I have no idea how long it would take me to get a job, but I've been scouring every rental site since my first night at Halen's, desperate to find *anything* within a decent price range the instant I have some money coming in. And unless I want to rent a single room for an astronomical monthly fee, my options are slim, even with Rosie's gracious pay.

I fall into the driver's seat and open the email. The newest listing is for a large vacation home off Crystal Lake, across town from Halen, on the high end side of Styx. It's set at a price that has me doing a double take. Less than half the rent of any home in the area and significantly cheaper than every other listing on my saved list. It absolutely has to be a typo.

And yet… what if it's not? If it feels scammy, I just won't go see it. If they made a mistake, my email will tip them off and let them know they need to correct it.

What do I have to lose if I just apply?

Before I can second guess it, I decide to cash in on my lucky streak and submit my information for them to contact me, then drop my phone into the cup holder so I can begin the short drive back to Halen's.

**12**

*The Lamb*

GABE WAITS two weeks before he comes to collect me from Halen and Kennedy's. The moment I heard the loud pounding on the front door, I knew it was him, and my body entered fight or flight.

"I need to talk to her, Hales," he pushes when she tries to kindly send him away. His heavy footsteps rush through the living room above my head anyway.

I hear the pitter patter of Halen's small steps as she chases after him. "Now is not the time, Gabe," she calls, out of breath.

I've locked the door at the bottom of the basement stairs, shoving a chair against the knob in case he decides to try and push his way through with brunt force. That seems to be how he handles things nowadays.

My restraining order was filed earlier this week. I have no doubt that's what brought on our sudden visit from the devil himself.

"Jo-Jo!" he calls down the steps, using the same nickname my mother gave me.

He thinks the nostalgia will tug at my heart strings, but it does the opposite, reminding me how they both have betrayed me. He stomps down the steps, and then tries to turn the knob, growling in frustration when he discovers it's locked.

"You have to give her time," Halen calls to his back.

"She's been given enough of that in that mental hospital. It's time for her to come home and get back to normal."

I roll my eyes, aggressively jabbing my middle finger up at the closed door with a scowl. It's just like him to try and declare what's best for me. To talk down on Sunnybrook as if he wasn't the one to send me there in the first place.

"You need to leave," Kennedy's voice says from the top of the steps, her tone low and serious. It's a warning more than a suggestion.

"Just give me five minutes, Jo-Jo," he yells through the door, ignoring Kennedy and Halen. The door rattles as his fist pummels it. "We can clear all of this up."

I don't respond. I know that giving him any shred of attention will only make this worse.

"Let us talk to her. We want things to get back to normal just as much as you do," Halen says in a weak attempt at negotiation. She's right outside the door now. Probably standing beside him.

I'd think it was just a tactic to get him out of her house, but I know there's truth behind her statement. She'd rather pack me up and send me back to his house than deal with me for a second longer, especially after this. When I've been fighting and bucking against every rule or ultimatum she tries to present me with.

"Leave, Gabe," Kennedy grinds out.

"Fuck off," he bickers.

There's the distinct sound of a struggle on the other side of the door. Gabe grunts, Halen shouts, and something slams against the door. Then, silence. I sit up on the couch, debating if I should unlock the door and hear him out for the sake of peace.

"Oh, my god. I'm calling the police," Halen cries out, her steps rushing back across the house. "Stay there, Ken!"

I'm flying off the couch, crossing the distance from the couch to the stairway in three quick strides.

Gabe begins apologizing repeatedly, his voice raising with every weak 'sorry' that leaves his mouth. My fingers wrap around the lock, ready to twist it and whip the door open to face my personal nightmare. But just before I do, I hear Kennedy's voice.

"You've got some balls coming here, trying to retrieve her like a piece of property after what you did to her," she growls. "Get the fuck out of my house, you piece of shit,"

"I didn't–" He starts, but his voice is cut off.

My forehead rolls against the wood, breaths erratic as I strain to hear every word.

"I know you did it," Kennedy snarls, her tone so severe, he doesn't bother trying to refute it. I can only imagine what her face looks like. How terrified he must be. He's already used his strength against her. That's the only defense he has.

"They're on the way," Halen calls from the front of the house.

"Save your bullshit excuses for someone who will believe them," Kennedy mutters, low enough so Halen can't hear. "Leave before I press charges."

Gabe sputters out a few more weak apologies, but there's no arguing with Kennedy when she's in this protective mode. Especially when she'll get him thrown in jail for trying. His feet climb the stairs, then cross the living room and out the front door.

I'm swinging the door open and falling to my knees on the floor beside Kennedy in the next breath. I'm so grateful for her, I could cry.

And I do.

"He won't be back here," she promises, pulling me into a tight hug. Halen appears at the top of the stairs, tears streaming down her cheeks.

**13**

*The Lamb*

I GOT the house on Crystal Lake.

It's a beautiful, fully furnished, sprawling ranch. The neighboring homes are so spread apart, I can hardly see them —a huge contrast from my old place with Gabe, where we could hardly park our car in the driveway without scraping against the neighbors brick. When the girl from the property management company showed it to me, I nearly passed out. It felt like home, yet still so out of reach.

Familiar, but unattainable.

I never realized those things could coexist.

We wrapped up the showing in utter disbelief that it was listed as low as it was. She even called the owner to confirm.

"To be honest, this is the first property I've shown for this company," she admitted sheepishly, adding that she had only been hired a few days ago. Even once it was confirmed by him firsthand, she seemed shell-shocked.

"Houses in this neighborhood are charging double this

price for a one week rental. I don't think he knows the gold mine he has here," she mused, running her hand along the marble countertops.

I was fully prepared to walk away when she told me there was a ton of other interest. How could I compare to any other applicant with no recent work history and no proof of income? But she encouraged me to apply anyway, and I knew I'd regret it if I didn't.

Getting my hopes up felt like setting myself up for disappointment. I spent an admittedly obscene amount of time trying *not* to think about it as I waited for a call back, which only made me obsess over it more.

Halen and Kennedy have no idea that I've already begun my search for a place, although their need to know every move I make has grown tiresome very quickly. Each time I walk out the door, I'm met with a string of questions from Halen about where I'm going and when I'll be back, as if I'm not a grown ass adult with full autonomy. Kennedy has reminded me several times that she does it because she cares.

"Those days you were living on machines practically tore her apart. She just needs time to adjust and recover," she always says.

It's not an attempt to guilt me. I honestly think Kennedy may be one of the few people who actually sees through Gabe's facade, especially after his last visit. But it has the same effect either way.

I'd never want to cause my sister undue stress. I know that if the roles were reversed, I might have reacted the same way. It just seems like neither of us are happy with the way things are right now, and moving out seems to be the only answer.

Six days after submitting my application, I received the email that I was chosen. I was in the middle of a morning shift at the cafe, and I shrieked so loud, Rosie came barreling in from the back office thinking we were being robbed.

"I knew you would get it," she shrieked with a smug smile, pulling me into a celebratory hug.

In the two weeks I've been working for her, we've become fast friends. Something about her makes me feel comfortable enough to easily share pieces of myself that some of the people I used to consider best friends don't even know. And she shares things with me, too. Her worries over her sister, her stress over the business, how she struggles to balance work life and personal life and has lost most of her relationships over all three.

I think it helps that we found each other through the one thing we each prefer to keep tucked away from the world: Sunnybrook—our dirty little secret. As much as she loves Ginny, she's not a topic that Rosie likes to discuss with just anyone, even the people who knew her before she went in. I only had to explain to her what happened to me once, and she immediately believed every word I said.

No sympathetic head tilt. No pathetic click of her tongue. No rationalization for Gabe or my mother. No doubt about my mental health.

None of the usual reactions I receive.

*"That guy sounds like he needs a quick punch to the throat and knee to the balls,"* was all she had said, scowling.

After that, we dropped the subject. Whenever something comes up with Halen or anyone from that point in my life, she's there as an ear for me to vent.

I think it's the most functional friendship I've ever had.

"I thought for sure they would go with someone else," I admitted to her, still shocked. "They told me they received several offers for more money."

Part of me feels like I don't deserve it.

"You can't lose something that's meant to be yours," is her

reply, and something about those words made me feel so much better about getting it.

Breaking the news to Halen and Kennedy goes a little differently.

"Off Crystal Lake?" Halen's shrill voice questions doubtfully. "Isn't that a gated community?"

"It's not gated, it's just private."

"It's full of expensive-as-hell houses," Kennedy scoffs.

"How are you going to afford this, Jovie? That coffee shop isn't paying you *that* much, is it?" Halen's nose scrunches in distaste.

She's had an issue with me working at Old Soul—and Rosie, specifically—since the day I told her about it. Supposedly, she doesn't agree with me taking a job through someone I met at a mental hospital. In truth, I think she's intimidated by the relationship I've formed with my new friend while ours seems to be falling apart at the seams. She can't stand that I've ditched our old friends and have still managed to make new ones, either.

Instead, she's reminded me repeatedly that I could work with her at the sports bar she bartends at. On random shifts with pay that isn't guaranteed. If I did that, I'd have to take on one, maybe two more jobs just to pay my bills.

*"I just want things to go back to normal. How can we do that if you won't move past what happened?"* She asked me one night, after I had turned down plans to go to dinner for the third time.

The control freak in her can't wrap her mind around the idea that her idea of 'normal' doesn't exist anymore.

"The rent is crazy low, and Rosie pays me decently," I start to defend, but stop myself before going any further. I don't need Halen's approval, and she doesn't need to know every detail about it.

"Are you sure it isn't a scam?" she asks, her tone serious.

As if I'm incapable of realizing when someone is manipulating me. The irony of that isn't lost on me.

"Halen," Kennedy warns, cutting her eyes over to my sister in irritation. "That's great news. We're happy for you, Jo."

"I just don't understand why you're rushing to get a place. You can stay here as long as you need."

*Yeah, where my ex can come barreling through the door at any moment and physically abuse all three of us.*

Rolling my eyes, I turn toward basement stairs to start packing, feeling even more justified in my decision to leave than I did before.

Kennedy hisses something at my sister, and then I heard her footsteps follow me down the stairs. "Stop, Jovie. You know how Halen is. She just takes a second to adjust to things."

I pause at my dresser and throw the top drawer open, grabbing up all the contents in my arms to throw them into a suitcase.

"How long are we going to make excuses for her childish behavior, Ken?"

"I'm not being childish, I'm being realistic!" Halen calls down the stairs, driving my point.

Dropping my things onto the bed when I realize my suitcase is still sitting in the closet, I throw my arm in the direction Halen's voice just came from and raise my brows at her wife incredulously.

"Why can't you just be happy for me, Halen? God, it's so suffocating here. No one can grow or move on in this environment," I cry out.

"*Suffocating?*" Halen screeches, her feet stomping down the steps. Kennedy attempts to intercept her, but she pushes past. "I'm sorry that our zero-dollar-a-month-rent that we've offered you doesn't live up to your standards."

"Halen…" Kennedy warns, but my sister purses her lips and crosses her arms, stubbornly refusing to back down.

I want to scream back at her that I almost preferred homelessness over staying with her. That ever stressful and unbearable moment I've lived over the past two months has been directly correlated to her need for control and support for my enemies. I want to roar every insult I can think of into her face and whittle her down to nothing, the way she's effectively done to me.

"We're finished. I'm not going to say something I'll regret," is what I say instead, turning back to my task. When they don't immediately leave, I throw over my shoulder, "I'll be out of here the instant I get my keys."

I'm not sure what silent exchange happened behind my back in the couple moments before I heard their footsteps climb the stairs, but I did hear them arguing later that night before Kennedy's footsteps shuffled into the living room, and then the house filled with cold, stony silence.

14

*The Lamb*

My new home is quiet and quaint—the exact opposite of the chaos I've always known and been forced to grow comfortable with. Even Halen and Kennedy's home had an energy that fought and thrashed against me while I lived there, desperate to exercise me from it like a poltergeist.

There's none of that here. Just peace and quiet, a neutral space, ready and waiting for someone to make it their own. For *me* to make it my own.

A sanctuary, perfect for healing.

Finally, the storm has settled and I can begin rebuilding from the rubble.

I've been moved in for a week. When I'm not working at the cafe, I'm tinkering around with the furniture and knick-knacks scattered around. I've found a hobby in visiting thrift stores alone and collecting whatever strange oddities I feel drawn to—mostly snowglobes. I've already accumulated an impressive collection.

It's been therapeutic. I've never had the chance to shop around and actually consider if something was *my* taste. Not for my mother, not to match whatever's in style. Just for me.

My social life has shriveled and died. Even if my supposed friends had bothered to reach out once I got out of Sunnybrook, I don't think I would have accepted any of their invitations. There's a new fear that's been activated—a lack of trust in all of those who I once thought would be around until the end. There's been a line drawn in the sand, with two distinct sides established.

Unfortunately, I looked up and found that most of the people I loved so dearly were standing on the opposite side, staring back at me like I'm the villain in their story.

It's just another step to finding myself. Attracting the people who call to me on a soul level and holding tight to them when they come. Dr. Forrest has made it clear that repairing friendships I didn't break should be low on my list of priorities.

So I thrift. And I work. I watch TV, journal, and for the first time in a decade, I draw. Anything to avoid people or the angry thoughts that always seem to find their way through the cracks of my weakly-laid foundation.

I take every day as it comes, careful not to plan too far ahead. As much as I resent what Gabe has done to me, I'm grateful for the way it's forced me to flip myself inside out and really look at what falls out. To compare that to the woman I want to be, and take note of how to close the gap.

But no amount of gratitude or inner peace can compete with the paralyzing fear that at any moment, it can all happen again. That Gabe could bust through my front door, tackle me to the ground, and take my life for a second time.

So, no matter how many ways I try to justify my reclusiveness with apprehension and self-actualization, it all boils down to one single thing: bone-chilling terror of losing control again.

Journaling has helped. Instead of numbing my mind with reality TV or social media, I've trained myself to reach for my notebook instead. That's what I'm doing when I see the figure in my backyard for the first time.

It's nearly pitch black outside. The tired Spring sun still tucks itself in early, taking time to rest before Summer begins to demand more.

He's nothing more than a shadow. A darker shade of black standing out against the glistening lake behind him. I can tell he's facing the house—can feel his eyes leering at me. The moment I see him, a chill runs through my bones, skittering beneath my skin. In a subtle move, I reach beside me and grab my phone, keeping my left hand poised against the journal like I'm still writing so he doesn't realize anything is astray. Hopefully, he'll assume I couldn't see him blended so well against the darkened sky.

Dropping my head, I keep my face turned into my lap and dial 911 from my peripherals, hitting the speaker button as my left hand draws lazy circles on the paper.

"9-1-1, what's your emergency?" The operator's calm voice fills the room.

"There's a man standing in my backyard. I think he's watching me," I explain on a shaky breath, tucking my chin further into my chest so he can't see my lips moving.

"Are you alone, ma'am?"

"Yes."

She asks for my address and I give it to her.

"We've got a squad car on the way. Is there anywhere you can go in the home to stay safe?"

"I-I don't know. He's just standing there, watching me. I'm afraid he'll follow me if I move."

She asks me to stay on the line as we wait for the police to arrive, and makes her best attempt at small talk as she tries to get more information from me about the man.

I'm trying to focus on what she's saying, but my eyes stray back to the window and land on him. I'm startled at the soft glow that now illuminates his face, casting shadows across sharp, masculine features.

My phone vibrates against the couch with an incoming text, and my head is immediately whipping around to check it.

Unknown: Welcome home, Stardust.

That's it. That's all it says. When I look back to the yard, he's gone.

Grabbing my phone up, I stand from the couch and bravely go toward the window, scanning the backyard for any sign of him.

It's like he's disappeared out of thin air.

When the police arrive, we go through the footage that my brand new security cameras picked up together, but none of them seem to have caught him walking around. Even the one facing the back, directly where I swore I saw him standing comes up short.

The officers shift uncomfortably on their feet, sharing a look as the realization dawns on them that I'm probably out of my mind. They saw the footage themselves—no one was there at the time of my call. It's because of their quick dismissal that I keep the text to myself. There's no proof that it came from my yard. That could have been anyone playing a prank on me, and I'm not willing to sacrifice my sanity trying to explain anymore.

Still, they continue their investigation, asking each question half-heartedly so they can fill out their paperwork.

When they leave, they'll chalk this up to another crazy out of the loony bin, and move on.

*What was he wearing? Did you notice any strange vehicles parked near your home? Have you gone anywhere today that he could have followed you home from?*

None of it matters. They can't do anything to someone who can disappear with no notice, like he's slipping behind secret doors. Who evades all the security cameras and strolls completely undetected past them on the street.

They can't save me. Not from him, and not from Gabe.

He knew I was calling the police on him. And yet, he still sent the message. Still watched me. Still waited to see my reaction to his message.

He's not afraid of them, and that's even more terrifying.

**15**

*The Lamb*

I'M HALFWAY through a slow shift at Old Soul the next day when a woman strolls through the door, her blonde hair blowing all around a narrow, heart-shaped face as the crisp autumn air meets the warmth of the cafe. Something about her instantly feels oddly familiar, though I can't put my finger on *what*.

It's another one of those things—the memory blips I seem to keep having. Where a person or place will ignite an aching in my chest, screaming that I've *been* here before... *seen* them before. But my memory always seems to fall short when it comes to recalling how or where.

Each time it happens, my fears that Gabe's attack altered my brain in some way always come rushing to the forefront, desperate to dig their claws in and steal me away, back into that dark place I was in at Sunnybrook. It takes more effort than I'd like to admit to pull myself back to the present, though I get better at it each time it happens.

The woman practically glides through the small space, shoulders back, even with a backpack slung around them, and chin held high as if she doesn't have a care in the world. She screams wealth. From her professionally manicured nails—a simple nude—to her practically airbrushed makeup and neutral, high-end clothing.

She stops before me and offers a broad, friendly smile, revealing a perfect row of pearly white teeth behind her full, red-painted lips.

"Hello, Jovie."

She greets me as if we've met before, and that odd feeling grows even more intense. But just as the awkwardness settles in as I realize I *don't* remember her, those green eyes flick down to the name tag pinned to my pink apron, and it dawns on me that she must have read it as I ogled her while she made her way through the door.

Clearing my throat, I pretend to arrange the display cabinet beside me to hide my paranoid blush. "How can I help you today?"

"Can I get a large black coffee with triple cream and sugar?"

Nodding, I turn my back to her and begin pouring the coffee. Anything to avoid those intense eyes boring directly into me so unashamedly. Once the simple drink is made, I enter it into our system and tell her the total.

"That's a beautiful locket," she compliments, handing her credit card over to me.

"Thanks."

"I used to have one just like it. I've somehow misplaced mine though." She makes a show of shaking her head with self-deprecating eye roll as she grabs her card and receipt back from me, followed by a broad smile, as if to say, *you know how it is.*

"That sucks. I hope you find it," I tell her lamely, immediately wishing I had taken a second to come up with something more clever to say.

This is just one of those charismatic women who seems to have everything come naturally to her. Simply being in her presence shines a light on all my flaws and shortcomings, leaving me floundering and insecure. Although, based on how friendly she's been through all my awkward stuttering, she seems like the type who would never hold any of it against me.

A stiff nod is all she leaves me with before she grabs her cup and settles into one of the seats farthest from me, where she spends the rest of the afternoon.

When I get home that night, there's a scribbled note sitting on my table. It's been ripped out of the notepad I keep on my fridge, the pen still sitting beside it like the person who wrote it had to quickly run out.

*Sorry I missed you. I'll be back soon.*

Just a few rushed words, and my blood goes still. He was here, inside my house.

Waiting for me to come home so he could do... *what?*

Confront me about calling the police? Hand me another fig?

Murder me like Halen says?

It's equally as unsettling as it is comforting. Now, I know I'm not going insane. There was a man in my backyard, and he's likely tied to the figs inside my home.

But then again... *there was a man in my backyard, and he's likely tied to the figs inside my home.*

I can't call the police again. Not until he shows himself and there's no denying his presence. For now, I'll wait.

That night, I slip a knife beneath my pillow and don't sleep a wink.

## 16

*The Lamb*

HE'S BACK AGAIN.

I can feel his presence before he bothers to show himself.

It's always this way with him now. He slinks around in the shadows, stalking me like the predator that he is—learning my patterns and behaviors—before he feels comfortable enough to step into the light and reveal himself. I've tried calling out to him, screaming obscenities his way and demanding that he show himself. It never works.

My mystery man only reveals himself when *he* believes it's time.

That doesn't stop him from still leaving notes and figs behind. As if the weight of his very existence doesn't give him away, he wants to make sure I'm well aware of when he's been here. Especially on the off chance that I happen to miss him.

The notes are always filled with odd, cryptic messages

that are scribbled in sloppy, masculine writing on random pieces of mail or post-its. As if they're thrown together in a rush—an afterthought.

I can't figure out his schedule. He doesn't even appear to have one. But he *has* to have a job or a family or friends. He has to have *something* outside of watching me, and I can't figure out how or when he fits those things in. I can tell he comes from money, just in the way he speaks of things. You just know when a person hasn't had to worry about when their next meal would be, or if their electricity will be cut off that month. This man has never experienced those hardships. And if I couldn't tell by just looking at him, I'd know the instant he opened his mouth.

Everything he thinks and says feels like he comes from a completely different world. Perhaps that's what he finds so alluring about me. Like watching a wild animal in their natural habitat, he observes me as the lower class, over-worked single woman with open interest and intrigue. It would make me uncomfortable if he were anyone else, but something about him rips away that awkward layer that sits between me and other people. Probably the fact that he's already violated my privacy so thoroughly, there's not much else for me to lose when it comes to him.

And while that fact alone should make me want to kick him in the balls and call the police on him, it doesn't. Because for every piece of information he steals from me, he leaves behind breadcrumbs about himself for me to follow. Each interaction is a transaction, where we carefully share more and more about ourselves. It drives me absolutely mad that, for the most part, he holds all the power in this exchange.

I've done my own due diligence and attempted to stalk him. I'm embarrassed to report that my best attempts have come back fruitless. Mystery man seems to be just that—a mystery. A figment of my imagination. If he didn't leave physical, tangible evidence of his visits, I would be fully convinced that he wasn't real.

**17**

*The Lamb*

I FEEL like I'm going insane.

That seems to be the only explanation for why I'm seeing and hearing things that clearly aren't there. The creaks and groans of my old cottage-home have morphed into footfalls and quieted movements in my mind. An entire being has taken root in my imagination, haunting and stalking me.

The figs that keep mysteriously appearing on my table are not helping. Nor are the letters.

I thought it was whoever I saw standing in my yard that first night here, but the figure hasn't returned, and there's been no trace of anyone else besides me coming into the house on the cameras.

It feels like someone is playing a sick joke on me. I wouldn't put it past Gabe to wage a psychological war, but everything about this feels odd. He isn't patient enough to pull something like this off for so long.

Admitting these things to Halen and Kennedy is out of the question. If either of them catches wind that I'm in a dangerous situation, they'll be moving my things out before I can even muster up the breath to protest. Worse, if it turns out that this is all in my head, they'll send me back to Sunnybrook.

No, I'm on my own in this, which is probably for the best, considering it all appears to be symptoms of my overactive imagination. Most likely from so much isolation.

Working at Old Soul Cafe has proven to be enough to pay my bills, thankfully. I've been pinching pennies and cutting coupons just to ensure that I don't have to take on a second or third gig, the same way I would when I was living with Gabe. When your entire life is only filled with temporary, dead-end jobs, you tend to lose your motivation for much else. In fact, working three jobs is part of what caused the people at Sunnybrook to believe I wanted to off myself.

Luckily for me, Rosie pays well and my tips make up for the rest. The only downside is that I'm ready to pass out by eight every night. Even on my days off.

It provides a great excuse to get out of being with all the people who only want to question me about Gabe and campaign for him. Tonight is no exception.

My phone sits on the coffee table before me, dancing across the glass with the vibration of Halen's third phone call. She's gone out with a group of our friends for dinner and drinks and they want me to meet them. They've been begging for hours, and the calls only get more desperate as the night wears on. But I don't have the energy to defend myself or thwart off their attempts at rationalizing things they have no capacity to understand. I tried once to give them the benefit of the doubt, but they refused to listen to me.

Even Halen, who I've made great strides with, jumps on their delusional bandwagon and begins spewing the scripted bullshit that sounds a little too much like Gabe's words for my comfort.

Lightning steals my attention from my phone screen as it splits the sky in half, followed by booming thunder that rattles the glass knick-knacks sitting on the shelf across from me. My lamp flickers, my electricity holding on for dear life.

Who would want to be out tonight, anyway? The weather channel is claiming that this will be the worst thunderstorm we've gotten in years.

I hate storms. I've hated them for as long as I can remember, and my fear only blossomed into full-blown terror when a tornado passed over Sunnybrook one night and they didn't even bother having us take shelter. The surrounding neighborhoods were completely destroyed and the news outlets didn't stop talking about it for a week straight. It was a miracle that it jumped right over us, then touched back down a mile away.

That's what they said. *A miracle*. And the administration at Sunnybrook never even bothered to move us out of our rooms, away from the windows.

There were no other incidents while I was there, but the storms this summer have been incredibly dangerous. Especially being off of Crystal Lake, where the water seems to rise and tease me with its surprising depths. They cut off my electricity and leave me cowering in the dark, curled in a ball until the sun rises and I can breathe again.

So for them to say this one will be the *worst*... that has me frozen to my spot, listening for any small change in case I need to take cover.

I think it would take a truly insane person to admit that they were grateful to have a stranger or ghost lurking around their home in the middle of the night, but I've accepted that my sanity has long since abandoned me. I'll openly confess that if there were a time I would want to be haunted, it would be tonight.

Lightning strikes again, followed by a loud crashing noise from somewhere down my street. Seconds later, my electricity flickers out, blanketing the room in complete darkness. Gusts of wind rattle the large window panes, practically bending the old, thick trees lining my yard in half. Hail slams against the glass, threatening to shatter it to pieces.

My breath quickens, chest tightening as panic begins to sink its claws in. I pull my knees to my chin, rocking in my seat in an attempt to calm myself. It works for a moment, soothing the ache in my chest until another bolt of lightning illuminates the room, thunder crashing right behind it.

The hysteria engulfs me, so quick I can hardly conjure up a breath. Tears freefall down my cheeks as a sob breaks free from my lips, and just like with everything else in this sad excuse of an existence, I lose control. Emotions roll through me like waves in a tsunami, cresting and crashing over one another until they drown me. I'm so overwhelmed with them, fighting for breath—fighting for *release.*

Release that comes in the form of more cries, more sobs, more tears.

The panic tightens its fist on me, squeezing until there's no more air left in my lungs and I'm dry heaving.

I'm out of control. Everything has fallen apart, breaking me open until I'm nothing but a shattered shell of a human. This is what Gabe wanted. What my mother wanted. They strived to control my life, and I thought that getting away would prevent it. That a restraining order would stop Gabe. But even without contact, he's succeeded.

He's won.

*He's won.*

"He's won."

"No, he hasn't."

I don't realize I'm saying the words out loud until their rebuttal is murmured into my ear. Large, strong hands slip beneath my arms and legs to pull me up from the floor—*when did I get on the floor?*—in a cradle position. A solid chest hits my left side as my rescuer breathes soothing words into my ear.

"You're safe. You won," the deep voice repeats through the chaos that's swirling around in my mind. They're a lifevest thrown into the depths of my thoughts, pulling me to the surface so I can finally stop this spiral.

I'm being carried somewhere I think. My feet slide against the doorway to what I believe is my room, then I'm taken a few more steps before I'm being gently laid down onto the bed.

"He won," I repeat the words, because they seem to be the only ones my mouth is willing to form at this point.

The soft cotton of my comforter is draped over my shoulder right before the bed dips behind me, and the same strong arms that carried me here are wrapping around me again, pulling me flush against a warm, solid chest.

A man's chest.

But not Gabe's. I know that for certain.

"Shh, he hasn't won, Stardust," the deep voice coos. "No one will ever violate you again."

This stranger somehow knows what's happened to me. But how?

I turn my head to look back at him, but all I can see through the pitch black of my room is dark hair lying in disarray against my white pillowcase.

The same messy, silky hair that I've been seeing in my dreams since I was in the hospital. How is that possible?

*Who are you, dark angel?*

"Relax, baby. I'm here." His arm tightens across my chest,

and despite my best efforts to hold my eyelids open—to shift and turn my body against him so I can get a better look at his face—I'm completely depleted. My mind fights it, but my body gives out, and within seconds, sleep pulls me under, the sound of rain slapping against my windows a distant memory.

**18**

*The Wolf*

I PROMISED myself I'd take a hands-off approach with her. To look, but never touch. I can rationalize the stalking and meddling so long as it's done for her benefit. I can't say that would be the case when I finally get my hands on her. But she makes it so fucking impossible when she's clearly drowning and no one—not even her useless sister—has come to pull her out of the depths of her mind.

Can't they see her fading away right before their eyes?

I started staying in her spare bedroom to keep a close eye on her. Remotely running a multi-billion dollar company while creeping around in the shadows, dodging creaky floorboards to remain undetected in a house I technically own hasn't been ideal, but I'll do anything to keep her safe.

The figs were once so symbolic for us—a representation of how forbidden and taboo this whole thing once was. And I suppose that's still true, considering she has absolutely no clue that I exist. But no matter what memories her mind decides to hold onto or omit, no matter what twisted lifetime we find ourselves dropped into, she'll always be *mine*. Her soul belongs to me. Nothing about my love for her is taboo or forbidden—it's simply misunderstood by most.

So, while they don't hold the same meaning for me that they once did, I leave the figs to let her know that I'm here. That *someone* is here. And if they happen to spark some sort of recognition in her mind that leads her to remember us, then I would consider that a happy accident.

In true Jovie fashion, she's denied my entire existence. Thrashed and fought against it with all her might. She's allowed them to convince her she really is insane, and it's withered my beautiful little stardust into nothing but black-ened soot.

Thus began the letters. Quick, scribbled musings that I hope will appeal to some deep part of her that may recognize my words.

A quick, *sorry I missed you* or *you looked beautiful today*. A physical token for her to hold in her hands and feel how real I am. To make it impossible for her to deny my existence. It's counterproductive, given my hands-off approach. I have to do something to stop her from self-destruction, though. To turn her away from insanity.

If I could walk into that cottage and bare my soul without terrifying her, I'd do it in a heartbeat. But I owe her space and time. If she's going to find her way back to me, it has to be on her own accord.

Tonight, though… Tonight, I had no choice. She was hurting so deeply and breaking apart right in front of me.

She scared the hell out of me, slipping into a near comatose state as thunder and lightning crashed around her. I had no choice but to pull her into my arms. To feel her and let her know that she wasn't alone. That *he* didn't win shit. And when she finally calmed beneath my touch, I laid with her as she rested. For the first time since I woke up in this hell, I was finally *home*.

I make sure to leave her bed before she wakes. As much as I'd love to look her in the eyes and have her recognize me in the light of day, this doesn't feel like the right time to test her. Not when she's been through so much. Instead, I roll away from her sleeping form and sneak off into the spare bedroom, where I work and monitor, invisible to her eye.

**19**

*The Lamb*

LIGHTNING STRUCK one of the transformers at the end of my street, completely obliterating it. My backyard is filled with tree limbs, leaves, and debris that got caught up in the wind and discarded all around. The electricity company told me they won't be able to get my power back on for at least a week, which gives me no choice but to stay with Halen and Kennedy until it's fixed.

I don't want to. Everything in me is screaming against it, but I could hardly last one night alone in the dark. How am I going to survive a week?

The bright side is that this gives me a chance to take time away from the cottage to sort out my thoughts. It seems the longer I'm here, the more jumbled everything becomes. It's like the old home has a life of its own.

The man was gone from my bed by the time the sun peaked its head over the horizon, stealing away any opportunity for me to get a good look at his face. Not that I was even close to being awake until close to noon.

The more I think about it, the more confused and scared I become.

How did he know I was having a panic attack alone in my living room in the middle of the night? How did he have any idea what I was talking about when I was rambling about Gabe? And how the hell does he look exactly like the elusive figure that's haunted my dreams?

I saw his hair, and I just knew exactly what it felt like. His scent was like a distant memory—a word that sits on the tip of your tongue, but never materializes. I know it, and then I don't.

It makes absolutely no sense, and yet it feels like it's all coming together a little too easily.

The figs… the letters. For some reason, they were easier to digest when there wasn't anything else attached to them besides a mysterious figure in my yard that the police don't even believe is real. Just random objects appearing in my path every once in a while. They could have been for anyone. Now, things feel a lot more complicated. Way more dangerous.

Because he's real. I *know* he's real. I felt him—smelled him. And instead of sending me further into my panic, his presence calmed me. He tethered me to the ground enough for me to gain my footing through the chaotic thoughts.

So, as much as I'm dreading the thought of being back under Halen's watchful and controlling gaze, I'm looking forward to the chance to sort this all out in my mind.

"We had a ton of fun last night. You should have come," Halen tells me, shoving a slice of the pizza that she insisted I bring on my way over into her mouth. Her bloodshot eyes roll to the back of her head in hungover euphoria.

Kennedy just laughs at her, dipping her slice in ranch before delicately taking a bite of her own.

Mine sits untouched beside me on the table.

"Everyone was asking where you were. They miss you," Kennedy says around her food, and Halen grunts her agreement.

"You haven't been answering their calls either, apparently." My sister pins me down with a look that has me shrinking into my chair, ashamed.

"I've been busy with work. It's just me now, and the bills need to be paid."

It's a weak excuse, and they know it. But they can't argue with me. Not when they really have no idea what's been going on in my life. Besides, neither of them have ever had to carry an entire house full of bills on their own. They've always had each other.

"You're just working at that coffee shop, right?" Halen asks, raising her brow at me. When I nod my response, she says, "Your schedule can't be that strenuous."

Something about her tone as she says those words rubs me the wrong way. They're an accusation. A challenge. She doesn't think I've given her enough justification for ostracizing myself from everyone.

She's trying to force me to explain myself like a child who was caught breaking the rules.

Kennedy tenses, tilting her head at Halen like she's reminding her that she's gone off script.

I'm so tired of my sister thinking I owe her my life for what she's done to me—stealing my autonomy and sending me off to a mental hospital so that she didn't have to face the truth. I'm sick of everyone acting like they're just playing along with my temper tantrum before I come to my senses and stop the charade. Like they're holding out for me to crawl back to Gabe with my tail between my legs and an apology on my tongue.

"It's not, actually."

"Then why is it so hard to return a phone call? Or to make time for a dinner date?"

I lean back in my chair, crossing my arms over my chest with a challenging smirk and Kennedy mumbles a curse under her breath. She's been between us for enough arguments to know exactly where this is heading, but she has no idea how much harder I'm willing to fight now. Usually, I'd entertain it for a few minutes before backing down.

That's not me anymore.

They all stole my freedom away. Halen and Kennedy may have done it with good intentions, but it was done all the same.

It's time that they know just how I feel about it.

"It's not hard, Halen. I just don't want to, and given the fact that I fucking fought death to be here, I'm really not interested in wasting my time doing things that don't make me happy anymore."

"Look Jo, we never want to make you uncomfort–" Kennedy begins to soothe, but Halen speaks over her.

"Really? You think hanging out with your sister and friends is *wasting your time*? Get off your high horse and come back to reality, Jovie. We all know you took those fucking drugs yourself. Quit trying to pin it on Mom and Gabe."

Kennedy's gasp fills the space between us—space that feels like it's grown so large, it might as well be a canyon. I rear back, her words slapping me in the face harder than any physical blow she could have delivered.

I knew she felt that way. Every action she's taken since walking into that hospital room has proven as much. But to hear her openly admit it?

*Damn, it hurts.*

I want to throw this kitchen table across the room and shove her face into the wall, screaming every toxic, poisonous word that's rushing through my mind. I want to force her to look at me and just *see* me for once—see the toll that this has taken on me. To force her to *hear* me and believe my story, because every word of it is true and it tears me apart to constantly rehash and relive it, only to have everyone look at me like I'm just a reincarnation of my addict mother.

There's this new rage living inside of me that wasn't present before. One that's begging to be let off its leash.

But then I'd be stooping to her level, and I've worked too hard on healing for that.

Instead, I slowly stand from my chair, grab the duffel bag from the floor beside me, and walk to the back door I just entered less than an hour ago. As I pass my sister, I hold her gaze, realizing how much she looks like a complete stranger.

Siding with the devil has made her so ugly.

"Fuck you, Halen," I grind out, focusing on keeping my head held high.

I refuse to let her witness the way her words sink in and destroy me.

**20**

*The Lamb*

I'M WRITHING against the sheets, my comforter kicked off the side of the mattress, exposing my heated skin to the crisp night air. When I can finally pry my eyes open, I'm met with the bright light of the full moon shining in on me through my bedroom window. My hand moves between my legs on its own accord, swiping my arousal all around my center before I yank it back out, embarrassed.

I haven't ever been this worked up before. I certainly haven't ever woken in the middle of the night with my hand stuffed in my pants on the edge of an orgasm.

Falling asleep was hard enough without a fan or any other white noise to drown out all the random sounds of the house. Once I left Halen's house, I considered asking Rosie if she would let me crash with her, but it felt like too much. I don't want to overwhelm her and chase her off, so I returned home, lit some candles, and worked on my journaling.

When I finally did fall asleep, *he* was in my dreams. The

mystery man who seems to haunt and entice and terrify and electrify me all at once. It's not that I think he's attractive—I've yet to see his full face—it's just the way he holds himself. The way he supports me unconditionally and calms the storm inside of me like no one else can.

I wish so desperately that he were real. And if this is more than a dream, then I wish he were normal. That our paths crossed in a more conventional way, so I'm not left doubting every interaction we have. That whatever version of him that I'm getting is the one he presents to everyone else too, and not just a ruse.

My left hand slips back beneath the waistband of my shorts, fingers slipping into my slit as my right hand reaches into the top drawer of my nightstand for my vibrator. I've only ever used it a handful of times. Gabe never liked that I had one. He shamed me for it the moment I brought it home with hopes of spicing up our sex life.

*"Am I not enough for you?"* He had asked condescendingly before throwing it back into my nightstand.

I wanted to tell him no. That the three times he ever got me off, it was more from my own hand slipping between us than anything he was doing.

Now, I can use it whenever I want. But while Gabe is no longer in the picture, his shameful words still ring in my eyes each time I switch it on.

Tonight is no exception.

After a few moments of rubbing it against my clit, I can't get myself worked up enough to push his ingrained judgment from my mind and enjoy myself. Sighing in defeat, I flip the switch and set it beside me on the bed.

"Don't you dare fucking stop," someone growls low from the darkest corner of my room.

I startle, sitting up on my elbows to peer into the shadows just as he steps forward, revealing the familiar masked face that got me here. His shoulders seem broader in the dark, the shadows clinging to his back like they belong to him. My eyes fall to his unbuttoned jeans, exposing boxer briefs and an impressive bulge beneath.

"Pick that back up and keep going," he instructs firmly, his voice heavy with lust.

I don't move though.

Instead, I stare at him like a deer caught in headlights, my muscles stiff with humiliation as it dawns on me that he's been watching this entire time.

Could I have said anything that would indicate it was my weird attraction to *him* that has me up this late?

When it's obvious I'm not going to obey, he closes the distance between us in two quick steps, digging his knee into the bed beside my hip as he leans forward—over me. His fists land on either side of me, warm skin rubbing against my elbows. The position puts his face a few inches away, and more importantly, his groin hovering above mine.

"If you don't lean back on that pillow, grab the vibrator back up, and run it along your pussy in the next thirty seconds, I'm going to do it for you," he growls, shifting forward so our foreheads connect.

My brow kicks up at the thought of him using it on me. How erotic it would be to have his fingers working against my clit, pleasuring me. It's a sick fantasy that's chased away by common sense a little too late.

I'm already soaked again.

He moans, reading my thoughts far too easily. "Such a naughty girl… Imagining your cum all over a stranger's hand."

Leaning his weight back on his knees, he puts his fingers over the spot I imagine his chin would be, pretending to think. "Or should I use my mouth?"

I squirm beneath him, desperate for friction against my

throbbing center. When he notices my discomfort, he brings his hand down to cup me, applying the smallest amount of pressure that sends shockwaves through my aching core. I let out a yelp, my hips bucking forward. Deeper into his touch.

He snickers at that, shaking his head as he points to the vibrator.

"Use it. *Now.*"

All my self-preservation flies out the window when my hand glides across the sheet and follows instructions, flipping it on. And any humiliation I felt before disappears as he pushes my shorts aside for me as I run the cool tip against my clit.

"Holy shit," I garble, throwing my head back into the pillow. The mere brush of his fingers against my pelvis is enough to send me over the edge, I'm so desperate.

"Ah, that's it, baby. I've been waiting so fucking long for this," the startling admission slides off his tongue in a sultry, smooth voice.

I don't have the capacity to obsess over it right now, though. Not when he guides my hand to push the vibrator up with my center, rubbing it in lazy circles before gently nudging it inside of me.

"You're so fucking wet," he muses, leaning his weight forward to hover over me once again.

Then, without any sort of warning, he pulls the vibrator out of my grasp and brings it toward his mouth, pushing the mask up enough for me to watch as he opens his plump lips and runs his tongue along the hot pink silicone, tasting it. Tasting *me*.

"Mm," he moans, bringing it back down between my legs.

Instead of pushing my shorts aside again, I slip my hand beneath the waistband to set the vibrator against my slit. A low growl rumbles in his chest as he shoves my shorts and panties down my legs in one stroke, nearly ripping them in half with the force.

I kick them off my ankles, sending them flying to the floor as he wraps his palm around each of my thighs and spreads them apart.

This is crazy. Absolutely unhinged. And it's sending me into the most mind-numbing orgasm I've ever experienced.

What does that say about me?

What does it say about him?

"Relax, beautiful," he coos, sensing the shift in my demeanor.

He takes the vibrator and runs it along my slit, then back up toward my stomach in a teasing motion.

It's enough to pull my back out of my head. I squirm beneath him, but he uses his forearms to pin me to the bed as he increases his speed. Then, in one long stroke, he drags the vibrator from the top of my pelvis all the way down to my center, and plunges it in as deep as he can. Until the tips of his fingers nearly sink right with it.

The soft silicone curls inside of me at the perfect angle, reaching the spot that makes my eyes roll into the back of my head. I yelp, pushing my hips forward and the vibrator further in until my orgasm begins to build.

He sits back on his ankles again, pulling himself out of his briefs at the same time he slides the vibrator out of me. I peek down my body long enough to watch him stroke it one time before he pushes the vibrator back inside of me, and I let out another moan.

We only repeat the pattern three more times before I'm falling into euphoria, my screams of ecstasy filling the room so loudly, I'm sure my neighbors will be calling the police over to see what's wrong.

My back arches, center pulsating and twitching as he continues to work the toy on me through the most powerful orgasm I've ever experienced with one hand, while stroking himself with the other. Just as I begin to come down from the high, I hear him groan my name, and then feel his cum land all over my pussy in hot spurts.

He falls forward onto the bed, his weight shifting on his left palm as the other works out the rest of his arousal, sending it flying all over my slit.

"Holy fuck," he groans, out of breath.

His arm gives out, sending him careening into the bed beside me, his head landing directly onto my pillow.

I can hardly focus on that when he's this close to my face, his bright green eyes boring into mine like he sees me beyond whatever physical realm we're in together right now. We're more than just two bodies sweating and rubbing against one another at this moment. We're two souls connecting. Greeting one another after time away.

What just happened between us was the most intimate, erotic thing I've ever experienced with a man, and he hardly laid a finger on me.

I haven't even seen his face.

My eyes drop down to the mask, the fabric rising and falling in quick waves with his erratic breathing.

"You taste so fucking delectable," he muses quietly. "I nearly forgot."

*I nearly forgot.* What does he mean by that?

Reaching my hand down to swipe up some of his cum from my center, I quickly bring my finger to my mouth and suck it clean. He rears back, eyes widened in what I assume is a look of surprise. Or disgust.

"I didn't get to taste you," I explain, taking great care in licking all sides of my finger clean.

The motion doesn't go unnoticed by him, and I don't miss how he shifts himself away from me so I can't feel his arousal.

"And?"

I shrug, pretending to look up at the ceiling in disinterest. "It was okay. Salty."

Another low groan, and he props his head up on his palm. "Be careful, or I'll make you lay back on this bed and take my cock down your throat to give you a real taste."

"Promise?" I tease, licking my lips.

I want him to do exactly that. There's this feral side of me that activates the moment he enters a room. One that can't get enough of him. One that craves the darkest things.

But instead of following through with this threat, he wraps his arm around me and melds his body against mine, cuddling in close.

"Get some rest, beautiful girl. You can take me down your throat another day."

**21**

*The Wolf*

"WHAT IS THIS?" Eliza questions me the following Monday, bursting through my office door without any warning.

She's holding up a piece of paper, shaking it around so furiously, I can't see what's on it.

"I have no idea," I answer honestly, abandoning the spreadsheet I was reviewing to lean back in my chair.

"It's a contract drafted with Hugh Kensington. Isn't he the leader of that boy's club your dad runs?"

Hugh Kensington is the highest ranking Grand Master of the Order. He's also my grandfather's closest friend, and very intertwined in the Lancaster family investment business. He's always treated me more kindly than my grandfather, who will likely go through this whole night mingling with everyone but me.

I have no idea how she recognizes the name without the Order's name associated with it. People usually don't have any idea who he is unless they see him in his environment.

"Yes, he is," I confirm, deciding there's no point in lying to her when she clearly knows more than I thought. Either way, I have no knowledge of a deal with Hugh. "Can I see the contract?"

She flings it onto my desk, then points her finger in the spot where it says his name.

"I respect you, Sebastian, and I care about this company. But please don't tell me you're doing business with those snakes." She wrinkles her nose at the last word, giving away that she knows a little too much about the Order than her pay grade.

Most people have never heard of them at all.

"I don't have any plans to work with Hugh or the Order," I tell her, skimming the document for any indication of what it's about. It's a proposal from him to buy a stake in Lancaster Tech, which is even more odd. Those almost never cross Eliza's desk.

What the hell kind of test is this?

"I thought you were staying away from that crowd," she accuses, pursing her lips.

Dropping the contract, I lift my eyes back to her. "What do you know that you aren't telling me, Eliza?"

Shaking her head, she pushes her chin up in a stubborn pout. "Nothing besides that they're trouble, and the last thing you need is more trouble on your hands."

I shoot her a pointed glare. "I'm a legacy to the brotherhood. My whole family is a part of it and if I wanted to join them tomorrow, they would have to let me."

"What's your point?"

Pushing back into my chair, I point one finger at her. "First, my point is that you don't dictate what I can and cannot do." I hold up a second finger. "Second, you clearly know something that you aren't telling me."

She blanches, crossing her arms over her chest. "Are you

such an arrogant bunch that you don't think other people talk? They might as well be another street gang that everyone avoids for the reputation they've got around here."

I watch her for a drawn out moment, deciding if there's more to her outburst than a simple worry over mixing my business with the Order. She's too good at keeping her expression schooled, though, offering zero tells. We're far too alike than I like to admit.

"You're a good guy, Sebastian. I don't want to see you go down with a bad crowd," she finally says, breaking the silence with her softened tone.

"I don't have any plans to work with them," I assure her, tossing the contract back across my desk to prove my point.

I will, however, be investigating what this whole thing is about. They aren't allowed to touch my business. I've made that crystal clear. Not when there wasn't a single one of them who supported me when my grandfather and father revoked my inheritance to prevent me from starting it.

Eliza rushes out, mumbling something about getting back to her desk for a meeting, and I dial my father's number the moment she's gone.

**22**

*The Lamb*

MY FIRST DAY off from Old Soul is long and lonely. The power was restored after only three days, and by the time my lights flickered back on, I had overcome my irrational fear of being alone in the dark.

Darkness was my enemy. It strangled and choked me, gnawing at my heels and forcing me to relive the night that I was consumed by it. And by some miracle, with the help of this elusive and terrifying figure, I've conquered it. I've forced my eyes to adjust to it long enough for me to see that everything looks the same in the dark as it does in the light—the only difference is fear, and fear is a weakness I refuse to have.

By the time my lamps click back on and light floods the space, I hardly notice it anymore. I've slayed those demons and moved on to bigger problems.

Halen has continued her silent treatment, purposefully ignoring every call or text I send, begging for her to talk this out.

We've argued before—what sisters haven't?—but she's never held her ground this long. If I allow myself to think about it too deeply, I start to resent her even more. Her need to control my every move and emotion is what has gotten us here, and it rivals Gabe's absurd, abusive behavior.

I'm three martinis deep by the time I get the courage to drunk dial her. When the call goes straight to voicemail, I set my drink down on the coffee table, stand up on my couch, and scream into the microphone.

"Get over yourself and call me back, you stupid bitch!"

Satisfied with that message, I end the call and throw my phone onto the floor, bending over to grab my glass back up and take a huge gulp. Music blares through the small speaker I put in the kitchen, and I find myself swaying my hips and singing along in my own silent dance party.

*Fuck friends. Fuck my family. Fuck a boyfriend. All I need is myself.*

When the song ends, I clumsily climb off the couch and grab up one of the figs sitting on the table before me, rolling it around in my hands.

Who does he think he is, coming and going whenever he pleases? Haunting me like a ghost? Following me around like a creepy stalker?

"A ghost?" a deep voice calls from the kitchen just before the music is cut off.

He strolls into the living room, confident and smug. "Clever assessment, I suppose. But a ghost couldn't make you climax the way I can, beautiful little lamb."

My mouth clamps shut, jaw sealed tight. *Did I say those things out loud?*

My mystery man leans against the wall across from me in his usual black attire, only this time, he's left the mask off.

It's got me stunned silent.

"Come on, let me have it," he goads, closing the distance between us. When I do nothing but stare up at him, my mouth wide open like a fish, he smirks. "Oh, now you've got nothing to say?"

"How long have you been here?"

"Long enough to watch you down four of those glasses. I was going to stay away, but I'm afraid you'll drink yourself into a coma if I don't interfere."

*Four glasses?* I could have sworn this was only my third. Come to think of it… maybe I lost count altogether.

His dark chuckle fills the room, the sound so smooth and addicting. I doubt someone like him laughs often. I doubt he even smiles. There's no way he's managed to perfect that sexy, smoldering look without ample practice.

"Dance with me," I blurt out a little too aggressively. I want to take the demand back, but the look of surprise on his face has me biting my tongue.

*Good.* I like keeping him on his toes. He's starting to find me too predictable.

Wordlessly, he obeys, strolling toward me with his hand outstretched. I take it, and he guides me off the couch, catching me just in time before I nearly fall face first into the carpet. Once I'm steadied, he places my arms around his neck, circling his own around my hips.

A fast-paced song begins to ramp up in the background, but he guides us in a slow circle, completely ignoring the tempo bumping around us. When it becomes too much, I lean over and switch the song to one that's much more appropriate.

"This is nice," I mumble to myself.

The alcohol blocks any embarrassment I'd usually have at speaking so candidly. It is nice. Like hitting pause on all the chaos surrounding me and taking a moment to catch my breath without anyone else trying to control my every move.

I look up, and I'm instantly consumed by those light-green irises gazing down at me. So carefully. So lovingly.

He watches me like I'm the only other person in the world. Like every move I make is the most interesting, most outrageous thing he's ever witnessed. The way I always hoped Gabe would look at me, only to turn and find him looking elsewhere.

He watches me like a man in love.

And I'm drunk enough to believe it. To fool myself into thinking this is normal.

My gaze falls to his uncovered lips, grateful that he's finally decided he can trust me enough to take his mask off. He's utterly beautiful. The kind of man that is painted into masterpieces and printed on romance novels. Where every part of me is so average, he feels completely unique. Unattainable. A man who should be with supermodels.

Yet somehow, it's *my* home that he's dancing in on a Saturday night. *My* waist that his hands are tightening around. *My* face that he's admiring so fondly.

"Quit looking at me like that," he quickly mutters.

"Like what?"

Narrowing his eyes, he hums, "like you want me to throw you over my shoulder and take you to bed."

I bite my lip, mind filling with fantasies of us together, the same way they have been since he used my vibrator on me.

His palm presses against my back, pulling me flush against him. He drops his chin on top of my head, his chest rumbling against my ear as he lets out a deep growl.

"I'm trying to be good, little lamb."

"Why would you want to do that?" I ask into his shirt, smirking when his muscles tighten around me in response.

He inhales a breath, pausing for exactly one second before he disappears from against my cheek, and I'm suddenly scooped up into the air. The room spins as he tosses me over his shoulder, slapping his hand against my ass with a loud crack, and then we're off.

I try to wiggle against him but his grip only tightens across my legs, rendering me defenseless.

Moments later, I'm carefully thrown down onto the bed, and then he's climbing up my body, forcing my back against the sheets.

"I only have so much restraint," he grinds out, dipping his head to place a kiss behind my ear.

Then, just as delicately as he held me in the living room, he wraps his fist around my hair and pulls it back, his mouth clamping around my ears right before he bites down, pulling a squeal out of me.

"Please," I beg.

"Please, *what?*" he asks, tugging my hair even harder to force my chin up, exposing my neck. "Say it, little lamb. Tell me how badly you want me to fuck you right now."

"I want it. So much."

"Are you going to be a good girl and do what I say?"

"No."

Another tug, and this time, he nips at the soft flesh of my neck.

"Yes. Yes, I will," I cry out, squirming beneath his weight.

The alcohol blurs my vision and the room spins around me, but I grab onto his torso to center myself.

Sliding down my body, his fingers slip beneath the band of my leggings and tug them down, exposing my legs to the cold air. I shiver, kicking out of them as he rips the pants off my ankles and flings them across the room. His hand caresses up my thighs, squeezing and kneading my muscles as he passes them.

When his fingers reach my panties, he slithers them just beneath the edge, rounding my hip before he pulls them back out and continues to trail them upward—teasing me.

My shirt rises as he places his hands beneath it, moving them upward until they graze the bottom of my bare breasts.

I hiss out an erratic breath, desperate for him to touch my most sensitive parts. To grab my breasts into his hand or reach down and cup my center, the way he had done before.

But he doesn't do any of that. Instead, he flips us over on the bed so I'm straddling his waist. I smile, happy to finally have some semblance of control. Right when I begin grinding my pussy against his erection, he clicks his tongue and lifts me up as if I weigh nothing, then turns me out, away from him.

"What are you doing?" I whine, and then yelp as he smacks me on the ass again—a punishment.

His hands wrap around my hips, pulling them back until my center is perfectly lined up with his face, my knees digging into the bed on either side of his chest. He pushes down on my back, shoving me forward so hard, I have to brace myself on his knees.

With a satisfied hum, he hooks his thumb into my thong, pushes it over, and swipes his tongue along my center in one long, tantalizing stroke.

"Holy fuck," I cry out, leaning further into his knees to give him better access.

He's through with teasing. His tongue plunges deep inside of me, fingers working against my clit and deep into my center as I writhe against him in pure ecstasy. It only takes a few moments for my orgasm to begin building up. My muscles tighten, breath stopping as it rolls through me in waves of pleasure that have me whimpering into his lap.

"That's it, baby. Come on my face," he praises into my center, lapping up every drop.

His grip tightens on my hips to steady me, fingers digging so deep, I know there will be bruises peppering my skin tomorrow. They'll serve as a reminder of how euphoric this is.

Of how *real* he is.

His tongue tirelessly works against me until my muscles relax and the pulsating stops, stringing my orgasm for longer than I've ever managed to do. Once I'm finished and the only noise in the room is our labored breaths, he lifts me up and spins me back around, placing me directly against his solid length.

I lean forward and capture his soft mouth into a grateful kiss that quickly morphs from delicate and appreciative to needy and feral. There seems to be no in-between with us.

Reaching between my legs, I unbutton his jeans just in time for him to shove them out of the way, along with his black briefs. His erection springs free against my thighs and my hands grab it up immediately. It feels so much larger than I remember it being when I watched him stroke it over me.

I pump my hands up and down, making a point to gently caress the tip when I notice how he twitches the first time my palm brushes it. His hips move beneath me, sending him further into my touch with each stroke.

"Sit on it," he instructs, swiping his fingers through my center to check my readiness.

When I don't move right away, he shifts beneath me, grabbing himself out of my hands to line his head up with my entrance.

"I said…" his other hand wraps around my hip to push me backward, giving him full access.

"Sit." His tip swirls around my pussy, spreading my cum around.

"On." It slips inside, and then he throws his hips forward, filling me in one stroke. Large hands wrap around my shoulders and push them down, forcing himself deeper inside of me.

"My cock," he groans, finishing his command before he lifts me up off of him, only to slam himself back inside.

My mind finally catches up, hips rolling with his as he grinds into me, his tip hitting a spot deep inside my pussy that has me throwing my neck back in pleasure.

He grabs up my breast and kneads it, pinching my nipples between his forefinger as his cock slides in and out of me at a faster pace.

"So fucking tight, baby," he muses. "You look like a goddess riding me like that."

I smirk, placing my palm against his chest to steady myself as my hips move with his. The new position provides enough friction against my clit that I start to feel an orgasm build again. This time, I want him to finish with me.

"I'm going to come," I warn him hoarsely.

"Not yet." He pauses his movement, stilling inside of me.

When I scowl down at him in disappointment, he lifts me off and throws me onto my stomach. Seconds later, an arm slips beneath me and yanks my hips upward, positioning me so my ass is up and my face is buried into the pillow.

I'm too drunk to keep up with his quick movements.

There's a loud *smack,* and then my ass burns. "You'll come when I tell you to come. Understand?"

"How am I supposed to stop it?" I whine, my hand instinctively going for my now-throbbing center.

But he swats it away, grinding his own two fingers into my slit as his stiffened cock rubs between my ass cheeks.

"You come when *I* tell you, and not a second sooner," he repeats, his tone more severe.

"Fine."

He gropes my ass, grabbing it up and using it as leverage as his tip finds my center and pushes inside, much slower this time. I can feel every ridge of him as he enters me, then again as he pulls himself out.

And my body immediately reacts.

I try to fight off the building pressure. I attempt to distract myself from what he feels like inside of me, bringing my mind back to my argument with Halen and random tasks I have to do at work and smelly old socks after a long day. None of it works, especially as he picks up his pace and my cheek is ground further into the pillow.

"I'm going to come!" I warn, because it feels completely out of my control.

But I should have kept my mouth shut and taken whatever punishment he planned for me later, because he responds to my warning by pulling out of me completely. Instead of the orgasm my body so desperately craves, I'm left feeling empty and frustrated.

"Goddamnit," I growl, slamming my fist into the bed.

"Should we stop here, or are you going to be a good little lamb and obey my fucking orders?"

Irritating, egotistical man.

"I'll be good," I promise, pushing my ass into the air, because all I want to do is come and I don't think my body is going to get there by my hand alone. "Please."

"Mm, that's right," he coos, rubbing the raw spot on my ass cheek where he's been slapping me. "I'm so close, baby. Just wait for me. We'll come together."

He plunges back inside without another warning, and my orgasm immediately catches back up with me, my center throbbing with the new stimulation. There's no way I'm going to last much longer if he keeps edging me like this.

"Not yet," he warns when I cry out, wrapping his hand around my hips to block my hand from rubbing my clit.

"Please," I beg again, because I'm so fucking desperate to release this pent up energy.

"Ah, fuck," he mutters into my back as his fingers begin working against me again.

"Can I come?" I ask breathlessly, nearly ready to explode.

A second passes without his response, and he pushes himself into me as deep as he can, applying more pressure against my clit. It's my tipping point. I can't hold onto my orgasm any longer.

And just as I begin to release the reigns and let myself freefall into a euphotic abyss, his cock begins to pulsate inside of me.

"Come with me," he says, and I do.

My orgasm rips through me like a tidal wave. So powerful, my legs give out and nearly collapse onto the mattress before he catches me up and pumps the last bit of his arousal deep inside my pussy.

Once he's finished, he gently lays me down on the bed and rubs my back as I process the aftershock of such a powerful orgasm.

"That," I breathe, turning on my side to face him. "Was the hottest thing I've ever experienced."

I've never had a man finish inside of me. Gabe refused to have sex without a condom, even once he confirmed I was on reliable birth control. I thought it was weird that he didn't trust me to go without after years of being exclusive, but I never pushed the subject.

Now that I know how it feels to take a man without anything interfering, I'm addicted. And for some reason, having him fill me with his seed feels a thousand times sexier.

"You need to work on obedience," he mutters beside me, a teasing lilt to his voice.

I reach over and shove his shoulder back, sending him flying into the mattress. He laughs—a beautifully breathy, smoky sound—and then rights himself.

"Give me a few minutes, and we can practice again."

And we did. Twice.

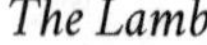

**23**

*The Lamb*

THE BLONDE WOMAN has returned to the cafe every day this week.

Sienna is her name. I learned it on the third day she came in, when Rosie took her order during a rush and scribbled it onto her to-go cup before she handed it over to me.

I think it suits her.

The familiarity I felt on that first day remains unshakable, and I spend more time than I'd like to admit thinking about her. I just know that something isn't right—there's a piece missing from the puzzle lying before me.

It's the same unsettled feeling that the mystery man who haunts my home each night leaves me with.

They both feel like people I've met before—people I've shared experiences with—and yet, I know for certain that I never saw either of them before I went into Sunnybrook.

Sienna always sets herself up at a table with her laptop and a notebook, and then stays for hours at a time. When it's just her and me, she'll strike up random conversation—anything from letting me know she likes a certain song that comes on or rolling her eyes if she thought a customer was rude to me. Other times, we'll sit in silence as I clean up or she types away at something.

I assume she's a student at the university down the street. That would explain why her class and demeanor seems so out of place in our impoverished little city. Unless she's working remotely. Perhaps she can't afford internet, and this is the only place she can do her job.

*No, there's no way that's true. Look at her.*

These are the things I begin to obsess over as I try to work. I've even gone as far as considering she's stalking me, just like the mystery man appears to be doing in my home. They could be in it together. Maybe they're friends with Gabe, and this is how he's managed to keep tabs on me all this time.

"Mmm, I love this one," Sienna calls out, interrupting my spiraling thought process. She bobs her head to the beat of a random song by The 1975. I can't sort through my panicked thoughts enough to identify which one is playing from my personal playlist, but it acts as a bucket of ice water, quickly pulling me back to reality.

I offer her a tight smile, mostly because it feels impossible to form words right now, and then grab my phone to turn the music up a couple notches. Sienna smiles back, unaware of my internal struggle, then goes back to writing in her notebook.

Thankfully, Gabe hasn't made any attempts to reach out to me since that day at Halen's. He has, however, created an entire smear campaign against me with all of our old friends to destroy my credibility.

As horrible as it sounds, I really can't find it in me to care. If anyone truly believes that I'm more capable of attempting suicide than he is of trying to overdose me to gain more control over my life, then they really weren't paying attention to all my silent warnings before. The small crumbs I would leave behind in hopes of someone—*anyone*—finding them and realizing how trapped I really was. I'd do it unintentionally, as if my instincts were acting on their own accord, skirting past my conscious thoughts to sound off warning bells to anyone who might recognize and listen.

That's what my therapist in Sunnybrook told me. She's helped me heal through so much more than just the event that brought us together. We've worked through years of childhood trauma and neglect, and have recently begun digging into the reasons why I am the way I am.

I haven't told her anything about my stalker or Sienna yet. I'm afraid of what she'll say to shatter the illusion I have of them.

Ignorance is bliss, and all.

Anyway, just because he's been staying away doesn't mean he's given up. I've learned that lesson with Gabe the hard way. Although, is it possible that he would go as far as hiring two people to watch me day and night? Especially when the night watcher has also been sticking his tongue inside of me?

Not likely.

And Sienna doesn't seem desperate enough for money to babysit some boring batista. She's clearly here for something else.

*That's all it is. No one is coming to get me. No one is watching me.*

Reminding myself to breathe, I realize I'm just being paranoid.

The song changes to something a little more loud and upbeat, and Sienna stops moving in her seat as I turn the volume back down. I realize a little too late that she's staring at me from across the dining room, brows pulled together in worry.

"Are you okay?" She asks once the music is low enough to hear her.

Nodding a little too fast, I try to smile at her again. When her face falls even further, I'm certain it turns out to be more of a grimace than anything close to the assuring gesture I intended for it to be.

"You went somewhere…" she accuses, shifting her legs around the chair so she can fully face me.

She says those words in a way that makes it sound like she knows me enough to differentiate between me being *here* or *somewhere else.* Which is impossible, considering she's practically a stranger.

"I didn't go anywhere. I'm right here," I stupidly counter, wrapping my hand around my neck instinctually.

"You know, I do the same thing. Certain songs or words will remind me of something and suddenly, I'm taken back to that place…" Her eyes shift somewhere above my head as she speaks, and it appears she's done just that. She's here, sitting before me, but her mind has drifted off.

"I just got caught up in my head," I dismiss.

Sienna appears to snap out of whatever memory she was just pulled into, offering a sheepish smirk identical to the one I attempted earlier.

"If you ever need to talk, I'm here."

*Yeah, right.* The last thing I'm going to do is unload all my baggage onto a random customer. Rosie would probably kick my ass. Then, she'd fire me on the spot. But I won't admit that to Sienna and make this exchange any more awkward than it already is.

"Thank you," I tell her instead.

She sits there for a brief moment, warring with herself over something before finally opening her mouth to speak.

"My brother is one of those fancy business-types in New York," she begins hesitantly, eyeing me closely for a reaction to her opening up. When she takes in my schooled, neutral expression, she allows her face to loosen and light up as she goes on more candidly.

"We're twins, but we couldn't be any more different. He's so serious, and I'm so… *not.*" A chuckle falls from her lips easily, like she's remembering some running inside joke. "But it paid off for him. He skipped college and created the fastest growing tech company in New York. He's probably lounging in his penthouse while I'm stuck here, studying for some useless exam so I can graduate from here and continue into doctorate hell."

"Everyone has their own path to success."

She scoffs. "Yeah, Bash has always followed his own path." There's a small pause, and I assume she's finished speaking, but instead of turning back to her computer, she stands from her chair and walks over to the counter, stopping right across from me.

Her chin dips into her chest as she vulnerably explains, "he went missing a couple months ago. Just disappeared out of thin air for weeks. We didn't know if we should be searching for him or mourning him. The police warned us to prepare for the worst. And then one day, we got a phone call from a hospital just outside of Styx, claiming they thought Bash was their John Doe."

My eyes widen as a gasp leaves my lips before I can stop it. Sienna just nods, as if she's used to that response, and then continues on.

"We never even thought to check this far. He *hates* Styx, and almost never leaves New York anymore. But alas, it was him. I can't even begin to describe the relief I felt when I walked into that hospital room and saw his face." Shaking her head, she drops her gaze to the counter, where her fingers are drawing lazy circles.

"Anyway, those weeks without him were pure torture. It was like I was moving outside of my body—like I was here physically, but my mind was somewhere off with him, wherever he was. And even though he's back and he's safe, sometimes a certain song or smell will catapult me back into that agony. I don't know what kind of demons live in your past, but I'm no stranger to the chokehold they can have on your psyche."

There's a pause—a silence between us that should be awkward, but isn't somehow. She's extending an olive branch toward me. This stranger, who has absolutely no idea who I am or what I've been through, has managed to relate to me better than anyone I've considered a close friend in the past. The bell above the front door jingles as a couple walks in, but I don't react right away.

Sienna does. She straightens, her eyes flicking between me and our new company, and her brows pull together in worry, as if she's only just realized what she's done.

I call out to the couple that I'll be right with them, and then I focus my attention back to Sienna, softly grabbing her wrist just before she turns to walk back to her table.

"I'm sorry that happened. Your pain must have been unimaginable."

"It was."

"Thanks. For making me feel less like an outcast." *For making me feel* normal, *even though I know how far my life sits away from it.*

She purses her lips, nodding. "Anytime, Jovie. We've friends. You can't get rid of me that easily."

*Friends.*

Are we friends? That seems like a generous term for a few conversations in a coffee shop. Perhaps these random, meaningless encounters *have* added up to a small, budding friend-ship between us without me realizing it. I can't figure out if that's good or bad.

Before I can fall too deep into my head about it, I step over to take my new customer's orders. By the time I'm finished with their drinks and they're on their way out the door, I realize Sienna has somehow slipped out without me noticing.

**24**

*The Wolf*

THERE ISN'T an opportunity to ask my father about the contract with Hugh Kensington until the following week at family dinner. My first attempt to bring it up over the phone only led to him brushing it off and playing ignorant. I know that if the conversation is had in person, I'll be able to tell if he's lying or not.

Eliza remains oddly concerned about it. For some reason, she wants nothing to do with Hugh or the Order, and she's made it clear that she doesn't want me involved with them, either.

"Hugh has his hands in everything," my father says dismissively when I ask again over dinner. He holds his phone out in front of him, eyes squinting at whatever is on the small screen.

My mother grows visibly uncomfortable with the mention of Hugh. The moment I brought it up, she rose from her seat and began nervously clearing the table, her hands moving in a blur. Sienna senses the shift and stands to help. He pays her no attention, too focused on his phone.

"I just find it odd that he attempted to draft up a contract requesting an exclusive stake in my company while I was missing," I point out suspiciously, relaxing back into the chair.

"I'm sure he's too busy to bother with whatever you're insinuating, Sebastian," he mutters, looking over at me from beneath a furrowed brow.

Something crashes onto the table, and then my lap is soaked with water. I stand so abruptly, the metal chair I was seated on falls backward as my mother apologizes profusely, grabbing up our discarded fabric napkins to soak up the puddle on the table before it leaks onto me any more. Sienna runs into the house to grab more towels and my father barks out a string of curse words.

"Come on, Sylvia," he angrily berates, pulling his drink out of the soaking mess. His hostile tone only makes her nerves worsen, and she stutters out even more self-deprecating apologies under her breath.

"I just don't like this talk at the dinner table," she mumbles to herself, grabbing up the wad of dripping napkins into her hands.

"It's fine, Mom," I soothe, dabbing at the spot on my pants. "I'm sorry I brought it up."

Sienna rushes back out with more towels and begins sopping up the rest of the mess.

The rest of the night with them is tense and awkward as my father struggles to drop his irritation at my mother for her accident. The conversation about Hugh is effectively dropped and never revisited by the time Sienna and I are walking through the elevator doors to leave.

## 25

*The Lamb*

Styx Thrifts is by far the best hidden gem my hometown has to offer. Jammed into the basement of an old dry cleaner down the street from Old Soul Cafe, it's not usually packed with random tourists or college students, the same way the store near my house is. Most people have no idea it exists. In fact, it took me weeks of working at Old Soul to discover it, and that was only from Rosie mentioning it in passing.

Naturally, they have the most unique and valuable treasures.

I try to stop in after work at least once a week and almost always walk out spending far more than I should on snow globes and random knick knacks. Wendy, the owner, has even started setting things aside for me if she thinks I'll like them. This week, she's showing me a beautiful, fully-crystal snow globe with a metallic-green hummingbird sitting in the center.

"The moment I pulled it out of the box from this estate

sale, I knew it was meant for you," she explains, her eyes lit up in excitement.

She twists the music key three times, then sets it down on the counter as the melody begins, glitter falling lazily around the hummingbird. It's my favorite part of collecting these globes. I wish I could crawl into one of them myself and quietly spin in the peace and calm.

"You always did have a thing for hummingbirds," Gabe's voice startles me from behind.

I do my best to suppress the chill that creeps across my skin, lifting my gaze to Wendy in a silent plea for help when I realize it really is him standing there, mere feet away.

She doesn't catch it, though. Instead, she smiles up at him, nodding her head like she thinks we're friends.

I've never had a thing for hummingbirds. My mother has, though.

"I told her this one was meant for her," Wendy says, eyes bouncing between us as I shrink further into the glass display case behind me.

Gabe just stands there, hands stuffed into his pockets innocently. He allows his gaze to slowly rake down my body, making a show of pretending to be surprised by my cold shoulder.

"I didn't know you two knew each other," Wendy goes on, awkwardly filling the gap in conversation where Gabe and I should be happily greeting one another.

"Of course," he says, smiling over at me sadly. "Jovie and I used to be in a relationship."

Wendy nods once, as if she finally understands the awkwardness between us. She grabs the snow glove up from the counter and mutters something about wrapping it for me, then turns and shuffles away.

"Wendy and I have gotten to know each other pretty well these past few weeks," he explains, shrugging. "I heard that you come in here pretty often. I've been hoping to run into you eventually."

My heart spasms in my chest, stomach sinking. *I've been hoping to run into you eventually.* Gabe doesn't thrift. He doesn't even like used things—always told me they were beneath him. He's been coming here to find me. To pretend we've only happened to cross paths, instead of admitting he's been hunting me down.

Who the hell has betrayed my trust enough to tell him where to find me?

Scowling, I cross my arms over my chest. "You're violating your restraining order."

He scoffs, finally pulling his hands from his pockets to reach out for me. But I step back, escaping his touch.

"Come on, baby. Let's get back to how things used to be and forget about all of this."

Shooting him a narrow look, I drop my hands down to my side, flexing my fists. "I thought my lawsuit against you would be enough indication of what little interest I have in doing any of that."

"I forgive you," he mutters condescendingly, well aware of how much he's testing my patience.

My nostrils flare as angry heat floods my cheeks. I can barely speak. He's got me cornered in the back of this shop, his body positioned perfectly in my way so I can't drop my head and leave the way I want to. He thinks he can force me to have this conversation with him right now. That he can convince me to throw myself at him and beg him to take me back.

He senses it—my need to escape. My stomach coils in terror as his entire demeanor shifts, eyes darkening and muscles flexing as he anticipates the fight I'm planning to put up.

"Is there anything else you had your eye on?" Wendy's

voice calls from the back just before she breaks through the doorway.

Gabe slightly jumps, and I sigh in relief. "That's it, thank you, Wendy. I have to get going. I'm already late meeting a friend."

I come up with the lie on the spot, hoping that if he thinks someone is expecting me, he'll be discouraged from trying to grab me up as soon as we leave and drag me over to his car. Would he be willing to risk it?

She announces the total and I hand over the cash, telling her to keep the change so I can get out faster. I don't have time to wait for her to go into the back and run my card or pry the register open and count out the cash.

Gabe pretends to busy himself with random things around the shop as we complete the transaction, conveniently placing himself by the front door by the time we're finished.

"I'll walk you to your car," he says as I pass him, loud enough for Wendy to hear. With a quick wave to her over his head, he follows me out the door.

Once we're closed off in the dark stairway, he grabs my arm and slams my back into the wall.

Leaning his body against mine to pin me to my spot, he places his lips against my ear and whispers, "You need to drop the act and come home. It's been long enough."

I try to lift my hands to shove them against him, but he quickly wraps his thick fingers around my wrists and holds them down, sending the box with my snow globe crashing to the floor.

"What are you going to do, Gabe? Tie me up and throw me in your trunk?" The words come out in a vicious snarl, but my lungs constrict as the panic settles in.

He could do just that. He *would*, if it meant getting his way.

"Consider this your warning. If you don't drop these bull-shit charges and get rid of the restraining order, I'm going to be forced to take extreme measures."

"Or, you could fuck off and leave me alone," I spit, fighting against him.

"I didn't go through all of this just to let you go that easily. I'm going to make this right."

With one last squeeze around my wrists—so tight, my hands nearly go numb—he throws them against the wall and steps back. I'm frozen to my spot, eyes wide as I wait for whatever he plans to do next. It feels like I've been electro-cuted, my anxiety and panic zapping me through the chest as I enter fight or flight, the way I always do around him now.

Gabe turns to take the first step, swiveling his head to glare at me, teeth bared. I've gotten under his skin. At the last second, he starts toward me again, slamming his foot into the box sitting beside my feet. The snowglobe explodes, glass splintering all around as the liquid and glitter spill on the ground. I jump, shrinking further into the wall with a wince as I anticipate a second blow that never comes.

When I open my eyes again, he's already climbed halfway up the stairs, shoulders pushed back in confidence. My cowardice has only inflated his ego.

I wait until he's out the door before I slide down the wall and crumple in on myself, allowing the tears to fall.

## 26

*The Lamb*

Sobs wrack my body as I shove my face into the pillow, hands frustratedly clenching the sheets beneath me.

*I'm broken.*

That's what they all think. That's the excuse they use to explain away my behavior instead of listening to me. Instead of hearing the words I've been screaming from the top of my lungs and *believing* them.

They want me to be suicidal. They think it's easier to accept that I'm an addict like my mother than to admit they may have misjudged Gabe's character. My insistence that they've got it wrong makes them uncomfortable, so they avoid and deny. And in the process, they invalidate my entire experience.

I'm so tired of it. I'm exhausted from explaining myself to people who I shouldn't need to explain to. So, I pull away, and that makes them angry too. There is no right answer anymore. Not unless I want to shred myself apart to fit in the tiny boxes they want to shove me into.

That is absolutely not an option.

The bed dips behind me, and I panic for a fraction of a second, before the calm sweeps in and chases it away.

All of it.

The hurt, the sorrow, the betrayal.

It's like his spirit is a repellent fog, lazily flowing through the room until everything is clear and I can breathe again.

"Shh, you're safe," his low, soothing voice coos against my ear as long, gentle fingers brush through my hair.

I remain silent for a few moments, enjoying his presence before I'm bombarded with more intrusive thoughts. Like wondering who he is and how he's here? And crucifying myself for allowing this to go on.

"The last man I trusted ended up trying to kill me," I admit quietly.

"I'm not like him," he mumbles into the back of my head, his arm stiffening against my hip.

He speaks as if he knows what I'm talking about. *Who* I'm talking about. Heaving out a sigh, I allow myself to believe him. Just for now. For the sake of this moment.

My thoughts stray to this morning, when Gabe stopped me outside of work. He looked different than I remember—so angry and ragged. Where I've concentrated my efforts on forgetting about him and moving on, he seems to be doing the opposite, his feet stuck firmly in the past.

"I wish I never met him." I surprise myself by saying the words out loud.

Everyone has gaslit me into thinking Gabe is a good man. That this was an isolated incident—if they even bother calling it that—and alluding to the fact that he may have a part in any of it. They want to overlook every warning sign he's thrown up and blame me for all of it.

But he isn't a good man. He used and abused me for years, taking advantage of my desperation and fear of losing him to exploit me. Ending our relationship was the best thing that could have ever happened to me. Even if it only happened because he killed me.

"I wish that, too," a deep voice grumbles into my back, reminding me of his presence.

And I don't know what it is that makes me say it—perhaps it's the candidity of the moment, or the vulnerability I'm feeling from the freshness of his visit, or something else entirely—but I open my mouth and utter the words I've been stamping down each time they claw their way up into my throat.

"I wish I could have killed him instead. Or at least been able to take him with me."

His head lifts from the pillow, and I feel his eyes boring into my hair. But I'm too afraid to turn and face him after what I've just said.

"You think that would have made things easier?"

"Easier than having to face him whenever he chooses to ambush me? Than relying on some piece of paper to keep him away? Yes, it would be way easier if he were dead and gone."

The admission is poison stinging my tongue. I shouldn't have said it—I know that. Those kinds of things are better kept to myself, especially if you don't want them to come to fruition.

But holy shit, do I mean it. I hate him. I can't fucking stand what he's done to me and how he's imploded my entire existence for a shred of control over me. As if what I already gave him wasn't enough. In true Gabe fashion, he took and took and took, until there was nothing left for me to give. Until it was my *life* he was greedily reaching for, and even then, he didn't stop.

I wait for the reprimand to come. For the guilt and shame to be cast upon me like it always is.

*You shouldn't wish ill on people like that, especially someone who loves you.*

That's what Halen would say. She'd berate me until I took it all back and apologized, betraying my own feelings to seem like less of a problem.

The mystery man never does any of that. He remains still behind me, hardly breathing. It's to the point where I doubt he's there anymore. I would think he got up and left if it weren't for his weight against my back. Just before I muster up the courage to look behind me and witness what I assume will be his horrified expression, he finally speaks.

"He came to see you?" He grinds out, fingers paused at my neck before he inhales a long breath and moves them down my back in a long, comforting caress.

"Of course, he did. Because that's what he does. He pushes and pushes and ignores every boundary I put between us until I break down and give him whatever he wants," I ramble, throwing my hands around in frustration and opening the floodgates when it appears he's giving me the space to do so. "God, I hate him so much."

"He would be better off dead," my mystery man agrees grimly, and I nod my head, ignoring the feeling that I shouldn't speak such things about a man I claimed to love for years.

"I'd certainly be happier if I didn't have to deal with him."

We drop the conversation after that. I feel like a weight has been lifted from my chest after admitting all the horrible things I've been feeling since that night Gabe tried to kill me. I know it's dangerous to allow this man so close to me—in my bed, against my skin. There's just something about him that stops me from pushing him away.

He doesn't judge me for the things I've had to do in order

to survive the mess that has become of my life. In an unexpected, twisted way, he's become my safe space to admit my worst, most toxic thoughts out loud. How is it possible that a complete stranger—a man who has helped himself into my home against my will—has become my sanctuary? I truly don't know, and I don't have the mental capacity to overthink it, either.

After a few minutes of silence, I turn in my spot to face him. Those ethereal, green eyes blink at me unassumingly, patiently waiting for me to decide my next move.

"Touch me," I whisper weakly, my self-consciousness forming a lump in my throat.

He doesn't hesitate or question me. Instead, his hand lifts from the spot it was resting between us and cups my cheek.

"You're worthy of so much more than he was willing to give you," he mutters under his breath, fingertips grazing against my jaw and over my chin before his thumb caresses a circle around my bottom lip.

With one subtle shift, his thumb is pushed into my mouth, stealing away my breath as it moves past my teeth and toward my throat. I tighten my lips around his knuckle, swiping my tongue along the pad of his finger and pulling a groan from deep inside his chest.

My hands reach up to catch his wrist and guide his fingers across my skin, but the moonlight catches the bruises Gabe left on my wrist and he pulls away from me. He shifts on the bed, gripping my arm to hold it further into the light.

"He did this." Not a question.

There's no use in lying. "Yes."

"Did he attack you when he came to see you today?"

"No, he just wanted to scare me," I openly explain, because I don't feel like I need to filter things with him anymore. Not since I've already admitted so much.

"I'm sorry," he mumbles sadly, dropping my palm.

I shrug, numb to all the terrible things Gabe has done by now. I just want him out of my life. "He's a controlling asshole. I knew my restraining order would piss him off."

He lays back into the bed, disappearing into his head. He doesn't pull me to his chest or cuddle me like usual. In fact, his whole mood has shifted, and the intimate moment we shared before is long gone.

I lie onto my pillow next to him, each of us staring up at the ceiling as we process.

"I don't want him to hurt you again," he tells me softly, draping his arm across his forehead.

"Neither do I," I agree.

It's the last thing I said to him before drifting off to sleep.

**27**

*The Wolf*

GABE IS easy to find once I slip away from Stardust's sleeping form late that night. I've been tracking his phone since I bought the Crystal Cottage with the intention of having her move into it, too afraid to risk having him sneak back in and take her from me. If I'm completely honest with myself, I should have done this the moment I got Sienna off my back after I left the hospital. For some reason, I felt like I needed Stardust's permission to kill him, though. Like I couldn't take the option away from her if she wanted to do it herself.

Not that she'd ever want to take a life.

When she admitted that he tried to see her today, I nearly lost it. Where she is light and love and everything good in the world, I bleed black. I crave revenge and flourish in darkness. Where she breathes life, I breed death.

He's breaking her spirit. Picking it apart piece by piece in a methodical way that makes her feel like it's happening naturally. Like she's going insane. I refuse to allow it to go on. Not after I've seen what can happen if I wait.

I park outside his house and pull up my map, following his dot drive home from a local pub a few minutes away. It's the same house I sat in front of *before*, when I watched him through the window as I pleasured myself to thoughts of Stardust. Too many times, I've considered where we would all be right now if I had just walked through his front door that night and slit his throat then.

Would I still have been catapulted into this hell?

My car idles across the street as he pulls into the driveway like a bat out of hell. I hide behind my tinted windows, watching in disgust when he falls out the driver's side and stumbles up the porch steps, walking right through the unlocked door.

This will be an easy kill, I can already tell. Not exactly who I would have chosen to break myself in, but he's been high on my list for a while. Might as well knock it out.

It'll be cathartic for me—an easy transition back to the Serpent Slayer.

Back to myself.

I linger in my car for a few moments, allowing him time to settle in before I'm squeezing between his car and the house on my way to the side door. I've scoped out the place enough to know that this is the door he usually comes through. The bedroom—*her* old room—sits on the opposite side of the house, down the hall and to the left. Sneaking in through this side gives me a chance to get eyes on him before he realizes I'm here. Although, based on how intoxicated he was when he walked in, he'd probably hardly notice me either way.

The door creaks as I open it and slip into the basement stairway, immediately pushing myself into the dark corner when I see that the kitchen light is on.

Two people stand against the sink together in a tight embrace. I immediately recognise Stardust's sandy hair, tied up into a messy, loose ponytail. It takes a moment for me to realize that isn't her wrapping her arms around his neck, practically sucking his tongue down her throat. The limited view I have of the woman's profile slightly shows more weathered, aged skin.

This must be her mother.

Locking lips with her ex boyfriend, further proving Stardust's story to be right.

My fists flex at my sides, fingers brushing against the knife I secured in my pocket before walking in here. I should slaughter them both right here. Carve their bodies up and leave them to bleed out beside one another, so the truth of what they've done is impossible to deny anymore. So their sins against the woman I love are finally paid for.

But she didn't say anything about wanting her mother dead, and I don't want to take something from her that she's not ready to lose.

Gabe pulls away, swiveling his head around to stare into the dark stairway, where I'm standing. His eyes squint, then widen, a forced attempt to focus through his intoxicated state.

"Did you hear that?" he asks the woman, who has moved her attention down to suckling on his pale, freckled neck.

"Mmm?" she mumbles into his skin.

He grabs her shoulders and shoves her backward, not even bothering to see if she's okay when she loses her balance and her ass slams onto the floor. She grunts, then moans as her hand crosses her chest to caress her elbow, which seems to have taken the brunt of her fall.

Gabe ignores it, stepping over her sprawled-out body to approach the back door. I'm positive he's about to find me, readying myself for a fight, when at the last second, with only a few inches separating us, he stills in the doorway. Llistening.

I could kill him right now. All I'd have to do is swing the knife around the thin wall that is concealing me from his view. He wouldn't have any idea that it was coming. Stardust's mother is so out of it, I could walk right past her and to the front door, and she'd have no idea what happened.

But that's not how I wanted to do this. I need it to be neat. I need it to look like an accident—like he did it himself. I want to steal away all his credibility. To thoroughly humiliate him as he humiliated Jovie.

So, I wait with bated breath, tucking myself further into the corner so he doesn't realize I'm here.

Gabe's arm reaches forward, and I think there's no doubt that he must know I'm here. But instead of grabbing me up and attempting to pull me out of the shadows, he goes in the opposite direction and tugs on the screen door until it latches closed with a loud *click*.

All I can do is blink, too afraid to even exhale a breath onto his arm and expose myself before I'm ready as he leans even further to grab the storm door and slam it shut. The wind blows into my face, rustling my hair as he quickly twists the lock and then backs away.

"You need to be better about locking these damn doors," he berates the old woman, who is still groaning on the floor.

She's obviously too intoxicated to say much else.

"Anyone could walk through here," Gabe goes on. There's a loud scraping noise as he drags what I assume is a chair across the floor. The woman yelps, and then there's a loud *harumph* as he hoists her onto the chair.

"Jovie was never this much of a lightweight," he grumbles, out of breath.

"Jovie never drank," the feminine voice slurs, then hiccups. "Jovie wasn't fun like I am."

There's a loud *smack*, followed by a cry of pain. "Don't ever speak about her," he commands, his tone severe.

I step forward, ready to throw my entire plan out the window and carve into him the way I so desperately want to. When his swaying body fills my vision, I see that she's leaning forward, her head resting in her arms on the table. She's passed out. Likely been knocked out of consciousness with his hit.

He stands over her crumpled form with a syringe in his hand, the needle poised against her skin. All my self-control dissipates as the scene before me unfolds, nearly identical to what I assume happened to my beautiful little lamb on the night she was killed.

He's trying to do it all over again.

"Don't make another fucking move," I call to him, taking the step up into the kitchen to reveal myself.

"Who the fuck are you?" he barks, tripping backward, into the wall.

I don't answer. It doesn't matter who I am. I'm not going to give him the benefit of knowing. When I take his life, I want him to be just as confused about what's happening as he ensured Stardust was. Instead of responding, I rush toward him and rip the syringe out of his hand, turning to grab the vial he left sitting on the table.

This seems like the perfect way to end him, and he's practically handed it over to me on a silver platter.

Dipping the needle in, I suck up the rest of the liquid to fill the barrel, then throw the glass down onto the ceramic floor. It shatters around my boots, landing in tiny little shards on top of Stardust's mother's bare feet.

Gabe turns to run, slamming his shoulder into the wall before he moves over toward the doorway and breaks free of the kitchen. Heavy footsteps shake the floor and rattle all the photos lining the walls of the tiny living room. I leisurely follow behind him, stopping when my gaze shifts away from his receding back to look into Stardust's smiling face beside me.

They appear to be at a wedding in the photo. Gabe stands behind her, his reddened face resting on her shoulder as his arms wrap tightly around her waist. She's wearing a light pink, silky dress that hugs all her curves. It matches his tie. They must have been in the wedding party together, because there's a group of people dancing behind them in the same shade of pink. The smile she's donning doesn't seem to reach her eyes at all.

In fact, if I were to cover the bottom half of her face completely, she would look more terrified than excited.

There's another one beside it of them sitting at a bonfire with four other people. Everyone is smiling at the camera, holding their drinks up in *cheers*. Except for Stardust. She's facing the camera, but her eyes are twisted on Gabe, who is holding an iPhone over the flame, threatening to drop it in.

There's got to be at least twenty more lining the walls, each of them framed in collages labeled *Family* and *Memories*. Photos documenting small moments of their life together that they thought were happy or fun. And in every one, Stardust looks more uncomfortable.

This was her life before me. These are the people she's lost because of the coward in the other room.

There's a loud crashing noise at the end of the hall, followed by a string of curse words. Metal clangs on the wooden floor and I take the three steps into the small hallway to see Gabe on his hands and knees, scrambling to gather bullets before they roll beneath the bed.

He doesn't hear me approach in his panicked state. Doesn't even look up as I glare down at him from the doorway, my shadow looming over his pathetic figure. One step, and my boot is covering the hand that holds the gun, my weight pressing down until I hear bones crack and he cries out in agony. Oops. That will confuse the coroner.

When I pull my weight off, his fingers remain splayed out, unable to grasp the gun lying beneath them. I kick it under the bed, then crouch down beside the sputtering piece of garbage and grab his collar, yanking him up like a rag doll the same way he did to Stardust's mother.

"I'd love to take my time here with you, but I've got to get back to my girl," I tease into his ear before throwing onto the unmade bed.

He just looks up at me, eyes wide as saucers and spit flinging around his lips as he begs for mercy.

*I missed this.* The power and control over a situation. The weight of another man's shitty life in my hands.

I ignore his bumbling, leaning onto the bed to place my knee into the center of his chest and steady him. He tries to flail around and fight when my hand wraps around his thick arm and pins it to the mattress, but he's far weaker than I am, especially in his intoxicated state.

*What did Stardust ever see in this guy, anyway?* He looks like a toad, all freckles and blemishes and scabs.

I have no intention of ever finding out. Hopefully, his death will bring her enough peace to stop giving this waste of a human any more thought.

"Jovie looks positively miserable with you in all those photos," I mumble absentmindedly into his ear.

It bothers me more than I thought it would—seeing her with him. His hands pawing all over her body. I thought I could handle it, especially with the assurance that he'll never touch her again. But I didn't expect to see so much evidence of her being unhappy. I guess I assumed that her misery started when he tried to take her life to control her. Every inch of this house holds evidence that it went on much longer than that.

Which begs the question: has she ever truly been happy before? Or has her entire life been filled with hardships and torment?

Judging by what I heard come out of her mother's mouth earlier, I'd have to guess the ladder.

Gabe's glossy stare bores into me, and I can see it in there—the masculine urge to defend what he thinks is his. To break free from my grasp and piss in his property. It may have been a mistake to mention her name before I had a good grip on him.

Thankfully, he's inebriated. Even if he could somehow build up enough adrenaline to throw me off his thick, hump of a body, his reactions would be too slow to stop me from retaliating.

Almost as if he can sense this hopeless fact, he deflates beneath me. Bringing the needle up to his skin, I do a quick scan for any other track marks to let me know where he usually goes. There's a small scattering of red dots and scabs on his inner arm, so that must be the best spot to hit.

"She's so fucking beautiful when she comes," I muse, buying myself time as he half-heartedly fights against me. It's almost like he *wants* to die.

Such a disappointing, anticlimactic kill.

I continue in my own sick attempt at rousing him. I expected more of a fight tonight and he's giving me nothing. "Have you ever seen it? I doubt you have. The way her eyes roll to the back of her head... her sultry moans..."

*Fuck*, I'm getting hard just thinking about her.

While straddling another man. This is a new low for me.

I'll just have to find a new victim to have my fun with. He's pathetic.

I shift my weight, my knee pressing further into his chest as I squeeze his arm to swell his veins, then jab the needle into the biggest bulge.

"Don't worry, I'll take great care of her," I whisper into his ear as the liquid floods his veins.

There's a quick flash of recognition across his features before the drugs take over and his eyes shutter closed. When I'm sure he's knocked out, I climb off of him and step back, watching the rise and fall of his breaths as they grow slower and more shallow.

Witnessing the moment a soul detaches from a body is therapeutic for me. A special, quiet blip in time where free will is ripped away and the universe forces its hand. Death's sweet lullaby sounds from a distance, calling him toward her.

We're good friends, me and Death. I've kept her fed and she's given me another chance with the love of my life. I once thought us enemies. Back when Jovie was taken from me before I could truly have her. And again when I woke up in that hospital and Jovie wasn't there.

I was wrong.

With one foot in the physical realm and another behind the veil, I watch her grab Gabe by the hand and hug him into her side comfortingly, the two forms fading away as I feel myself returning to the living. At the last second, she swings her shoulders back to look at me, and I'm met with the most severe, most beautiful face I've ever laid eyes on. One that causes my heart to sputter and stop in my chest.

Because I recognize that face instantly.

It's Sienna.

*The Lamb*

> Halen: Gabe was found dead in his house this morning.

THE NOTIFICATION of Halen's text wakes me from a fitful sleep.

That's all she wrote. No explanation. No emotion. Straight to the point.

I try to call her, but it goes straight to voicemail. I don't get an answer from Kennedy's phone, either. It's the first form of communication I've received from either of them in weeks. Devastating, soul-shattering news.

My mind immediately returns to conversation from last night.

*"I wish I could have killed him instead."*

*"You think that would have made things easier?"*

He did this. There's no doubt about it. I told him I wished Gabe was dead, and he did it.

What have I done?

What have I *done?*

Somehow, as if my thoughts have conjured him into existence, his dark form fills my bedroom doorway.

"Did you do it?" I ask, too wound up to bother with dancing around the subject.

I know the answer, anyway. Even before the recognition flashes across his face, quickly morphing into unapologetic resolution.

His lips tighten into a thin line, refusing to admit his crimes.

"I told you that I wished he was dead in a moment of weakness, and you went and fucking *killed* him," I exclaim in disbelief, throwing my hands around.

Brow quirking, he stubbornly straightens his shoulders. "He was an open end that needed closing," he replies in that cold, detached tone he gets.

"He was a *person*! I loved him!" I cry out, hiccuping in a sob.

I should be surprised by the deep, severe scowl that he pinches his face into. By the casual way he shrugs his shoulders. The dismissal of a human life.

"You were terrified of him. There's a difference."

Swinging my legs off the side of the bed, I stomp over to where he stands. "You don't have any clue how I felt about him. He was the love of my life."

Even as I say it, I know that's not true. There was a point in my life where I thought Gabe was it for me. I wanted it all with him—the fairytale dream that every girl hopes for. It was so easy to wish for those things when he treated me like his queen.

There wasn't a crazy, deep dive into the abusive situation we ended with. Little by little, he started shifting. So subtle, I didn't notice the trap was being set until I was caught in it. And then, I fought like hell to get out of it.

Gabe may have been in it for the control. To prey on a woman he saw as weak and fallible. But none of that negates the feelings *I* felt—the love I had for him.

There's a quick flicker of emotion that I haven't seen him wear before, but it's gone before I can identify what it was.

"He manipulated and controlled you well before he put that needle in your arm. Don't allow your grief to confuse love with infatuation over the false reality you built in your head just to survive him. None of that was real."

"And which category do you suppose you fall into? Terror or love?"

His eyes flash, a conniving, evil smirk tugging at the side of his mouth. Closing the distance between us in one short step, he wraps his palm around the front of my throat, tugging my face toward his. Strong fingers press deep into my skin, threatening to cut off my air supply.

"You can pretend to everyone else that the terror you felt near him was love. That you stayed through all the abuse because you were the dutiful, obedient little girlfriend he painted you as. I don't give a fuck about that." I try to swallow, my throat flexing into his grasp as he pulls me even closer, grinding his forehead into mine.

"But don't try to tell me that *this* doesn't electrify you. That my hand around your throat doesn't have your panties soaked. You can't lie to me, Stardust. You aren't terrified. You're finally *living*."

Shifting my hips, I internally curse my traitorous body. He's right. I'm so fucking turned on by this. But that doesn't change what he's done.

"You *murdered* him," I grate through his hold.

*Focus on the facts, Jovie. This man is a cold-blooded killer with his hands around your throat.*

He sneers. "Trust me, it would have happened whether I was there or not."

"I had him handled."

His hand releases me from the hold he had, pushing me backward hard enough that I stumble into the dresser. "Did you? Is that why you've been sitting here alone, day after day? Trapped in panic attacks while he fucks your mom behind your back?"

My eyes widen, heart splintering into tiny shards. I want to pick one up and stab him in the neck for speaking such crass words to me. For being just like everyone else and weaponizing his knowledge against me.

He knew I'd be destroyed by that discovery. He timed his delivery perfectly for his own agenda. Just like Gabe, he traps and manipulates me.

*No more.*

"You're a monster," I seeth, rushing toward him to shove my palms against his shoulders.

He's taken off guard, tripping backward one step. When I come after him a second time, my vision filled with reddened rage, he catches my wrists into his hand, pinning them together against my stomach.

"Me? A monster?" He barks out a laugh as I struggle against him. "Oh, little lamb, you haven't even seen the worst of what I can do yet."

"Fuck. *You.*"

"Good. Get angry. Show your fucking teeth and use this rage against someone who deserves it. Stop lying down and taking all this bullshit from everyone who claims to love you and defend yourself for once," he shouts at me, twisting us around so my back is to his chest, his fingers still wrapped around my wrists to stop me from pummeling him. "Or they're going to trample you into dust."

"I can't!"

"Why?"

"Because…"

"Why, Jovie? Tell me why you won't bite back at them the way you do to me. Why do you allow them to treat you this way?"

"Because…" I search for an excuse, but only one comes to mind. The cold, hard truth. Once I'm faced with it, I can't get it out of my mind.

"I'm weak," I sob, falling onto my knees. "Because I'd rather be alone than be hurt by the people I love so much."

His feet shift against the carpet before he kneels before me. The same palm that has bruised my wrists now caresses my back comfortingly. I don't look up, though. My face stays buried in my lap, tears streaming from my eyes and gathering into puddles on the floor.

"You deserve more than that," he mumbles, his lips brushing against my scalp in a kiss.

"No, I don't," I quietly disagree.

"Yes, you do," he insists, snaking his arm behind my knee, the other one supporting my back as he lifts me into the air. "You deserve the world—the entire fucking universe. And I absolutely refuse to stand by and allow anyone to treat you any less. Consider his death a warning to everyone else in your life."

"Don't you hear how terrifying that sounds? How are you any better than he is?"

With his face still in the same stoic grimace, he simply says, "I have no limitations when it comes to you."

"You need to leave," I insist, coiling away from his touch when he reaches out for me with those deathly hands.

"Fine," he relents, dropping his head.

I silently watch with conflicting emotions as he turns for the door and walks out without saying another word.

And then, I allow the tears to freefall.

**29**

*The Lamb*

GABE'S FUNERAL IS TODAY. I've been torturing myself over the past week, cycling through conflicted emotions. It's my fault he's gone. Regardless of what the mystery man said about closing a loose end, it was my moment of vulnerability that caused him to go there and murder him in cold blood. It feels inappropriate to mourn him beside a crowd full of people who have no idea what the truth is.

Alongside all the grief and guilt is something I never expected to experience—relief. Every time the feeling comes sneaking in, I have to push it aside and remind myself that he was once my entire world. That I planned a life with this man, and his actions against me don't give me the right to be equally as cruel.

He was found in his bed, body stiff and eyes wide open. An overdose is what they're saying, but I know better. Even if those drugs were his, they were pushed into his system by someone else, the same way he had done to me.

The worst part? It was my own mother who found him in bed the next morning.

The mystery man wasn't bluffing when he told me they'd been fucking behind my back. Once word got out that she was destroyed over it, people began realizing how much sense my story made.

His mother opted to host the 'celebration of life' at the restaurant on the end of our street instead of a funeral home. I haven't so much as driven in that area since the day I was taken away in an ambulance. Even when I lived with Halen and Kennedy, I actively went out of my way to avoid being here.

It all looks the same, but couldn't feel any more different. These are the roads I took when I was fighting to survive each day. When I was operating solely in survival mode, following a gross pattern of wake up, work, suffer, sleep.

It was complete misery. I realize that now more than ever.

I have no intention of staying long enough for a reunion with all the people who abandoned me when I needed them most and listening to their whispered apologies as the truth dances around right before them. Gabe was my first true love, but he was terribly abusive and he caused more harm than good in my life. Mourning with his friends and family feels incredibly wrong.

Instead, my plan is to get there early, offer condolences to his mother and brothers, and then leave within the half hour.

Unfortunately, my own mother is there, helping his family set up when I enter the restaurant. She's the first to spot me lingering awkwardly in the doorway, debating whether I should turn and run or follow through with the original plan.

"How nice of you to show up," she sneers, abandoning the photo poster she was hanging on the wall to stride over to me. It falls to the floor in a heap, knocking some of the photos off. I can tell within the first three steps she takes that she's using again. Gabe seems to have had the exact influence on her that I thought he would.

"I wanted to pay my respects," I explain meekly, waving at his mom when she turns to see who my mother is addressing so harshly.

I've always gotten along well with his family, as much as he wished I didn't. Gabe was of the opinion that he was better than his single mother and blue-collar working brothers. He always tried to inflate our financial situation to make it appear like we had more than they did. I thought they were kind enough people, regardless of their wages.

Gabe was hardest on the people who loved him most.

I can only imagine what sort of lies he spun to them about me.

"That's ironic, considering how you abandoned him," my mother slurs into my face, stepping over to block my view of Gabe's family.

They just tuck their heads down and get back to whatever they were doing before, avoiding the altercation.

Focusing my attention back on her, I fake a grimace. "It seems like you didn't waste any time taking over for me."

"He certainly enjoyed the upgrade." Running her eyes up and down my body in a cruel assessment, she crosses her arms over her chest, proud of the sick insult.

*This was a mistake.*

I've hardly begun to scratch the surface of the damage they've done. Putting myself in a position to be abused all over again before I've come up with effective defenses against them was premature and stupid on my part.

I can't blame my mother for being exactly who she has always been.

I blame myself for thinking I could handle it.

Holding up my sympathy card, I gesture my head toward Gabe's mom. "I'm just going to give his mom a hug and be on my way."

"No one wants you here," my mother snarls venomously, and behind that nasty, jealous expression, I can see the hurt she feels.

As with everything else, Gabe has poisoned my relationship with my mother to exercise his control. I had the rude awakening when she sat beside him as he pressed the fatal dose into my veins, and I'm being forced through it again now that she's staring at me with a hate in her eyes that could have only been placed there by someone spewing lies.

What sort of emotional torture was she put through when I left? What kind of mind games has he played to turn a mother against her own daughter?

I want to grab her hands and apologize for leaving her behind in a situation that I knew was toxic. Hell, for even introducing Gabe into our lives in the first place. I want to tell her that I forgive her for what she's done, and remind her that time is fickle and never guaranteed.

And that's when I realize that I'm more healed than I thought. It's when it becomes glaringly obvious that weeks in a mental hospital and therapy have actually amounted to something. The old me would have allowed her words to sink in and fester inside of me. They would have taken hold of my emotions for days and convinced me to spew the same venom back at her.

I've spent enough time in peace that the anger I held inside of me over that fateful night and everything that came of it has dissipated. If they want to believe the lies Gabe told them or doubt my intentions, then that's a conscious choice they're making to remain stuck in the past—a past they have no true understanding of, if their information comes from my abuser.

"Fine," I relent, setting the card down on the nearest table. "I'll just go."

I wait for her slurred comeback or for her to come to her senses and see what a mistake she's making, but she just wrinkles her nose, her brow raising impatiently when I don't move. With a heavy sigh, I cast one last look at Gabe's family before turning away.

Officially ending that chapter of my life for good.

**30**

*The Wolf*

SIENNA HAS MADE it increasingly difficult to keep tabs on her since she realized I've been watching her. It happened on accident. A quick slip of the tongue where I mentioned her being somewhere without doing a mental check of whether or not she shared that information with me, and she blew up.

Now, there's long stretches of time through the day where she disappears into thin air, only to randomly pop back up at her apartment hours later. The mere fact that she goes through the trouble of turning her location back on each night proves that she's fucking with me. Unless I'm willing to commit to following her around all the time, I'm stuck being blind to her whereabouts.

I can justify my obsession with Stardust. I'm not ready to cross those boundaries with Sienna just yet.

Logan has been making more of an appearance in her social circles, always finding a way to be in the same place as her. She thinks it's because he can't take no for an answer. Of course, I'm well-aware of how far he'll go if she continues to reject him, especially with support from the Order to push their own agenda. Explaining that to her has been impossible.

Every day, the idea of joining the Order to gain inside information becomes less ridiculous.

I can't slay the beast with a simple sword and shield. It has to be done from inside. Otherwise, I'll always be three steps behind them.

But when I mention that I'm considering the idea to Sienna, she throws a fit.

"You've been adamantly against those chauvinistic pigs since you were a kid. Now, you randomly have an interest in joining?"

She showed up to my work one slow afternoon, effectively pissing Eliza off by not making any sort of appointment. I'm just thankful she picked a day I'm actually here to do it. Explaining that I was in Styx would only reopen the Jovie debate, and I'm through speaking with her about that.

"I can change my mind," I point out.

"Why does it feel like this is brought on by me admitting Logan won't leave me alone?" She kicks her hip out, arms crossed over her chest.

"Don't be ridiculous. I wouldn't base a lifelong commitment on something as trivial as your dating life," I lie.

*Yes, I would.* If it means preserving her life. But she can't know that.

"Don't lie to me, Bash."

"Dad has been hounding me for years to consider it. After what happened, I think it would be nice to have a brotherhood at my back."

Her sour expression matches how I feel muttering those false statements, but I need to work on making this newfound interest believable. Sienna isn't the only one I've expressed my distaste to, and she certainly won't be the first to question me on it.

"I think you're making a mistake," she nobley declares, as if that will somehow change my mind.

"It's a good thing you don't get a say then, isn't it?"

"Why are you being such an asshole?"

I blow out a breath, turning back to my computer to dismiss her. She can argue with me all she wants, but she won't disrespect me in my own building.

"I don't have time for this. Why don't you go back to Styx and worry about whatever club you're going to this weekend? Leave the grown-up stuff for me to deal with, like you always do."

I regret the words the instant they leave my mouth.

Her face screws up into a hateful sneer, eyes wild with rage as she swings my office door open.

Before she leaves, she looks over her shoulder and says, "you know what? On second thought, you'll fit right in with the Order."

Then, she storms off.

**31**

*The Lamb*

Sienna is in a mood today. It's one of the rare times I've seen her with anything other than the friendly smile she usually wears, and it's managed to completely throw me off. I didn't realize how much I relied on her optimism to make my shifts at Old Soul more bearable.

"Just an argument with my brother," was all she vaguely offered when I asked about it. I dropped the subject, still unsure of how to handle conversations surrounding her elusive twin. An hour later, she appears to be in a better mood, but mine has taken a nose dive.

"This is a good song," she comments, dancing in her seat.

I move in sync with her from behind the counter, dramatically gyrating to the beat to make her laugh. It works, and I continue to make up silly moves until the song ends.

"Ooh, I like you," Sienna snickers, pointing her pen at me when the song is over like she just got a brilliant idea. "I bet you'd be a riot to go out dancing with. My best friend can't dance to save her life."

Rolling my eyes, I focus on the rag I'm swiping in circles on the counter. "I doubt that."

"Not your scene?"

"Oh, it's not that. I used to be a waitress at a few bars downtown. My friends and I knew all the best spots. But I don't get out much anymore."

"Ah, this is when I discover you're a murderous recluse." She teases, her tone light and unintrusive. Not the usual prying I'm used to.

"No, I just don't talk to anyone from those days anymore. A lot has changed."

With a knowing smirk, she shrugs. "So, your ex got the friends in the breakup?"

Pausing my hand, I look up at her disbelievingly. "Yes, actually." *And my mom. And my sister.*

And just when I start to get uncomfortable with how quickly she was able to come to that conclusion—*am I that transparent or is she some weird, obsessive stalker?*—she shakes her head and clicks her tongue.

"I've been there. I've only got one real friend. As much as Mallory gets under my skin, she's never let anything come between us. I can't say that for anyone else."

"You're lucky." I can't even get my own sister to give me that.

"You should come out with us this weekend." When she can tell I'm about to decline, she rushes to add, "Just because he got the friends doesn't mean you have to miss out on all the fun."

"I don't know…" What excuse do I really have?

*Sorry, can't. I have plans to sit home in my dark house and wait for the scary, not-so-imaginary dude to come carry me to bed?*

A night away from that place might be exactly what I need.

Swiping her hand in the air dismissively, she tells me, "Ah, that's the people-pleaser in you, Jovie. You can tell me no without trying to make up an excuse."

She laughs then, and it consumes her entire face in a way that lifts all the tension from my shoulders. This is what I like about her. I don't have to pretend or make excuses. She seems to accept me exactly where I am.

"No, I think you're right. I could use some fun."

"Perfect," she exclaims, clapping her hands. "I know the perfect place."

Ignoring the weight dropping in my gut, I attempt a smile as the realization of what I've just agreed to dawns on me. The rest of the afternoon has a constant flow of traffic that makes it difficult to hold a conversation, and Sienna seems too concentrated on whatever she's doing for me to voice any of my concerns over our plans. Before I know it, she's packing up her laptop and I'm busy with the closing chores, our plans long forgotten.

32

*The Wolf*

Stardust is planning a night out.

I've been darting between Styx and New York to make it into work every day after spending my nights with her. It's complete misery. Ordinarily, I would have just stayed in Styx and worked from her spare bedroom, but we're putting together another merger at Lancaster Tech—one I hadn't been presented with *before*—and my whole team has been struggling to prepare.

"I don't know what you do when you leave here, but you need to cool it. You look like ass," was the greeting Eliza gave me this morning. "They're going to reject the deal solely based on the fact that you look like you crawled out of a dumpster."

An odd thing to say to someone wearing a thousand dollar suit, but I laughed it off with her. She's not wrong. I had hoped to rest tonight with Stardust when I arrived there. Of course, those plans changed when I saw her closet ripped apart.

I have no idea who she's planning to spend her night with, and that fact alone is driving me more insane than anything else. I've dropped the ball. The entire reason for me doing this—following her around, tracking her phone, violating her privacy while she's in the shower—is to keep her safe. How the hell am I going to do that when I have no idea who she's interacting with all day?

Although, the small shreds of fabric she's laid out for herself on her bed before hopping in the shower are following in close second for driving me to insanity.

She has no idea I'm out here, mere feet away as she stands naked in there. I've held her in my arms each night this week, but I swear she still doubts my existence. Leaving her alone feels impossible at this point, especially when she's clearly formed an attachment to whatever she believes this thing is.

I want to step in there with her. To take her from behind and rub my hands along her body, filling her with my seed. The thought alone of her standing there, completely naked and unaware, has me achingly hard. But if I interrupt whatever plans she has, she might back out of them, and then I'll still have no idea who could have pushed her out of her depressive state enough to step out of her comfort zone. Instead, I shuffle out of her bedroom when the water turns off, lingering in the dining room as she gets ready. When it's time to go, I slip out the front door as she goes toward the garage, where her car is parked. Within minutes, we're pulling off our street and onto the main road.

Stardust's run-down car hobbles through the worn down streets of Styx and toward the city's center, where there's a small handful of businesses crammed together as a poor excuse for downtown. We weave around cars together until she quickly pulls into the entrance of a parking lot. Circling the block, I check my phone, the screen still pulled up to show her location.

It's grown still right beside mine. My eyes track her down on the sidewalk as I enter the cramped parking lot beside The Vault, a night club built into an old cotton factory. Something about this whole thing feels off. Stardust *never* goes out. She hardly leaves her house to do anything outside of work or visiting her sister. And after the week of panic attacks we've had together, I'm surprised she's willing to leave the couch.

So, who the hell could she be meeting? And how did they slip under my radar?

There's something I'm missing here.

I hardly have time to climb out of my car before she reaches the middle of a long line of people waiting to enter, balancing far better than I would have expected her to on the black, three-inch heels she's decided to torture me with tonight. It hits me that as much as I've memorized her daily patterns, I've never taken the time to fully get to know her past any further than what that waste of skin did to her. It seems as if my little Stardust may have had a wild streak. I'll have to make an effort to dig into that.

I'm finally within a few feet of her, my eyes never leaving her back, shivering from the cold air hitting all of her exposed skin, when she shifts on her feet and reveals who had been holding a spot for her in line.

And to my absolute horror, my gaze locks with my sister's.

**33**

*The Lamb*

To my disappointment, Sienna and her friend, Mallory, settled on a new club in downtown Styx. When she first told me, I was reluctant to accept. It created a new list of excuses for my anxiety to convince me not to go.

I've obviously never been to this one. I've never hung out with these women before.

The wave of excuses rolled in as my anxiety drowned me.

My mind is my worst enemy. It's been programmed since the beginning to default to ridicule and fear. I so desperately want to escape from the constant flow of intrusive thoughts that work overtime to convince me that a normal, healthy life is unattainable.

The only way I can even begin doing that is by obliterating those limiting thoughts one by one.

As much as I hate my mystery man for what he's done to Gabe, he opened my eyes to how much I've been letting everyone else win.

So, while going out to an overstimulating, crowded club with two people I've never met before seems like such a trivial thing to have to overcome—if I'm *that* uncomfortable, I should just back out—I know it's the first step I have to take into my new future. The one I've earned through literal blood, sweat, and tears.

I see it as practice.

I didn't give myself enough time to obsess over any of the ways the night could go wrong. Once I finished covering the afternoon shift at Old Soul for Rosie so she could visit with Ginny, I went straight home and started getting ready.

One thing I've noticed about Sienna is that she pushes me out of my comfort zone, but in a way that makes it feel like I'm only being nudged. She talks about life and makes it sound appealing and exciting, a stark contrast to the dull and daunting way I've always viewed it. It's addicting. And dangerous.

"My roommate comes off as a bit of a bitch, but she's harmless," She warns as soon as I walk up to her in the long line to get into the club.

"I'm sure she's not that bad."

Said friend appears at Sienna's side from somewhere around the corner, a serious look on her face.

"Mallory, this is my friend from the coffee shop that I was telling you about," Sienna introduces, and something about her tone and the odd way Mallory reacts tells me that they've spoken about me in more depth than just the coffee-shop-girl. It instantly makes me uncomfortable.

Where Sienna is all natural beauty and curves, Mallory looks like she took a photo of Sienna into her plastic surgeon's office and told them to copy it. She has bleached, platinum blonde hair and plump red lips that are obviously more filler than anything, with makeup caked onto her face and chest that's a shade off. And as I'm taking her in, I realize she's staring at me with the same amount of disgust.

"Okay," is all she says.

"Okay…" Sienna chirps, widening her eyes at me to say, *I told you so.*

Mallory looks down at her phone, typing out a long message. When she's done, she quickly locks it and rolls her eyes. "Your brother hasn't been answering any of my messages. What is his deal lately?" She whines to Sienna, whose eyes flick to me nervously before she shrugs.

"I think his attention is on someone else at the moment," she vaguely explains. The line moves, and we each step forward.

For whatever reason, it appears they don't want me to be a part of this conversation, so I busy myself with my phone the same way Mallory had done. Except, I don't have anything to do, so I end up absently scrolling Facebook as they speak.

"Don't tell me that," Mallory warns. "You know how jealous I am."

Sienna giggles. "I don't think he cares if you're jealous, Mal."

"He may not, but whatever whore he's with will have a rude awakening."

I lift my gaze to Mallory, who is all skin and bones with almost no muscle. Watching her fight *anyone* would be comical. When I turn toward Sienna to see if she's thinking the same thing, I'm shocked to find that she's already staring at me, head tilted like she's trying to figure something out.

The line moves again, and Sienna snaps out of whatever trance she's in.

She seems a little spacey today.

"Bash will come around," she tells her friend, but her eyes oddly remain on me.

"If he doesn't, I'd pay to watch the cat fight," I joke, looking to Sienna to laugh with me. But she doesn't even crack a smile. In fact, she isn't even looking at me. Mallory looks like she smells something foul.

As if the joke finally hit her, Sienna finally releases a strained giggle, mumbling something to Mallory about betting on the other girl.

After a few long, awkward moments, I turn away from them and move with the people in front of us, thankful for the distraction of the doorman, who is demanding my license so we can enter the club next.

This is going to be a long night.

EVEN WITH MALLORY'S immediate dismissal of me and the awkward moment before we walked in, we managed to have a great night. Thanks to her and Sienna's shameless flirting, we each had a drink in our hands at all times. When we had to set them down to dance, a new one appeared within minutes. We laughed and joked and danced, and for the first time since I got out of Sunnybrook, I was… *happy*. Genuinely happy.

No one brought up Gabe or that night. No one looked at me like the sad suicidal girl who can't be left alone for five minutes. No one tried to convince me to speak to my mother or drop the charges. Because no one here knows any of that, and they couldn't care less.

And as I'm jumping up and down, flailing my arms around in some ridiculous dance with two women who hardly know me, but have treated me more human than any *friend* I spent my life growing up with, I realize something. I don't have to tuck myself away in a remote corner of Styx to find peace that I've earned. I don't have to stay in environments that I've outgrown.

I'm not the fucking problem here, and I'm sick of being treated like I am.

My drunken, wobbly gaze catches on a dark figure standing against the back wall, eyes cast out into the crowd menacingly. As if he can sense my attention on him, he shifts and those eyes snap right to mine. My breath hitches in my throat when his brow raises in a challenge.

I turn toward Sienna to ask if she can see him too, but she's grinding her ass against some guy who she introduced to me as an old friend a few minutes ago. When my head swivels back to find the figure again, my heart drops into my stomach.

He's standing right in front of me now, inches from my face. I stumble back a bit, but he remains still, irises practically glowing above a black mask that hangs down his chest.

And I know that it's *him*. The same man who keeps appearing in my house. The one who appears at the most random times.

"Hello, Stardust," his gravelly voice says from beneath the mask, confirming my suspicions. I shouldn't be able to hear it so clearly over the music—no one else appears to even notice him—but I do.

I reach down deep in my chest, searching around for the panic and fear that should be rearing their heads at the sight of him. But as always, I come up short.

It seems that no matter what this man does, I can't find it in myself to be afraid of him.

That threatening gaze flick over to my friends before he takes one step closer to me, leaning forward so his masked lips are against the side of my head.

"Come with me."

The song blends into the next one, and my head spins a little at the change in pace as everyone around us begins dancing faster. Sienna is still with that guy and Mallory has disappeared somewhere deeper in the crowd.

I shouldn't go with him. Every survival instinct I have screams against it. But my head is swimming with all the alcohol I drank and the room is getting stuffier as more people begin to swarm the dance floor. Even if I don't walk away with him, I need to get out of here.

As if he senses my sudden lack of balance, he reaches his hand out just in time to catch me before I topple over as two girls rush past us, slamming into my shoulder.

My stomach churns, all the alcohol I've consumed threatening to spill out. The man wraps his arm around my waist and guides me through the thickening throng. I attempt to look back at Sienna to let her know that I'm leaving, but we're moving too fast, and she's already too far away.

*This is bad.*

I can hardly move my arms or legs to kick or punch my assaulter as I'm stolen away, and all the terror that should have crept in since the moment I locked eyes with him floods my system.

This isn't just from the alcohol. Someone has obviously slipped something into one of my drinks and the only person I can think who would do it is currently shuffling me into the passenger seat of a black sedan. He carried me out the front doors and past security like some lightweight drunk, mumbling something about me having had one too many drinks.

"I'mmm calling… th-the copss…" I drawl once he has his door shut, reaching into my bra to grab my phone that I thankfully had the brains to stick in there the last time I peed.

The engine roars to life and he reaches his hand across

center counsel, snatching the phone from my hand way too easily.

*Shit*. This is pathetic. I can't even move my arms to lean over and grab it back.

"What have you had to drink?" He calmly asks, pulling the car out of the parking lot.

I try to watch out the window to catalog any unique landmarks I can follow back when I make my escape. But we're driving too fast, and my mind is too sluggish.

"You should know," I think I say. It comes out as one long, slurred mess.

He doesn't bother responding, which pisses me off. "I don't know why you're doing this to me," I look back to sneer at him, but the fast movement has my drink coming back up, spilling into my mouth.

"I didn't do this to you, Stardust."

My eyes cross. "Who is this Stardust? I've got news for you, buddy… I'm not her. I'm Jovie. So you can stop acting like you know me."

Was any of that legible? Who knows? Slouching into my seat, I cross my arms over my chest.

He isn't listening to me. Or if he is, he isn't bothered by my tantrum. When that doesn't get a rise out of him, I try the door handle, shocked to find it unlocked.

It opens, and the fast-moving cement rushes beneath me, wind whipping my hair into my face. I contemplate jumping for a full second before I decide that since I can't feel my arms or legs anyway, I might as well do it. Just as I go to swing my legs over, his arm drapes across my chest, pinning me to the back of the chair. The tires screech as his foot drives down on the brakes, forcing the heavy door to slam shut.

"What the fuck are you doing?" he barks, pulling over to park.

"Trying to get away from you."

"Trying to kill yourself is more like it."

I flinch, the words cutting a little more deeply than I'd like for them to.

Rubbing his hand down his face, he blows out a breath, nearly ripping the mask off. "Look… you need rest. I'm not going to hurt you. I'm trying to get you somewhere safe while whatever drug those assholes slipped into your drink earlier wears off."

"You saw them do it?"

His brows pull together, casting shadows over his light eyes. "Yes."

I sit back, wading through my chaotic thoughts to consider the options I have.

I could still try to break away from him. We haven't been driving for very long… I'm sure I could find my way back to the club. Sienna is hopefully looking for me by now.

*Sienna.* If I was drugged, she could have been, too.

"I have to get back to my friends. They'll be worried," I tell him.

"Your friends are fine without you, trust me."

*Trust him.* As if that's even plausible, given the circumstances. He's a murderer. He killed Gabe in cold blood. And he's going to kill me next.

"I'm not leaving you here. You can't drive home in this condition. And you sure as hell aren't going back to that club, where the people who did this can drag you out of there as easily as I just did."

Well, there it is. He's effectively ripped away every option I have.

"I have an apartment in the city. You'll stay in my spare bedroom until this wears off. I won't even talk to you if you don't want me to."

Locking the doors, he shifts back into drive and takes off,

his eye flicking back and forth between the road and my hands.

I try to keep my eyes open, but they feel like they're being pulled down by weights. No matter how hard I try, they continue to close and within minutes, I'm taken under by sleep.

his eye flicking back and forth between the road and my

I try to keep my eyes open, but they feel like they're being pulled down by weights. No matter how hard I try, they continue to close and within minutes, I'm taken under by sleep.

34

*The Wolf*

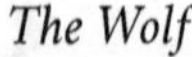

THE BOUNCER CONS me into paying him five-hundred dollars just to let me in without waiting an hour in the ridiculous line. Another hundred to the coat-check girl who didn't even end up servicing Sienna and Jovie, and I'm finally standing in the middle of the dance floor, surrounded by sweaty, gyrating bodies.

It smells like piss here. Piss and alcohol and cheap cologne. The sticky floor grabs at my shoes with every step I take, and three people bump into me without even realizing it on my way to the bar that sits in the center of the space.

That's where I see Mallory's blond head bobbing to the beat of the music, a pink drink in her hand and a random guy talking into her ear. Sienna is standing beside her, leaning over to say something to Stardust.

*Stardust.*

The relief I feel at seeing her, safely standing there with

an easy smile on her face, is palpable. I watch her lips move to say something, and then Sienna barks out a laugh.

I'm moving toward them before I can second guess it or come up with a plan, but by the time I make it around a group of handsy, cackling women who take special interest in the mask I threw on to conceal my identity, they've moved deeper onto the dance floor.

I can't stand these environments. Surrounded by people who are so wasted, they can hardly comprehend where they are. The music is always too loud, the lights are too bright, and they pack everyone in like cattle for slaughter. It's another way that Sienna and I contradict each other, because she thrives in places like this.

Pushing through the throngs of people, I carefully scan the sea of faces in hopes of catching sight of one of them, but just as I do, the DJ drops the beat and the lights go down, blinding me. By the time the colorful flashes begin again, I've lost track of them.

A large hand wraps around my shoulders and attempts to spin me in place. When I don't budge, Logan steps around me, that familiar, creepy grin plastered across his face.

Memories of his agonizing screams flash through my head, and I'm mentally jolted back to the night I killed him. For a split second, my mind can't keep up with the idea that I've already watched the life drain from his eyes, yet he's still standing before me, alive and well.

He's staring at me like he's waiting for a response to something, but I didn't hear whatever he said. I huff out a deep, "huh?"

"I said I'm surprised to see you here." He gestures toward his chin, touching an imaginary mask. "I didn't know you were into the mask stuff."

"Oh... yeah." Mask stuff? What the fuck is he talking about?

I'm disappointed he was able to identify me at all.

"I know some women go wild for it. You'll have to let me know how it works for you. Is Sienna here?" He looks around, ignorant to my murderous thoughts at the mention of my sister's name.

The sister he murdered.

Or didn't, I guess. *Yet.*

Fuck, I can't keep my thoughts straight.

"She's around."

"I'll keep an eye out."

It takes everything in me not to wrap my hand around his throat and insist he doesn't, but I have to remember to play the long game. Instead, I clap him on the shoulder and make up an excuse about going to the bathroom, then walk away before I can hear his response.

Luckily for me, that's exactly where Sienna has disappeared to.

My hand reaches out to wrap around my sister's arm, tugging her into the men's bathroom just before she can step into the women's. I shove her flailing body against the sink and lock the door behind us. Seconds later, someone tries the handle, then pounds on the door, screaming something about having to take a piss.

As if he can't do it right there on the dance floor like everyone else.

Sienna gathers herself, wrapping her arms around her torso. She needs to work on her defense if this is how she reacts to a man throwing her around.

"Bash?" she shrieks, squinting her eyes in disbelief. "What the hell are you doing here?"

"We need to talk."

Her brows compress into a scowl, mouth opening in shock as the truth dawns on her. "God, you really are stalking her, aren't you?"

Ignoring the disgusted look on her face, I press on. "What are you doing with her?"

"What's it to you? She's *no one*, isn't she?" She throws my words back at me, stubbornly hiking her hand on her hip.

"Don't fucking play with me. What is your angle, Sienna?"

"Okay, so you're finally ready to discuss the elusive *Jovie*?" her hands come up, fingers wiggling around in a petulant display.

"Fuck off. I don't know what game you think you're playing with me, but you have no clue what you're getting yourself into. Back off of her."

She moves over toward the mirror, pursing her lips to examine her makeup. "I asked her to come out with us. She seemed like she had to get her mind off of things."

Irritation crawls up my neck like a million little spiders, my patience wearing thin. I need to release this rage before it consumes me.

She did this because of our argument.

"Why the hell would she feel comfortable going out with you?" I ask in an even voice, determined not to fall prey to my own emotions and take this out on her before I get some real answers.

With all the time I've spent following these two women around like a lost dog, how the fuck did I miss *this*?

Turning around to face me, she leans her back against the counter, her perfectly-made-up mouth pulled down into a frown. "You won't tell me *anything*, Bash. I know she's somehow connected to whatever happened. I had to find answers."

I growl, fingers coming up to my scalp to pull at my hair in fistfulls. I'm going absolutely insane—losing control of every aspect of this horrible clusterfuck.

"Why can't you just leave shit alone, Sienna? It's none of your fucking business. When are you going to get that through your head?" I want to scream, but my words come out sounding far deadlier when I keep my voice even, tone low.

Someone else slams their fist against the door, and I know we've only got a few more minutes before an employee comes to unlock it.

She flinches, pulling her arms in to cradle her chest. "I care about you," she mumbles weakly, a stark contrast from the confident pain in my ass she's been these past few weeks.

"I don't give a fuck. This has nothing to do with you anymore. Back off of her, or I'll make you."

"*Make* me?" She shifts on her feet, her stance growing more defensive. "What does that mean?"

"It means that I'm not someone to test."

She gapes at me. "*What?* I don't even know who you are anymore, Bash. Since when do you speak to me like this?"

"Since you began shoving yourself into places that you don't belong."

"I'm just trying to help you."

"I don't fucking need your help," I snap. "And I don't need you sniffing around Jovie. She's not some pawn for you to use to get to me because you're bored with your own life."

"I know she isn't just some pawn. We're friends now, and I care about her. She's clearly been through some shit."

"*Friends?*" I scrub my hand across my face, completely exasperated with her. The last thing I need is for her to bring more attention to Stardust. "You don't make friends."

Ignoring my jab, she schools her face. "Why does she have my locket?"

My spine goes straight as an arrow. I completely forgot about that. Stardust has had it strung around her neck since I saw her in the hospital. If Sienna has been hanging around her, I should have realized that was the first thing she'd notice. Especially when Stardust is such a mystery to her.

Drawing out a long breath, I roll my shoulders and look her square in the eye. I have no explanation for how Stardust has the necklace, even if I wanted to give her one.

So, I settle on a quick, condescending dismissal.

"There are a million necklaces out there that look exactly like that one."

"I know that it's mine," she insists, stomping her heel against the tile like a child.

"How can you be so sure?" I push, a weak attempt to annoy her and deflect.

"Because I can, Bash. And I want to know how this seemingly random woman who has no clue who you are, somehow has a family heirloom that I just so happened to lose the night you went missing."

Shaking my head, I grab my nose and look down at my feet, searching for some way to explain all of this without sounding insane. When I come up short, I just say, "I told you, this is not something you want to get caught up in."

"I'm not accepting that as an answer anymore."

"What the fuck do you want me to say, Sienna?" I push out, exasperated.

"I want you to tell me who the hell she is to you. Explain why you're stalking her in the shadows like some insane freak. I want to know how she ties in to your disappearance. You have to tell me *something*."

"No, I don't."

"Then, you can stay away from her while I figure it out myself."

"That's not happening," I scoff, hissing out an irritated breath. "I'm taking her home. You should leave, too. And what the hell are you doing with Logan?"

"That's none of *your* business," she bites back. "You can't just drag her out of here. She's having a good time."

The lock on the door rattles and turns as someone sticks

a key inside. Sienna and I turn to face the irritated employee at the same time, each of our expressions so severe, his steps falter.

"You can't be in here together, and the door cannot be locked..." he sputters out, his words trailing off as Sienna steps toward the door.

She doesn't acknowledge him. In fact, she walks by as if he isn't even standing there, pausing in the doorway at the last second to throw one last irritating remark over her shoulder.

"Fine, take her home. I'll be going home with Logan tonight, anyway."

With that, she steps back into the club, leaving me alone with the disgruntled employee and a full line of men waiting to take a piss.

"You need to leave," the employee tells me, hitching his thumb over his shoulder.

I don't bother arguing. Not with him, and not with the rest of the assholes standing outside filled to the brim with liquid courage. Instead, I make a bee-line for the dance floor, determined to grab my little lamb and get her out of here.

**35**

*The Lamb*

I WAKE in a dark room splashed with deep reds and purples—a dark contrast to the stark white of my bedroom that I've grown so used to. The bed is like a cloud, fluffy and soft, but my head still feels like it's about to explode across the crimson pillowcase.

The last thing I remember about the night before is dancing with Sienna and Mallory. Everything else is a blur, and no matter how many times I attempt to reach out a mental hand into the dense brain fog, I come up empty.

I barely had a chance to drink the cocktails Mallory was shoving into my hands before Sienna was pulling me onto the dance floor. But someone must have drugged me. That's the only explanation.

And whoever it is seems to have brought me here.

When I manage to muster enough strength to sit up, I force myself to take in the space.

It's bland and impersonal. A guest room, I suppose. The

rich colors of my comforter are splashed across the walls and on random pieces of thoughtfully placed decor. When my eyes swing over to the nightstand beside me, I notice the glass of water and two white pills sitting there with a scribbled note.

My blood runs cold in my veins the instant I see the familiar, masculine handwriting.

*Drink this. Breakfast is waiting for you in the kitchen. Your car is parked in the street.*

I'm in *his* house. But how?

Could he have been the one to drug me?

I wouldn't think so, based on how gentle and caring he's been this far. But I don't know him well enough to say that he *couldn't*. How else could I have ended up in his house, though?

There's a vibrating sound beside me, and I have to search through the blankets for a solid minute before my phone pops out from beneath a pillow.

Sienna: Did you get home okay last night?

She thinks I went straight home.

I don't answer the text. Instead, I exit out of my messages to bring up a map and see where I am. It has to be somewhere close by if it's *his* house. How else could he be showing up in my room every night?

My heart does a flip in my chest when a street somewhere in New York shows up.

So, not a house, but an apartment. An apartment over an hour away from my house…

How could he have driven me this far from home and I can't remember a thing about the ride here? What could he do for a living if he has an apartment in the city? With a guest bedroom?

Unless, this is *his* room…

*I genuinely have no clue who this man is.*

The reality of my situation settles over me like a thick blanket, and I'm consumed with bone-shattering panic within the blink of an eye. I've never been to New York. I have no idea how to get around this city. I could be in the middle of a dangerous neighborhood and not even know it.

"Fuck, fuck, *fuck*," I whisper to myself, scrubbing my hands across my face.

How could I be so stupid? I bet he walked right up to me and I melted into his arms like the spineless jellyfish that I am.

I have to calm myself. I can't fall into an uncontrollable panic attack in the middle of a stranger's home. For all I know, he could be waiting for me on the other side of that door. And then what? He wraps me in his arms and calms down the storm that he's created?

No. I have to play it cool until I get home.

*So the full panic attack can begin, and he can crawl into bed with me and make it better.*

Yeah, I'm a fucking idiot.

With a deep breath, I flip the covers off of me and check myself out, pleasantly surprised to find I'm in the same clothes as last night. He made no attempt to undress me. *This time.*

I drag my feet into the large attached bathroom to relieve myself and splash some cold water on my face. The deep hues thoughtfully carry on in here, and I get the distinct feeling that it was decorated by a woman. The floral shower curtain and abstract artwork doesn't feel very masculine.

Could he be married? What are the chances of me walking out of this room and finding an angry, scorned woman waiting for me on the other side?

God, this is such a nightmare.

But the only way out is through.

Making quick work of tidying up the bed, I grab my phone up and square my shoulders, then swing open the door.

To reveal a wide open, brightly lit hallway that's twice the size of the one in my house. Confused, I slowly shuffle toward the stairs at the end, making note of the other two closed doors on the way. When I reach the top of the steps, I gape down at the spacious living room below, my jaw practically dropping a whole level.

Okay, scratch what I thought before. He doesn't live in an apartment. He lives in a fucking *penthouse*.

What does this guy do for a living?

My grip on the curved bannister tightens with each step down, my nerves so high, I can barely breathe. All I can do is hope that no one else is around to catch me sneaking out of here like his pathetic one-night-stand. The easy girl he brought home who passed out before he could have his way with me.

*I hope.*

No one is around, though. When I reach the bottom stair and start toward the elevator, something in the huge, black and white family room catches my eye, and my feet are bringing me toward it before my mind can catch up.

I have this nagging feeling like I've been here before. Something about this room—the uniquely carved cathedral ceilings or the contrasting decor—feels so familiar. But that's not even remotely possible. I've hardly ever left Styx before this, and I know for a fact I've never been to wherever the hell my map shows I am.

There's an abstract art print above the sofa, so large, it nearly takes up the entire wall. A splattering of thin, light yellow brush strokes sits in the mirroring position of thick, black and dark brown against a stark white canvas. It's like the yin and yang symbol, only messy and chaotic.

The yellow in the painting is the only speck of color in the otherwise black and white room. The way the yellow spread across the canvas, so thin and docile like strands of hair or yarn, feels familiar. I can't place my finger on what it could be, though, and I've spent enough time staring that I'm worried someone may walk in and see me. Clamping my mouth shut and forcing my eyes away, I turn toward the dark hallway off the family room that I can tell leads to a kitchen.

The most startling part about this place is that there's not a single personal memento to indicate anything about him. No family photos, no quirky fandoms, no books…. Nothing to indicate he's even a real *person*. That painting is the only thing that feels remotely personal, and it very well could just be a random piece of art he picked up somewhere.

This penthouse is more like a museum than a home.

The kitchen offers more of the same bland, impersonal decor that he either had an ex pick out or hired someone with absolutely no taste. As promised, there's a large plate of food wrapped in plastic sitting in the center of the island. There's no chance I'm eating anything he prepared. Not when there's a chance he's the one who drugged me and took me here.

Instead, I meander further down the unlit hallway, toward the two black doors sitting across from one another at the end. Wrapping my hand around the first gold knob, I'm disappointed to find it's locked.

I should turn back. I *really* should get out of here before he returns from whatever hellish black hole he's disappeared into. Instead, I try the other knob, pleasantly surprised when it turns with my palm and unlatches.

The heavy door swings open into a grand master bedroom. The walls and ceiling have been coated with matte black paint that absorbs all the sunlight shining in from the floor-to-ceiling window. A large mahogany four poster bed sits across from me, neatly made up with a fluffy black comforter and a mountain of pillows.

That feeling hits me all over again.

Familiarity. Recognition.

My mind fights the memory off, blurring it and chasing it away before I can grab hold of it. Before I can fully recall.

I step further into the room, allowing myself time to take in the space without worrying about being caught. Scraping my mind, desperate to recall *something* that can explain why I feel so comfortable here.

"This isn't the kitchen," a patient, even voice says from behind me.

I spin in place, heart hammering in my chest when my eyes land on *his* face. All I can muster is a sheepish smile.

I've been caught.

"This is your room." A dumb statement from a nosey, annoying girl.

Obviously it's his room.

"It is," he agrees, leaning his shoulder against the door frame.

He's not dressed in his usual black jeans and hoodie. Instead, he's wearing a dark gray suit with a black dress shirt, his charcoal tie loosened around his neck.

The mask is once again absent from his face, and I wonder what makes him decide whether to wear it or not.

He hasn't stepped into the room with me. Hasn't grabbed me by the wrist and dragged me out. In fact, he doesn't even look irritated with me for violating his privacy.

"I was just looking…" I begin to explain, placing my hand over my heart to stop it from beating out of my chest.

He shakes his head to stop me, tucking his hands into his pockets. "I have nothing to hide from you, Stardust."

*Nothing but your true identity*, I want to say, pointing out the obvious.

"Why did you bring me here?"

His response is immediate. "To keep you safe."

"Safe from *what*?" My voice hitches, arms spread wide. "The only common threat that seems to always be around is you."

We haven't spoken since the night I found out that he murdered Gabe. If he's been around me, he's stayed tucked into the darkness, where I can't see him. I still don't know how to feel about what he said to me then, or the passion he wore as he delivered his declarations.

"*I'm* not the threat that was around you last night."

"Are you trying to say my friend is a threat? Because that's bullshit."

Blowing out a breath, he rolls his eyes to the ceiling, shifting away from the doorway to walk into the room. Toward me. "Sienna isn't one, either. Yet."

My mouth goes dry.

"How do you know her name?" I ask in a whisper.

For some reason, this seems like more of a violation than anything else he's done thus far. It's one thing for him to stalk and haunt me. I don't think I can justify his behavior if it's bleeding into someone else's life.

That, and I may be a little jealous. But I stuff that feeling right back into whatever psychotic pit it came from.

He strolls past me, ignoring the way my muscles stiffen as he passes, then continues over to the window, where he stops to gaze out at the New York skyline. I was so entranced with my Deja Vu in the room, I didn't even attempt to look outside.

Stupid, easy prey.

"Of course, I do," he looks at me over his shoulder and chuckles like there's some kind of sick inside joke that I'm missing. When I shoot him a disparaging look, his smile falters. "I know everything about you," he amends.

I'm not sure how that is supposed to make this any less uncomfortable. I'm afraid that getting close to Sienna while I'm entangled in whatever this is with him may cost her dearly. I'll have to figure out how to keep the two completely separate. Although, if I can figure out a way to control when he comes around, I should end it all together.

He doesn't turn to look back out the window again. Instead, his eyes bore into me, a vulnerable sadness crossing through them before he blinks, and it's gone.

"I should get going," I tell him, awkwardly hooking my thumb over my shoulder. He hums his agreement, but neither of us makes a move to go.

"Did you drug me?" I blurt out before thinking it through. As soon as the words leave my mouth, I don't regret them. I want to know.

He shakes his head, turning his shoulders to fully face me. "I wouldn't ever hurt you," he rasps, eyes crinkled in hurt. "I carried you in from the car, laid you in the guest room, and left you to rest. If I'm being completely honest, I checked on you more times than I'm comfortable admitting, but I didn't cross any boundaries. I have no idea who spiked your drink. I'm just happy I got you out of there before they did."

My head drops, eyes cast down to the floor in shame. I should have known it wasn't him. It's too easy to blame him when something bad happens, simply because of the unconventional way our paths crossed. Because of his refusal to admit who he is while still being unashamedly himself.

Who is this mysterious man, and where did he come from?

"Thank you," I mumble into my chest bashfully.

He strolls over toward me silently, stopping a few inches

away. I only know because his feet appear in my vision, black leather against the dark, crimson carpet.

"You'll make it up to me," he coos, reaching his finger out to tuck under my chin, then pushes my head upward, forcing me to meet his darkened stare.

I search his face for the calm, docile man that walked into this room a few minutes ago and come up short. His entire demeanor has shifted again. He's back to that dominant predator who takes me in the middle of the night and kills those he thinks have wronged me. The one who absorbs all the ugly and unspeakable things I hate about myself, dirtying his soul in the name of cleansing mine.

I don't know how he does it so quickly, like flipping a switch and changing personalities.

"Will I?" I tease playfully, far too turned on by his shift than I'd like to admit.

This game between us has become addictive.

"You will," he assures, brows pinching together to cast a shadow over those odd greens as he sucks that beautiful, plump lip between his teeth.

"On your knees," his low voice growls.

"Now?"

"Right fucking now."

I obey, falling to the floor before him. My pussy is already heating up in anticipation.

Deft fingers slowly unlatch the thin leather belt wrapped around his waist. I lick my lips, swallowing down a lump in my throat just as he flicks his wrist and yanks it out in one swift move. The leather flies into the air with a loud snap and I jump at the sound, causing his eyes to widen in quiet excitement.

He grabs the other side of the belt, bringing the ends together to form a loop, which he wraps around my neck. I gaze up at him, my hands hanging at my sides as he tightens it behind me, only stopping when I whimper.

"Open your mouth," he commands, sticking his finger between my lips before I have a chance to accept the order.

I have to fight the urge to gag when it hits the back of my throat, curling against my tongue before he pulls back. The tip of his fingers swipes circles over my lips, spreading my spit around.

"Such a dirty little lamb. Let me cleanse you."

I don't know what it is about him that makes me enjoy this so much. Maybe it's the mystery behind his identity. Maybe the drugs from last night are still lingering in my system, influencing my reactions. Perhaps it's a kink I never knew I had.

Or maybe… there's a part of him that speaks to the darkest parts of me, encouraging them to step into the light and be seen like they never have before.

It's comforting. And it makes him impossible to deny when doing so feels like I'm also denying a piece of myself.

My hands come up to unbutton his dress pants, and he allows it, slightly loosening his grip on the belt to make room as I push them down and pull his erection out. I wrap both my palms around his length, covering him from base to just below his tip, and begin to pump them up and down. The movement earns a satisfied hum as he shifts his hips into my grip, causing more friction.

"Put your mouth on me," he instructs.

I don't hesitate.

Flattening my tongue, I swipe his tip along the surface, then slide it down the underside to the base of his shaft and back up again.

His approval is conveyed in the tightening of the belt around my throat.

I squirm on the floor, shifting my hips so my thighs rub

together against my throbbing center. I want him inside of me, as wrong as it sounds. An hour ago, I thought this guy had drugged me and dumped me in some random bad neighborhood of New York. Now, I'm wrapping my lips around his cock and shoving it as far down my throat as I can stand.

Life is funny like that.

He tilts his head back, pushing his hips forward to urge himself into my throat the final fraction of an inch that I thought I couldn't take. My lips meet his groin and I'm about to gag when he pulls back, and we repeat the process.

"Fuck," he drawls, pulling on the belt a little more. "Such a good girl, taking all of me."

The threat of my airways closing adds a thrill that has me moving faster against his erection so he can finish before I can't breathe at all. My free hand that isn't wrapped around the base of his cock and guiding it into my mouth slips between my legs and strokes my clit.

We continue this for a few more minutes, and he fucks my mouth so hard, I feel like my jaw is about to fall off by the time he stills for a second, and then his hot cum sputters into my throat. I don't dare stop them, though. Instead, I continue sucking, drawing out every last drop until his moans grow loud and it's clear he can hardly take any more.

My hand works against my clit the entire time, as right when he's fully satiated, I fall over the proverbial edge, throwing my head back in escstacy against his fist as my orgasm runs through me.

Once everything has calmed back down, I swipe the cum from my lips with my forefinger and suck it clean, gazing up at him through my lashes the entire time.

"You are the most exquisite thing I've ever seen, especially when you come," he muses, softly placing his finger against my chin to tip my head upward. "I'm so incredibly lucky that you're mine."

I want to protest that. To remind him that I don't even have a clue who he is for him to claim I belong to him.

Instead, I stay silent and he takes that as enough acceptance to swing the belt back over my head and readjust his pants.

"Let's get you home," he says once he's put back together, reaching a hand out to help me to my feet.

He leads me out the elevators and all the way to my car, even going as far as offering to lead me through the winding streets so I can get home safely. I decline, though. It doesn't escape me that I've officially become the discarded one night stand that I was worried about appearing as an hour ago, when I was trying to sneak away undetected.

"I'll see you tonight," he promises into my ear when he goes to kiss my cheek goodbye.

And for the first time ever, I'm looking forward to it.

**36**

*The Wolf*


DINNER at my parents is as boring as usual this week. The tension radiating between me and Sienna over Stardust makes it even more insufferable.

She pointedly ignored me for the first half, and then switched her approach entirely when our mother began talking about the Crystal Cottage, and she decided that glaring at me would be more effective to ensure I know how pissed she is.

As if *she* has a reason to be pissed at all.

We've survived the main course and I'm preparing my excuse to leave before dessert when my father leans back in his chair and throws his napkin onto the table. My mother tenses across from me before she drops her chin into her chest.

"I've got some news to tell you," my father begins. The wrinkles lining his face deepen with his frown, and I realize that for the first time in my life, he's struggling to speak.

"What is it?" Sienna pushes impatiently. I cut my eyes over to her in warning, but she doesn't look in my direction to see it.

"We've been trying to figure out how to tell you, but to be completely honest, there's no good way to do it."

He pauses again, his lips pressed together in a firm line. My mother finally raises her eyes, a stoney expression crossing her usually-happy face.

"Your father has been diagnosed with brain cancer," she utters, her tone cold and detached.

Sienna gasps.

"They can't be certain how much time he has, but it's not long."

"No." Sienna shakes her head. "They've got so much new technology for this sort of thing. We'll get a second opinion. We'll find something."

"The cancer is too aggressive. It's already spread too far."

"I'm sure there's something you can do for more time..." Sienna continues to argue, but my mother shakes her head and the words die off.

"We've looked into everything," she tells her in a grave tone.

"How long have you known?" The question is directed at our father now, the accusation clear. She wants to know how long they've kept it from us as we sat here, week after week like nothing was wrong.

"Three months."

"What?!" Sienna shrieks at the same time I say, "was this after I got out of the hospital?"

Ignoring Sienna's reddening face, my mother turns to me and calmly answers, "we got the test results the day you were discharged."

"This is bullshit. How could you guys sit here through these dinners for months and not say a word? What if we could have helped?" Sienna is visibly upset. She wears her emotions on her sleeve, in plain sight for everyone else to see. And right now, she's pissed.

And hurt.

And devastated.

All the feelings I'm experiencing, yet I'm incapable of mustering anything more than a frown.

"You can't help, Sienna. No one can," my father grumbles.

"Then, why wouldn't you at least want us to know so we could prioritize our time with you?"

"I didn't want you coming around out of pity. We've kept our dinners together. That's more than we had before."

Sienna just stares at him, eyes glistening with tears she refuses to let fall. My mother drops her head again, pretending to dab her lips with her napkin while my father keeps his expression blank—still too stubborn to show any emotion. We're so much alike, it makes me sick.

His diagnosis came in mere weeks after I returned here. Is it possible that with Sienna still alive and well, Mother Nature has taken it upon herself to claim his life instead?

This situation gets more confusing as time goes on.

My parents spend the next twenty minutes recalling everything they've been told about my father's prognosis in the past three months. And just as Sienna suggested, it seems like they've explored every option at their disposal. None of it is feasible.

"The cancer has spread into his bones and blood. Even if we cut the tumor out of his brain, it's still capable of spreading to more of his major organs. It's just not worth the risk of going through such a major surgery for such little payout."

Sienna peppers them with more questions over the next twenty minutes, until my father decides he can't take any more and scoots back in his chair.

"Come upstairs," he tells me, gesturing his head toward the stairs.

My mother bites her lip, looking between the two of us like she wants to object, but can't. Sienna rolls her eyes, sitting back in her chair and crossing her legs.

"Sure," I tell him, reluctantly standing from my seat.

"Play nice," my mother warns him, earning a condescending scoff as he slowly gets to his feet.

I follow one step behind him up the stairs and down the hall, waiting at his back as he unlocks the office door and swings it open, gesturing for me to enter first.

The memories flood in the moment I take my first step into the room—flashbacks of a time that I'm not even sure truly existed. Whispers of another life sing in my ear, and I could swear that as my eyes sweep through the space, there's still evidence of what happened here *before*. My mind convinces me there's blood splatters on the walls from the fatal shot he made. But each time I allow myself to check, every surface remains clean.

"Thanks for coming up here," my father says, oblivious to my internal battles. "I wanted to chat without any prying ears."

He rounds his desk and falls into the plush, leather chair. Just like before, I find myself assessing his sickly appearance. I'm not sure how me or Sienna missed that something was wrong with him. He's clearly been withering away right beneath our watchful eyes.

But I was fooled by this weakened illusion once before, and it cost me my life.

Before he realizes that I'm sizing him up, I pull out one of the chairs sitting across from him and take my seat, nodding my head for him to go on.

"I know this is a sore subject for us, given your obvious distaste for the Order..." he begins, just as I knew he would.

The only thing he isn't confident enough to speak openly about in front of my mother is his chauvinistic brotherhood.

Taking a long, steady breath, I wait for him to go on.

"You're my only son, Sebastian," he begins, the same way he always does when we broach this subject. He doesn't give a shit what I have to say about any of this. He just wants to get his side out so he can manipulate me into joining. "You're the last hope to carry on the Lancaster legacy."

"Sienna has the same amount of Lancaster blood flowing through her veins."

Shaking his head, he swipes his hand between us, dismissing me. "Sienna will be an invaluable asset to whatever family she chooses to join, but she'll have to continue her husband's name, not mine."

Ignoring his archaic logic and suppressing my eyeroll, I shrug. It's the only way I can think to release the tension that's building up without giving away how much he's already irritating me.

"What does this have to do with the Order?"

"You're the first legacy to reject the Order. Did you know that? Over one hundred years of our organization, and no one has ever chosen to forgo their rightful spot in the brotherhood."

"I've gone against the grain my entire life," I point out, resting my ankle across the opposite knee.

"Yes, you have. But I can't allow you to continue to embarrass me any longer. Not when there's a ticking clock against me. It's time for you to come where you belong."

My blood begins to boil, my heart kicking up into a dangerous rhythm. *Embarrassing him?* For my entire life, there was not a single thing I could do to make the man sitting before me proud. Acing tests, winning championships, earning awards—none of it was ever enough for him. I'm not delusional enough to believe that signing myself up for his sadistic brotherhood will be any different.

"I don't belong in the Order," I insist through gritted teeth.

He considers me for a moment, his mouth pressed into a hard line that deepens his natural frown. And I just stare back, challenging him.

"I want to show you something," he finally says, leaning over to open one of his bottom drawers.

As he pulls it open, he tenses, his face crumpling into a wince from whatever pain the movement has caused. I don't bother asking if he's okay, and he doesn't ask me for help. Instead, he pulls himself back up—much slower this time— and sets a roll of knives down onto the desk between us.

"These are my hunting knives," he begins, stating the obvious.

I've seen this set before. Years ago, when I was still too afraid to admit my hesitation to join the Order and he would drag me out to their father and son events. He brought these on a camping trip. I remember, because he pointed out the Lancaster crest that had been stamped onto the hilt and explained how they've been passed down for six generations.

"One day, I'd like to give them to you. But you have to earn them first."

Naturally.

"And how would I do that?" I ask, my tone flat and disinterested.

"We've got a small hunting trip planned with just a few of us. I can show you what we're all about, and you can make your decision then."

There's something sinister in the way he says it. As if going on this trip will make the decision for me either way. *This* is what he was hiding from my mother. But just as I go to decline, he stops me.

"Just take one last trip with your old man," he guilts, pushing the knives toward me.

Instead of gazing at them the way he expects me to, I lift my eyes to meet his, ignoring them completely as I consider my options.

This could possibly get me some inside information about them that I'd usually miss out on. I've already been considering recruitment. Would it be so bad to let a dying man think it was his idea? That I'm joining for his sake?

Brothers aren't supposed to discuss their business with non-members, but these assholes can't keep it to themselves, especially after they've gotten a few drinks in. If anyone is planning something sinister against Sienna or me, I'm sure they couldn't resist the temptation to threaten me with it. Especially now that they know how much I despise them. This trip might be what I need to get the information I've been craving, without the commitment of joining right away.

"Fine," I say without giving it much more thought. I'll stay one night, get whatever information I can gather, then disappear before they realize I'm gone.

His smile instantly broadens as he claps his hands together once in celebration. "You won't regret it."

Every instinct I have is screaming the opposite.

**37**

*The Lamb*

"MY DAD'S little boys club throws this charity ball every year," Sienna greets the next morning at Old Soul. "You should come with me. Mallory usually tags along, but she's got exams and I think she's in a fight with her boyfriend."

I go to shake my head and immediately decline the offer, but she holds her finger up in a silent plea to hear her out first.

"I know that last time we went out together, things ended up being a little weird," she breaks in with a pointed stare.

I still haven't fully explained what happened. Mostly because I have no clue how I left the club, but I also don't know how to describe my complicated relationship with the man who breaks into my house and watches me sleep. Admitting what happened the next day is almost worse than telling her I was drugged and driven an hour away to some strange man's penthouse. Not to mention the things we did after he found me in his room…

"But!" She continues, breaking me out of the memory. "This isn't the same as going to the club. It's a black-tie event. Super classy. And I won't leave your side the entire time. In fact, we don't even have to drink. Although, alcohol does make these things less insufferable."

"I don't know…"

"I'll buy your dress," she adds, clapping her hands together in a begging motion.

"I'll think about it."

Pushing out a long, dramatic breath, she leans over the counter and lowers her voice. "Look, my dad just told us he's got terminal cancer. This stupid ball is the last place I want to be right now, but I already promised I'd go."

"I'm sorry to hear that."

Waving her hand between us, she shakes her head. "Don't be. Just come with me."

And just like that, she's ensnared me. How can I decline the offer now?

"Fine," I relent, turning on my heel to grab her coffee. She's worn Rosie down enough to start getting them free every day.

I have no idea how she managed to do it, but that seems to be her superpower.

"I really am sorry about your dad." I hand her the drink, my voice breaking with sincerity.

Sienna shrugs. "Death is inevitable. Grief is a privilege. It means you've loved someone enough to want the impossible —for them to live forever." She takes a sip of her coffee, her eyes rolling in the back of her head at the taste. "He's old, so I knew it was coming eventually," she coldly adds before shuffling over to her usual table to begin her schoolwork.

But I can't get what she said out of my mind. *It means you've loved someone enough to want the impossible—for them to live forever.*

My dad is nonexistent. There's no doubt my mom and I have a rocky relationship. I'd never wish death on her, but could I say I want her to live forever?

If I'm being brutally honest... *no*.

The only people I can imagine feeling that way about are Halen and Kennedy, and I'm not sure they share the sentiment. My own mother didn't show up to the hospital when I died and came back. Even worse, she had a hand in killing me, so she definitely doesn't feel that way.

Sienna is right—grief is a privilege. How pathetic of a person am I that I hardly have it?

My eyes find her across the shop. She feels me looking and pops her head up from her computer, smiling broadly. I may have more people to add to that list than I realize.

Losing her would be devastating. I thought I was done forming friendships with people, completely content living alone in my own little bubble. What's the point of they're just going to leave the moment you do something they don't agree with? She's managed to sneak her way through the cracks and embed herself in my life.

Same with Rosie.

And as much as I hate admitting it... same with my mystery man.

Blood isn't the only prerequisite for loving someone. It's totally possible to find people in the most unlikely places and have them take enough space in your heart that you can't imagine life without them.

That you'd grieve them and want them around forever.

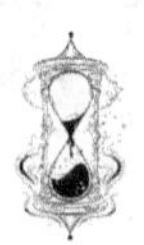

I ASSUMED that when Sienna offered to buy my dress, it meant we'd go shopping together and she'd pay the bill. When she texted me asking for my address and told me she was on the way after work the next day, I rushed through a shower, threw some makeup on, and panic-cleaned my house. I fully expected that she'd come by, do a quick walk through, and then we'd be on our way.

Instead, she pulled into my driveway and unloaded an entire clothing rack from the trunk of her luxury SUV, followed by at least twenty plastic-wrapped dresses.

"Did you buy all of these?" I questioned, holding the door open as she rolled it all into my front room.

"Well, I figured you'd have to work because Rosie makes you work every day," she grumbles, rolling her eyes.

She and Rosie have formed their own friendship from all her time at the cafe, and part of that entails Sienna harassing Rosie about my work hours.

"But my favorite store is only open until five and there's nothing in Styx that even comes close to suitable for an event thrown by the Order."

I follow her through the front room as she leads herself into the large grand room at the back of the house, never once asking me where to go. She parks the rack against an empty wall and starts fingering through the hangers.

"So, I took a ride to the city and grabbed these for us to try on."

Stepping beside her, I grab one of the price tags hanging out of the plastic wrap of a long-sleeved gown and check the number. My eyes widen in shock.

"This is a seven-thousand-dollar dress," I exclaim, quickly releasing the fabric from between my fingers before I ruin it. There's no way in hell I'll ever be able to pay for it if something happened.

Sienna shrugs. "I got it on sale."

"You *bought* all of these?" I step back, placing my hands on my hips. "I can't wear these." I can't believe she even thought that I could.

"Of course. How else do you think I was able to bring them here?"

"Sienna, this is insane."

"I told you that I'd buy your dress. What did you think I meant?"

"I thought we'd go to the mall and grab an evening gown off the clearance rack," my voice raises an octave as the reality of the inequalities between our two worlds comes crashing down on me.

We couldn't be any more different.

She gapes at me, plump lips wrapped in a perfect 'O' and nose scrunched as if that is the most offensive thing I could have said. "Did I do something to make you think I hate you?"

"These dresses are too much. I've never even seen this much money before. What happens if I spill something on it?"

"We'll get it dry cleaned…"

Dry cleaned. *Dry cleaned.* Growing up, we went through phases without a washer and dryer. And here she is, talking about *dry cleaning* a dress.

"It's really not that expensive to get something professionally cleaned," she continues, turning back to the dresses to pull a dark purple one off the rack.

"That's not the point."

"What *is* the point then? Because it seems like you're judging me for trying to do something nice for you."

"I'm not judging you. It's just…" I pause when she pulls the cover off the dress and holds it up to me, closing one eye as if she's imagining it on. When she decides it won't work for whatever reason, she puts it back on the rack.

"This feels like more than I'm worth," I finally admit as she turns away.

She stills, shoulders falling back. And I'm left nervously wringing my hands, waiting for her response to my ridiculous, insecure admission.

"How do you always manage to surprise me? Every time I think I've got you pegged, you pivot and throw me for another loop."

I blink, unsure how to respond to that.

When enough time has passed to make it awkward, I settle on quietly telling her, "I wasn't raised with money like you were."

"So what? How does that make you any less worthy of these than I am? I told you I'd buy your dress. I chose to pay for these particular ones because I think you deserve it and I want you to feel beautiful. But if you think you'll be more comfortable in a dress from JCPenney, we can go there right now and pick one out for you. I'll keep all these for myself."

My eyes catch on the midnight-blue gown on the end, then flick back to her. "I don't want you to regret it."

Sienna grabs the gown and rips the plastic off it, handing it over with a smug smile. "You're one of the few genuine people I've ever met, Jovie. I'll never regret being your friend. Go put this on and try to tell me it isn't the most beautiful thing you've ever laid eyes on."

## 38

*The Lamb*

THE STARGAZING BALL is held in a darkly lit, elegant ballroom overlooking the Hudson River and New York City skyline. Sparkling city lights flickering against the dark night sky serve as the backdrop to the black tie event. As soon as Sienna's driver pulled up to the curb of the hotel and let us out, I had the sinking feeling that I'd made a grave mistake in agreeing to come.

This isn't my scene. These are not my people. This is so far beyond my comfort zone.

She senses my discomfort just before we walk through the hotel entrance, gently wrapping her hand around my upper arm to lead me off to the side.

"You okay?"

"Yeah, I just feel a little in over my head." My attention catches on a couple walking by, dressed head to toe in designer clothes that probably cost more money than I'll ever see in my lifetime. Then, I look down and realize I'm wearing one of those ridiculously exclusive outfits as well. "You didn't mention how fancy this thing was."

"I told you it's black tie," she reminds, shifting herself to conceal me from view when she notices my worried expression. "Hey, if you want to leave, we can."

"No, no… I just need to calibrate."

Another group of people walks by, laughing about something the tallest guy said. One of the women notices Sienna and veers off from the group, stopping behind her just before tapping her on the shoulder to get her attention.

"I didn't think you were coming," she tells her, eyes flicking over to me for a second before she must decide I'm not worth being introduced to and I'm completely dismissed. "Is Mal inside?"

It's rude, but I'm oddly grateful. I hope everyone else regards me the same way, so I can get through this night without sounding like a bumbling idiot trying to relate to people who live completely different lives.

Sienna notices the dismissal, though. Her lips purse, eyes tight as she vaguely clips, "she might make an appearance later."

The girl nods, and someone from her group calls her over. She holds up a finger to them and turns back to us with a sheepish smile. "Cool. We'll catch up later."

"She's such a bitch," Sienna hisses under her breath, hooking her arm around my elbow to guide me toward the entrance. "Just hold your head high and remember that every single one of these people is too self-absorbed to bother with whatever you're doing."

"Thanks? I'm not sure if that's supposed to make me feel better or worse…"

She tips her head back and barks out a laugh as we enter a packed elevator, earning judgemental stares from the group of older people standing behind us.

"Sienna," one of them greets.

"Will your brother be gracing us with his presence tonight?" a man with short, graying hair asks.

Sienna turns back to him with a tight smile. "You can't ever be sure with Bash, can you?"

I remember her telling me about her brother—the one who disappeared and came back weeks later. She hasn't spoken of him much since that day we each opened up, but I can tell she's holding something back when it comes to him.

Could he be an addict like my mother?

A control freak like Gabe?

Why else would she be so tight-lipped about someone she clearly loves dearly?

Why else would they each think him so unreliable?

The man grunts, and I can tell he isn't pleased with her response. "I hope he does, for your father's sake."

Sienna's back straightens. She looks over to me, plastering on a playful, mocking smile, but I can see the tightness in her eyes. The crinkle between her brows. Her family is a sore spot, just as mine is for me.

We may come from different worlds, but our problems are more alike than I thought.

The elevator dings, opening right up to the grand ballroom, and Sienna leads me into the shark-infested waters.

## 39

*The Wolf*

As PART of our deal for the cabin, I'm attending the Order's annual Stargazing ball.

I know that I could back out now that the paperwork is filed and the house is mine. Find some excuse with work that he can't argue. But his new prognosis has left me feeling sympathetic. I don't want to cause undue stress for him or my mom. That, and I want the chance to rub elbows with the men who murdered Sienna and get a feel for where they stand now.

The last thing I expected was to find my sister sitting at our table beside my little Stardust. Dressed in a gown that mirrors the night sky behind her, earning her nickname even more, she's the epitome of beauty. She outshines every single woman here.

A beacon of light in this room of vile, twisted individuals.

And completely exposed to the monsters I've fought like hell to keep her away from.

I could strangle Sienna right in front of everyone for being such an insufferable menace. Never have I met someone who lives to press my buttons as much as my sister does. I have no doubt she knows exactly what she's doing to me with this faux friendship, and I hate that she's using Jovie as a chip in her little game.

She's infuriating. Even worse, she's dangerous.

As if she can hear my silent curses, her eyes find me across the room. I fix my face into the hardest glare I can muster. If her bullshit twin-telepathy theory is correct, I hope that every threatening and violent thought I'm having is blaring inside of her head right now.

But her only response is a shrug. A fucking *shrug*. As if we can chalk this up to a simple, "aw-shucks," and pretend she didn't just bring my girl into a lion's den waiting to devour her.

I can't sit at the table with them. Not after I've already shown Stardust my face. There's no way I'm capable of being that close to her without marking my territory, which will only raise more interest in her. The Order likes to take the things I care about, especially when I don't behave how they want me to.

Sienna has all but guaranteed my recruitment into this shitshow. There's no other way I can keep them both safe now.

An arm wraps around me, clapping my shoulder. "Glad to see you could make it," my father greets, swirling the whiskey around in his glass.

"We made a deal," I blandly remind him, turning my attention across the room so he doesn't catch me staring at Stardust.

"Yes, well… It still means a lot that you're here. I hope you're reconsidering your decision not to join. The Order would love to have you as a Lancaster legacy."

Charles Simon walks by Sienna, Jovie, and my mother. Logan trails closely behind, tapping Sienna on the shoulder in a quick greeting before he moves on to his own table.

He's set to initiate this year. We'll likely have our ceremonies at the same time if I decide to move forward with mine. His has been delayed this long so he can travel abroad without the rules and restrictions members of the Order take on when they swear in. Charles practically shit his pants when he came back and told him he was ready. He ran straight to my father and the rest of the masters to start the process.

"I am," I vaguely say as Hugh walks up beside us.

"Are my eyes deceiving me? Has Sebastian Lancaster graced us with his presence tonight?" He jovially greets with a broad smile, tightly shaking my hand.

"I had to bribe him," my father laughs, tipping back his whiskey.

"Good to see you, son." He says, dropping his voice. "We're always happy to have legacies around."

"We're hoping to get him initiated before this damn cancer takes me out," my father says, earning a sympathetic look from Hugh.

I'm not surprised that he told him before bothering to let us know he was terminally ill. My father had always been more loyal to them. That doesn't make it any less irritating.

"You're welcome to join the recruitment roster anytime," he assures me, then offers another sad smile to my father, who looks happy as can be now that he's proven his point and showed his hand.

"We can talk about it later. Go spend time with that beautiful family of yours while you still can." With that, he holds his drink up and walks away.

"Are you going to sit down?" My father asks me.

My eyes roam back to the table, where Sienna and Stardust's spots are now empty. I was so distracted with Hugh and refraining from pummeling my dad for his obvious agenda, I missed where they went.

Shaking my head, I hold up my empty glass. "I need a refill," I tell him. He nods, and someone else walks up from behind and pulls him into conversation.

I'm on edge the rest of the night, orphaned from my family and forced to wander around to avoid being seen by Stardust. During dinner, I escaped to the hotel bar and ate my meal alone, then rejoined the party once everyone was back up and mingling.

"Didn't I see Bash around here somewhere?" My mother wonders aloud, swinging her head around to search for me.

I happened to be walking near them, feigning interest in the silent auction tables. I move around the table to watch them, shifting around a couple to obstruct their view of me.

"He's around somewhere," my father mumbles into his glass, not even bothering to hide his smile at the idea that I'm actually enjoying myself at one of these functions.

My mother purses her lips, craving her head to look around him.

"Well, he hasn't bothered to sit with us and say hi for five minutes," she complains, finally giving up on her search.

I look to Stardust, who is trying to appear like she isn't listening to the conversation even though she clearly is.

I smirk.

*Is she curious about me?*

What has Sienna said about her elusive brother who never seems to be around?

Sienna must be on a mission to irritate me tonight. Where she usually ducks out of things like this shortly after dinner, tonight she keeps Stardust there until well after the last auction winner is announced. And since I don't dare leave them alone, I'm forced to sit through it all with them.

**40**

*The Wolf*

My FATHER's definition of a small, casual camping trip is far different than what mine is.

Members of the Order meander around the grounds, weaving and out of the line of campers parked in the empty field we drove over two hours to get to. I watch their familiar reactions, filling the void with meaningless conversation as they get their sites set up for the weekend.

There's got to be at least a hundred of them.

My father presses the button on our rig to get it to self-level while I hide away inside, unpacking the crate of food he brought so I don't have to pretend to be interested in anything the people who walk by and strike up small talk have to say.

Tonight is about settling in. That's what he told me when we backed the camper in. "Tomorrow will be when all the real fun is had," he promised.

It's difficult not to obsess over what Stardust may be

doing, or how Sienna could be pissing me off. The only way I was able to talk myself into following through with going was realizing that most of the people who I'm trying to protect them from are here, with me.

When I'm out of things to do in the camper, I reluctantly join my father outside on his makeshift patio, hopeful that the setting sun will keep most people away as they prepare for the day ahead.

Hunting is done during early morning hours, isn't it? They should be retiring early tonight if that's the case.

"I want to brace you for what you'll be experiencing tomorrow," my father begins, circling the base of his whiskey glass around the rim of the cup holder in his chair.

"I've been hunting before," I assure him.

My strategy has always been to linger in the blind and avoid killing anything, but it might be exactly what I need to take the edge off after going so long without killing.

My body may not have taken a life in this timeline, but my mind has. The urge to spill blood gnaws at me more as each day passes. Especially when those days are spent around the people who deserve it the most.

I can practically feel their blood dripping down my arms at the sight of them.

"Not like this," he insists, turning in his seat to fully face me. "These trips are usually only permitted for members, with the exception of a few trustworthy prospects…"

The words die off, but his sentence still seem to carry on between us, his expression conveying all the things he isn't saying aloud.

I'm neither of those things. Not officially.

Yet, here I am.

"I've assured them that you'll keep what you see here to yourself. I'm trusting that you won't make a liar out of me."

Raising his left brow, he works his jaw back and forth a

few times, then tilts his glass up to his lips and throws it back in one gulp. He's nervous. That much is obvious, even if I didn't already notice the stiffness of his shoulders or how he's looked over his shoulder several times in the span of a few minutes.

He's taking a risk with me here. One that he doesn't have full faith will pay off. But this cancer has forced his hand and pushed him into something he isn't sure I'm ready for.

*What the hell am I walking into?*

"You'll see what I mean when we head into the woods," he explains once his glass is empty, slamming it onto the picnic table beside us. "I just ask that you keep your mind open and your mouth shut. These are traditions that the Order has carried out for centuries. Generations of Lancasters have taken part."

"Gentleman," Hugh Kensington greets, and everyone turns forward to face him. Some men shuffle forward, forming a semi-circle around where he stands on the grass so they can hear better. I remain rooted to my spot, a few rows of people closing in ahead of me. Charles Simon, my father, and a few other higher-ranking members, including my uncles, sit behind him in camping chairs.

It took a half hour for us to hike out here through the dense woods. My father had to pause several times, clutching to nearby trees to catch his breath and rest his legs. His brothers passed by him without a second glance, leaving him for dead. After the third time, I was sure he'd want to turn back, realizing his body has become too weak to push through these conditions.

I wouldn't have opposed him. The closer we got to wherever we were going, the heavier the dread built in my gut. There's something seriously wrong with this place—with these woods. Horrible things have happened here, I can feel it. I only hope they weren't done at the hands of the men walking beside me.

He never asked to turn around. Instead, we waited together in silence until his breathing evened back out, and then continued on behind the rest of the group until finally, we reached a grassy clearing with a newly built, steel barn sitting in the center and a wood corral beside it.

The sight of it only made my trepidation double.

"The time has finally come for our Serpent Hunt to begin. For many of you, this is a long-awaited event. One we plan for throughout the entire year. For others, this is your first time." His steel-blue eyes scroll over the gathered crowd once we all filed into the clearing, stopping on me at his last statement. I stare back blankly, my expression schooled the way I would when my father looked at me with the same indignation.

"The rules are simple," he goes on, breaking our contact to continue his perusal of the crowd. "The prey is blindfolded. They'll be brought into the corral for exactly ten minutes for you to assess and pick through. Absolutely no touching, and no fighting with a fellow brother. The consequences will be worse than you can imagine. There's enough for everyone to have their fun. When the gun goes off, they'll get a five-minute head start. After that, the hunt is on. What you choose to do when you catch one is completely up to you."

His lips kick up in a sick, sadistic smirk, and Charles' gaze snaps over to mine when Hugh adds, "We've got good stock this time around."

There's some hooting from behind me as everyone's

adrenaline begins to flow and anticipation becomes too much for them to keep quiet anymore. Hugh allows it for a few seconds, smiling proudly at his constituents before he lifts his hands in a silent demand for them to settle.

When it's quiet enough to hear him again, he goes on. "Be sure to take your time and have some fun. This event only comes once a year, afterall."

He looks to someone in the back of the crowd and nods his head once before there's a sudden loud crashing sound, and we all turn to watch as Jeremy Bateman, a middle-aged investment banker who worked under my dad for most of my teens, walks backward out of the sliding barn door. He's slamming a metal rod into a steel bucket, eyes trained inside the building.

My stomach drops to my feet when the first one tumbles through the opening, falling hard onto her hands and knees into mud that has to be at least six inches deep with a bandana tied tightly around her head, obscuring her entire face. The rest pause at the wet, hollow sound of her fall, arms stretching out in every direction to blindly feel for some-thing—*anything*—that might direct them where to go to avoid the same fate.

The banging continues, louder and faster when they slow their steps. It's a demand for them to continue moving—one they obey hesitantly. I watch in complete horror as the rest of the men and women file out in a herd, quickening their steps and stomping the first woman deeper into the ground as she cries out in agony until she's nothing more than mud, bones, and blood.

Two men standing to my left chuckle at the gory scene, making a crass joke about *that one* having already been weeded out. I want to heave. It takes a concentrated amount of effort for me to turn my head toward the woods and bite my tongue, refusing to allow my body to expel the memory of what I just witnessed the way it desperately wants to. My fingernails dig deep into my palms until I feel blood trickle out from beneath them.

How the fuck am I going to fake my way this?

I can't.

I *won't*.

Maybe I can kill a few of them in the woods. No one would notice in all the chaos, would they? I doubt they'd be able to pin it on me if I'm discreet enough.

Inhaling a few deep breaths, I attempt to gather myself before anyone realizes something is atray. But Hugh's speech begins rolling through my head again, and the pieces start to click together.

*The prey is blindfolded.*

These men and women—they're the prey. Carefully curated to meet each member's sick desires.

*They'll be brought into the corral for exactly ten minutes for you to assess and pick through.*

They're going to circle these people like vultures, picking apart their appearance until they decide which one would be most suitable for their hunt.

*What you choose to do when you catch one is completely up to you.*

I shift on my feet, turning to watch as every member stares into the corral—rabid dogs with their mouths practically foaming in anticipation. They're going to torture and maim these people. For pleasure. For power. For *fun*.

And the last part—the one Charles made sure to look directly into my eyes as he said it—becomes apparent when my gaze accidently strays inside the corral, and I catch a glimpse of the soft, light brown waves I had between my fingers just last night.

*We've got good stock this time around.*

As if she senses my attention, her back straightens before

she blindly turns in my direction, face completely covered by the same tight, black bandana the rest of them are wearing.

But I know beyond a shadow of a doubt that it's her.

My soulmate.

*Stardust.*

## 41

*The Wolf*

My FEET TAKE me to her before my mind can come up with an inconspicuous excuse for it. I walk until my waist meets the wooden fencing separating us from them, my stomach tightening as I confirm my wildest nightmare.

She's been chosen for their hunt.

*This* is exactly why I was hellbent on keeping her away. *This* is why I wanted to strangle Sienna for even bringing her to that bullshit gala, parading her around like some new toy.

"Jovie," a voice calls from somewhere to my right, and Stardust's spine stiffens. "We're going to have so much fun today, Jovie-girl," the voice teases again.

The owner chuckles, and I immediately recognize that tantalizing sound from years of listening to Logan torment innocent people in school for fun.

I search for him, but there's too much movement between us as more members crowd around the corral to get a better look. Logan calls out another taunt to my little lamb, and I'm able to catch a glimpse of his buzzed, sandy hair.

I begin pushing through the people between us, ignoring all the grunts and groans as people berate me for my rudeness. I don't stop until I'm standing beside the man I should have killed the moment I walked out of that hospital.

"Logan." The name comes out like a curse. "What are you doing here?"

Stupid question. Obviously, he's here as a prospect.

His eyes flick over to me, brows pinched in confusion. When it's clear I'm expecting an answer, the side of his lip rises in disgust at my interruption.

"I could ask you the same thing," He barks, his voice unnecessarily loud. I've startled him.

His head swings over to the spot Hugh was standing a few moments prior, and I'm tempted to step between him and Stardust and demand an answer for why he's specifically tormenting her until I realize that Charles has stood up to witness the exchange with a wide, knowing grin.

"The Loyal Order of the Serpent is a closed society. Only a *select* elite and their legacies are welcome to join," Logan calls out, loud enough for everyone to quiet their conversations. "What is he doing here?"

The accusation is clear in his tone—I'm an outsider in his eyes, ineligible for membership.

"I'm just as much of a legacy as you, Simon. Moreso, considering my father and grandfather's rankings," I tell him, raising my brow when he trips over a loose rock and nearly falls backwards.

"That's debatable," Logan scoffs. "You've done nothing for the Order."

The scene has caused enough of a stir that most everyone has gone quiet. A few mumble their opinions to one another, shock spreading through them as my presence is quickly realized by the rest of the brotherhood.

But the more pressing issue is Stardust. I can't have him getting to her before I do.

"We've allowed the prospective member to join us in today's hunt so we can get to know him and make our decision. Same as you. Nothing is official, and he is *not* officially set to initiate this year," Hugh calmly explains before the chatter grows too loud.

He pins Charles with a punishing glare for his son's insolence, and the coward practically shrivels into the ground.

*Fuck.*

Logan looks at me with a murderous glare, his brows casting a shadow over his eyes that causes them to look near-black. I've thoroughly humiliated him. *Good.* That's the least I could hope for after taunting Stardust the way he did. Now, I'll have to repay him the favor for nearly killing her, too.

"She's mine," he mumbles under his breath when the focus has shifted enough for it to go unnoticed. His eyes ping over to Stardust, then back to me so quickly, I nearly miss it.

He's staking his claim. Or so he thinks.

"We'll see who gets to her first," I retort, winking at him teasingly.

Jeremy's loud banging starts up again, calling everyone's attention back to Hugh. The group in the corral startles, some of them actually pissing themselves out of fear for what's to come.

"Send them off," Hugh tells him, raising his arms toward the woods. Jeremy obeys, unlatching the gate to set the victims free.

But none of them move.

"Remove your blindfolds," Jeremy commands in a deep, authoritative tone. In one cohesive movement, each and every one obeys, rapidly blinking as they adjust to the bright sunlight. Some look over toward us, terror-stricken. Others mumble prayers into their chests, begging for salvation.

Before they can get too comfortable, Jeremy bangs the rod against the bucket three more times, then calls out for them to run.

And they do. They sprint off toward the woods, clutching onto their last shot at survival before they're hunted down like rabbits. Some trip, sending the others behind them flying face-first into the ground. To my relief, no one relives the same fate as the first woman, and each of them get back up to continue their run for their lives.

Stardust is no exception. She takes off to the left, sticking to the outside of the herd, where there's less of a chance for her to be trampled or tripped. My eyes track her as far as they can and I try to memorize her stride in case I have to track her footprints later. There's no telling if it will work, but I'm desperate for any advantage I can get over Logan, who has wasted his opportunity to track her by glaring at me the entire time she ran off like the egotistical piece of shit that he is.

The next few minutes are torture.

A hush has fallen over the campground as each of us wait the required time before we can catch our prey. I've fastened my mask around the bottom half of my face, and a few others do the same. Where I'm plotting how I'm going to capture Stardust and whisk her out of here before anyone notices we're gone, the men surrounding me are plotting the ways they'll torture and kill whatever unfortunate soul falls into their grips.

I don't have the capacity to let that bother me. Not right now, when all of my energy has to go to saving her.

But I know I'll agonize over this day for years to come. Every ounce of torture these innocent people endure will be etched into my soul—into the very fiber of my being. They can't be saved, though. Not by me alone.

With seconds to spare, I look up to thy sky and make a silent vow. I promise that I'll get retribution for what happens here today. I'll spill the blood of every single man who uses his power and status to inflict pain and suffering simply because they can—because they view themselves as more worthy of life than those who live below them.

I'll remember them. All of them. I'll keep their spirit alive, even if it's just a spark of what it should be.

A shot fires behind me, it's sound hallow and booming, and we take off.

The hunt has begun.

## 42

*The Lamb*

I'M SPRINTING the moment the gun is fired. There's no method or thought out plan for where I'm going, except *away* from wherever I just was.

They captured us all in broad daylight and shoved us into a van, driving endlessly until we reached a barn set in the middle of the woods. I was able to gather that much from the whispered, panicked conversations that were fit in as we waited for what was to come.

I'd just gotten off a morning shift at the cafe. My car was parked across the street, and I was only a few feet away when someone grabbed me from behind and tossed me into the back of a van. A burlap sack was thrown over my head before I could right myself to see who it was, and then I was hoisted up by my armpits and moved against what I assumed was the side of the vehicle. By the time I could relax against the cold metal, we were stopping again.

There was screaming and chaos, whispered threats, and

then someone landed beside me. They repeated the process three more times before the long drive began.

That evening, they came in wearing ski masks and stripped us of all our clothing, then wrapped our heads with blindfolds—so tight, I saw stars—ensuring we had no idea whether it was day or night. Those who fought it were beaten to death before our eyes and made an example of. The ones who cried or cowered were thrown around like rag dolls.

Then, we waited.

I'm not positive how much time passed before the banging and slamming began, but it couldn't have been more than a few hours. Once they felt that we were terrorized enough, they explained what was to come.

I thought that the mystery would be the worst part, but I was dead wrong. Knowing is far worse.

They're hunting us for fun. We were chosen at random as their prey and gathered together into a herd, then left to rot for hours like sheep waiting for slaughter. Well, I *thought* we were chosen at random. Until I heard my name being called out from a distance. My mystery taunter obeyed the rule that he was forbidden to touch me until the gunshot rang out.

I had five minutes to get as far away from him as possible, and I wasn't wasting a second of it seeking him out and trying to confirm what I already knew—that he wants to kill me like the rest of these people. The instant I can take my blindfold off, I'm shooting in whatever direction I'll find the least amount of obstacles.

And by obstacles, I don't mean tree roots or fallen branches. I mean people. *Humans* who have fallen and left on the ground to be trampled.

It's like a gruesome scene from a horror movie. Something I foolishly thought only happened in fiction. But these

monsters are real, their hunger insatiable. A living nightmare, worse than anything I've ever experienced before.

My feet ache and bleed as I tread over various sticks and
rocks that slice into them. My mind tries to cling to menial
details as I race past the foliage, survival instincts telling me
to pay attention to any unique markers that would tell me if
I'm getting anywhere, or if I'm just running in circles. It
doesn't matter, though. I don't know these woods as well as
they do, and even if the man who wants me dead doesn't
make his way out to me, one of the others surely will come to
collect.

There's no way they'd risk leaving one of us alive to
expose their operation.

I stop beside the thick, rough stump of an old tree,
hugging close to it in case I need to use it to hide. Slowly
sweeping my eyes across the foliage, I try to muster up a
plan.

Running is only going to get me so far. They've got to
have a way to catch up to us fast if they give us a head start.
That was just an illusion—a way to give us one last shred of
hope before ripping it all away for good.

I won't be fooled by something as fleeting and fickle as
hope.

There's a group of three pine trees about twenty feet
ahead of me, their branches low enough to the ground for
me to hoist myself up and climb onto. The needles are still
intact, offering a small amount of coverage to conceal me
from plain sight. Unless they knew to look up, they might
miss me completely.

It would make me a sitting target, but that might be my
only option.

The issue is my scent. They could have dogs they've
specifically trained for these hunts. Lifting my hands in front
of my face, then twisting my arms to do the same, I realize

I'm covered in tiny cuts from running carelessly through the forest. Blood still pools from some of them, while others have begun to coagulate and crust over. I don't feel any of it, my skin still numb from the adrenaline rush I had when they shot the gun.

There's no way I'll go undetected like this.

Spinning around, I look for something I can use to scrub the blood off. Maybe I can mask the scent enough to fool them into continuing on without checking the trees. I'm still completely naked, so I don't have to worry about my scent clinging to any clothing.

Ripping pine needles from the closest branch, I begin rolling them over my skin. Then, I grab up a handful of dead leaves from the ground, scrubbing them all over my body until I'm almost fully painted with the dark, dry dirt they were covered in. Before scattering them onto the ground directly below the tree I'll be sitting in, I get the idea to spread them out.

Five minutes have definitely passed by now. It's probably been closer to twenty, if I'm being realistic.

They'll be coming through here within a few moments. Whoever *they* are. Shivering at the thought, I push it far from my mind, promising myself I'll process all of this later. If I can survive until then.

I run the twenty feet back to the thick tree and circle the pines, rubbing more leaves on myself and then throwing them out as far as I can. When it seems like I've gone in enough random directions to confuse a dog, I sprint back toward my chosen pine and hop on, hoisting myself up the first branch.

My fatigued muscles scream with the effort. Each time I have to pull my body up another level, they quiver and shake. I'm only halfway when they begin to spasm, and it feels like they might give out completely. But I force myself to continue a few more feet.

Footsteps sound from somewhere below me, along with a few muffled voices. I still mid-step, awkwardly suspended a few inches away from the trunk between two branches. I make the mistake of looking down, my heart dropping at how alarmingly close their heads bob below me.

I should have climbed faster. I should have swung over to the next tree. I should have fucking fought harder when they grabbed me instead of submitting like some pathetic little girl.

*Should have, should have, should have.*

"I thought you said you saw her run this way," an older man accuses, his voice clear now that they're standing directly below me.

"I did," the younger one insists, spinning in a circle. "But she couldn't have gone this far. She's not in that good of shape."

Scowling down at him, I focus on keeping my breaths shallow and steady so they don't notice the small movement.

"We have to find her before he does," the man says grimly, staring back in the direction we all came from.

"What's the sudden interest in him? And how do you know the girl? You never explained that part to me." The younger one moves over to the tree I stopped at earlier and leans against it, pulling out a packet of nuts from his hoodie pocket.

I've seen him before. A few times, actually, with Sienna.

That revelation only makes this even more confusing.

"He's not important, but she's a liability. That's all you need to know."

"Well, our little disagreement earlier has stirred up a lot of attention already. I wish you had warned me that he'd be here."

There's another set of footsteps to our left, and I watch as both their heads swing in that direction, their spines stiffening enough to tell me they don't want anyone else involved. Reluctantly, I turn my own head to observe the new visitor.

Only to realize that no one is there.

But there were footsteps. We all heard them.

"We should go before someone finds us," the young one whispers. I can't, for the life of me, remember what his name is. "She isn't here."

The other man nods, then knocks the nuts out of his hands. He watches in shock as they spill all around, but follows behind obediently, his fists flexing at his sides.

While my back is screaming to lean against the trunk of the tree and relax, I don't dare move a muscle once they're gone. Not when I know there's someone else out there and I could risk being someone else's prey.

It doesn't take long for the visitor to step out from the trees and reveal himself, anyway.

I'm absolutely horrified when I notice the familiar black mask and dark, silky hair of my mystery man standing a few feet below me.

**43**

*The Wolf*

A HAND CLAPS onto my shoulder, squeezing tightly before it yanks backward, effectively turning me in my spot. My head remains facing out toward the woods though, despite my body swiveling to the side. My eyes don't leave Logan as he takes off with Charles in the same direction Stardust sprinted.

"I wanted to give you something before you head out for your first hunt," my father tells me when I reluctantly tear my gaze away from Logan's disappearing back and fully face him, shocked to find he's holding up a knife.

The blade sits in a brown, carved leather sheath that perfectly matches its wooden hilt. My father twists it around in his hands, rubbing his thumb over the spot where our family crest has been burned into the wood, same as the other roll of knives he presented to me in his office. He pushes it toward me, eyes lit up with a proud expression like I've never seen before.

"This is the blade I used on my first hunt. And your grandfather used on his. It's been passed down for six generations now." Sniffling, he drops his head, pretending to inspect the weapon. "You'll be the *seventh* Lancaster man to use this blade on your first hunt. The next man to carry on our traditions."

"I thought I was supposed to earn the roll of knives…" My eyes anxiously flick back to the woods.

"This is different. *This* knife is what you want for your first. The roll will be used later."

"You want me to use it… today?"

There's no way he thinks I'm fully on board with the shit-show that is happening here. How is he so obtuse, he can't see the disgust toward him and every single man here written all over my face?

I want to put a voice to the words he conveniently isn't saying. To scream how revolting and wrong I think this whole thing is. To call him out on the fact that he doesn't even have the courage to own up to what he's done and speak his sins out loud, the way a true killer would. Because he doesn't kill to seek justice or repent. He kills because it makes him feel powerful, and that kind of feeling can be addicting to a man with absolutely no control of his life.

It takes everything in me not to take the blade from his hands and jam it into his chest.

When he transfers it into my palms, I can practically feel the weight of the lives it's taken through the years settle in. As if the souls that were prematurely ripped from their bodies have clung to it over the years, cursing every Lancaster man who dared use it as a weapon for their own personal gain.

I can feel their dissent swarming me, buzzing around my head like an angry colony of bees. Their stirring fury stings me as the blade is symbolically passed down to yet another generation of weak-minded sheep.

*I won't use it like they did,* I want to tell them. *I'll find redemption for your suffering.*

My father—oblivious to my internal struggles—nods his head toward the woods and claps me on the back again. The tears from before still sit in his watery eyes, begging to fall. I know he won't let them. Not in front of me. This might be a step forward in his twisted mind, but it's not enough for him to show that much vulnerability in front of me.

"I saw you had your eye on one. Don't let that Simon boy steal your prey from you. Stake your rightful claim and join your brothers."

*Stardust.*

I almost forgot.

Doesn't he realize she's the same girl he sat across from and shared dinner with just a few nights ago? Of course not. They've completely stripped her of all her humanity to paint her as the animal they want to hunt.

Nodding my head at him, I shove the knife into my jeans and clamp my mouth shut before my thoughts find a voice of their own and take off running behind Logan and Charles.

His time will come. For now, I have to get to her before anyone else does.

I have to get her far away from here.

High-pitched screams filled with pain and terror echo off the trees around me from various directions. Each one sends a lightning bolt of guilt to my chest. Men I grew up with at dinner parties and school functions zip past me with crazed looks on their faces and weapons in their hands, so caught up in their hunt, they're oblivious to my presence.

They think I'm one of them. That it's safe to release the sadistic beasts lying dormant inside of them around me. Even worse, they think I'm doing the same.

None of them have any idea that their presence here today has signed their own death warrant. I'm coming after all of them—every single one.

A flash of shaved, brown hair appears ahead of me, stealing my attention away from the man who does my father's taxes lying in the dirt about fifty feet away on top of a weeping, naked man I saw in the corral. Once I see Charles' gray head bobbing up ahead, I take off in a sprint toward them, grateful that there isn't a third person in their grip.

**44**

*The Lamb*


HE CROUCHES to the ground where Gabe's nuts have spilled, leaning forward on his ankles to examine the area. But when he reaches out to touch whatever has caught his eye, it's not the nuts that he brings up to his masked face. It's a blood-smeared leaf. One I must have stepped on with my torn-up soles before hopping onto the branch.

The other men completely missed it, too caught up in their egotistical conversation to stop and look around.

He runs his finger along the smooth surface, smearing the crimson color further across the leaf. It's still wet.

I hold my breath as he swivels his head around, searching for more—tracking my path. But of course, there won't be any. Not unless he looks up at the branch beside him, where there's an identical patch of blood. I've accidentally led my hunters directly to me, despite my best efforts to confuse them.

I thought my worst threat was their dogs, so I focused on

confusing them. I had no idea he'd be so adept in tracking me.

He allows the leaf to fall from his palm and stares off into the distance, shoulders sagging forward with a defeated sigh. And just when I think he's about to give up—when I'm positive he's going to walk back to whatever corner of Hell he appeared from—the branch beneath my feet snaps under my weight.

My grasp tightens on the one above my head as it splinters off from the trunk and falls a few feet down before catching on the one right beside him. I'm left dangling awkwardly in midair, my arms stretched tight with my weight. Twisting my hips to the side, I wrap my legs around the trunk and scale myself up to the next level, completely forgetting about the man standing below me, his head tipped up in my direction.

Adrenaline rushes through my body again, swooshing through my ears as I finally right myself. It's so loud, I almost don't hear him when he sighs, "Stardust."

"Come down," he orders, pointing to the ground beside him.

"Fuck off."

A scream sounds off in the distance and we both tense, eyes snapping in the direction it came from. There's no way I'm handing myself over to him that easily and submitting myself to the same fate as the rest of the people I was brought here with. Not without some sort of fight.

"Please, come down," he begs in a strained voice.

"So you can maim and torture me? No thanks, you sick fuck."

"I promise, I won't hurt you." Holding his hand out, he steps further between the pine branches. "I can't help you if you're up there. I need to get you out of here. *Please.*"

I scoff, shrinking further into the center of the tree. "Fuck. *Off.*"

With a deep, frustrated growl, he grabs onto the first branch and starts pulling himself up. "If you won't come here on your own, I'm going to climb up there and drag you down against your will."

Gripping the next branch, I rush to hoist myself up another level, but my muscles are still fatigued from before, and he climbs much faster than I can. Within seconds, he's grabbing my ankle and pressing down, holding me to my spot.

"Don't," his dark voice warns as I begin to struggle against him, kicking my foot out to shake him off.

But he doesn't budge, and I almost lose my balance in the process. He swings himself up to the branch right below me, wrapping his arms around my bare torso to steady me. The knobs and peeling bark of the tree bite into my back, marring it even more.

"If you keep fighting me, you're going to fall," he grinds between his teeth, his mouth a few inches below my ear. "Please, just listen to me for once."

I reluctantly relax against him, but not because I trust him. Because he's right. If I fall from this tree, I'll break every bone in my body and he won't have to work at all to kill me.

"We have to get out of here before they come back for you with the dogs," he explains once he's sure I won't try anything stupid.

"What's wrong? You don't like to share?" I snark, wincing at what a sick, dark joke that was.

"No, Jovie, I *don't* like to share. I also prefer to keep you away from people who are actively trying to kill you," he retorts, his tone flat.

I hear the words, but my mind refuses to allow me to believe them. Why else would he be out here, in the middle of nowhere, with the sadistic, rich people who happened to steal me away and hunt me for their own pleasure? There's absolutely no chance this was an accident.

"We're going to climb down now. When we get to the ground, you can't run from me," he explains in a whisper, pulling me from my straying thoughts. "I know you don't believe me right now, but I'm trying to keep you safe."

There's no pause before he scoops me up and throws me onto his back. I have milliseconds to adjust, clenching my fists in his shirt to prevent myself from being flung onto the ground. A painful groan escapes my lips as he wraps one arm around my aching thigh, then slowly and carefully scales us down the tree.

When my feet hit the ground again, the sting from all my cuts has me hissing out a pained, agonizing breath. The adrenaline is fading away and with it, all the numbness is leaving my body until I'm left with nothing but aching bones and burning flesh. A shiver rolls across my skin, the cold air finally hitting me.

The man notices, then unzips his hoodie and wraps it around my shoulders protectively. He looks down at my feet and frowns at the bloodstained greenery below.

"I can carry you if you'd like," he offers, holding his hands up defensively when my face twists into a scowl at the thought of him touching me again. "Take my boots then," he amends, kicking them off his feet before even finishing his words. "They'll find us within minutes as long as you're bleeding like that."

I don't reject the offer, mostly out of sheer exhaustion, and he drops to his knees before me, his fingers moving quickly to transfer them over to my feet. They wrap around my calf, lifting it up to direct my toes into the warm shoe. Once he finishes tightly lacing the first one, he moves over and repeats the process with the other.

All I can do is stare down at him, a mix of appreciation and apprehension swirling together like a tornado in my chest. My body has completely relaxed in his presence, leaving fight or flight and entering a state of complete exhaustion, despite the threat my mind knows he still poses by simply being here. I need answers if I'm expected to fully trust him.

When the laces are double knotted and secured onto my feet, he lifts his chin and gazes up at me, his fingers skirting up my thighs in a slow, comforting pace. I don't see the malice or hunger in his eyes that I expected to find. There is no excitement at catching me or threat for what's to come.

All I see is… relief. Relief and fear. I can't seem to make sense of why either of those things would be present.

"I thought they got to you," he confesses in a hoarse whisper, fingers wrapping tightly around my upper thighs. "I followed your bloody path out here, and then I heard their voices. When the trail came to an end I thought…. I thought I lost you again. I was ready to burn this whole fucking forest down."

"Who are you?" I ask, my eyes flitting down to his mask, then back up to meet his tortured gaze. I haven't seen him wear the black scrap of fabric in a while.

*Who are you and why do you talk as if we know each other?*

Shaking his head, he drops it to his chest and allows it to hang between his shoulders. "The fact that you're asking me that is absolutely gutting," he mumbles into the ground.

There's a shuffling of leaves, and his attention snaps over to where it came from, eyes wide and alert. Our moment of vulnerability is over. These few minutes where we each seem to have forgotten where we are could end up costing us our lives.

Or at least mine.

"We need to go," his whispered voice rushes out as he climbs back to his feet.

Protectively wrapping his arm around my hip, he guides me into the opposite direction the noise just came from. But we're so distracted with what's behind us, we nearly miss the two men standing in the path before us.

"Hello, Sebastian," the old man from before greets darkly.

He cocks his gun and points it directly at my mystery man's head.

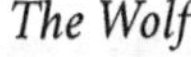

**45**

*The Wolf*

"Get out of my way," I growl, pulling Stardust against my chest.

"Oh, I can't do that, son," Charles coos condescendingly. "I have questions, and she has the answers."

"I don't even know who you are, you old fuck," Stardust spits from behind my arm, and have to stifle my laugh when Charles rears back, a disgusted look crossing his face.

She's gone feral, snuffing down the meek, polite woman I once knew—finally showing her teeth. There's a part of me that wants to laugh at the way she's handled this. To proudly celebrate the tenacity she's maintained as she stares her potential killer in the face. The other, more realistic side of me fears what might come from this traumatic experience. How will she cope when the adrenaline fades and she's left to pick through what happens here today?

While I'd love to skin the men standing before me alive

before plunging my knife into their flesh, I wonder if it would be too much for her to bear witness to.

What will the ramifications be when she wakes up and realizes all of it was real?

"She's as vile as we expected," he tells Logan, who hasn't taken his eyes off her once.

"I'm not asking again, Charles. Turn around and walk away, or you'll regret it."

His expression darkens, chin tucking down into his chest as he glares at me—*through* me—with hooded eyes. "What are you going to do? Tie me to a chair and slice me open? Douse me in gasoline and throw a match at me?"

I still, brows pulling together in confusion. Why would he say that? How could he know all that?

*Unless...*

"I don't know what you're talking about," I lie, fighting like hell to keep steady when there's a hurricane forming in the pit of my stomach.

Because he *remembers*. He knows I fucking murdered him. That I'm the Serpent Slayer—a traitor wearing the mask of his people, so I can learn their patterns and hunt them all over again, one by one.

He can't know that I remember, too. I'm well aware of how isolating it is to be in his position. The insanity he must battle every day, knowing there's something fucked up happening to us and having no idea what the hell it is. But if I admit to being like him, then I'm admitting to the crimes I committed against him and the rest of the Order *before*. I'd be further incriminating myself, confirming his suspicions. That's not something I'm willing to risk when I'm still not sure what kind of a role I'm going to take on this time in order to get close to them and find answers.

Narrowing his eyes, he glares at me in his best attempt to

gauge the truth of my words. I force my expression into neutrality, thanking God for the mask covering the bottom half of my face to make it that much easier. Once enough time has passed that his staring has grown uncomfortable for Gabe and Stardust, he shifts on his feet and brushes at his sleeve, face twisted into a bitter glower.

"Of course, you don't."

"Just come with us, Jovie." Logan reaches out for Stardust. She coils away from his touch, sending her one step deeper into my chest

"Fuck off," she tells him, repeating the words she used on me.

Logan rears back, his jaw twisting in an angry, contemplative circle. I watch carefully as his eyes flick down to her hands, then over to mine. He's assessing—deciding how easy it would be to simply grab her up and carry her off. He's so transparent, it makes me sick. There's one thing he isn't considering in his quick appraisal, and that's how fast I can slip the blade I'm carrying out of my pocket and into his neck.

"The rules state that brothers are not permitted to fight. There's enough *prey* to go around. I caught this one, fair and square," I remind them sardonically, wrapping my arm tighter around her torso in a possessive show of dominance that I hope also silently tells her I don't mean any of it.

I don't agree with this, but she's my priority right now. Her safety means more to me than anything else.

Charles huffs out a dry, mocking laugh. "You are not a *brother*, boy, and you knew we wanted her first."

But like Logan, he runs a contemplative scan over my body, assessing the threat I pose. Even outnumbered, I could take them out within minutes. I've already conquered both these men before, and I know their weaknesses. Logan is slow and predictable. Charles is old and frail. They'd be bleeding out on the ground before either could land a finger on Stardust.

"We'll get our answers another way. Let him deal with her mess. She's more work than she's worth."

Logan hesitates, eyes ping-ponging between Charles and Stardust as the reality of today—of the hunt—finally dawns on him.

"We can't just leave her for dead," he mumbles to Charles, feet rooted in their spot.

The old man pauses in his tracks, inhaling a long, frustrated breath before he turns back toward his son and shakes his head, holding his arm out toward me and Stardust.

"What did you think we were going to do with her, son?"

She shivers in my arms, holding her chin high in defiant contradiction. I look down at her, fixated on the soft tendrils of hair that have fallen out of her ponytail. They coil around her ear protectively, and I have to stop myself from leaning forward and running my lips against them, whispering promises that whatever they had planned for her will never come to fruition. I want to tell her she's safe and protected so long as she sticks with me. That I would never do the things these men are doing to innocent people. But I can't do that in front of Logan or Charles, who already know more than I want them to. They'll use her as a weapon against me.

Instead, I settle on covertly squeezing her hip beneath my hoodie as I lift my eyes back to Logan and Charles' receding forms.

Cowards.

Sad excuses of human beings.

*Dead.*

When they're far enough away for me to speak without being overheard, I grab her by the shoulders and turn her until she faces me.

"I know it's going to go against everything you want to do, but I need you to trust me. At least until I can get you out of these woods and somewhere safe."

**46**

*The Lamb*

WE HIKE for what seems like an eternity before the trees break and reveal a campground packed with various RVs and luxurious vehicles. He drags me along the perimeter, taking care in keeping us concealed from view until we stop behind a random site and he turns back, begging me to stay put while he grabs his keys and backs the white truck up to the woods for me to jump in.

If I'm going to run, now would be the time. When he's too distracted and trapped in the RV or the truck to immediately chase after me. His boots are like weights on my feet and my muscles are screaming in pain, but I could at least try, couldn't I?

Someone walks by the front of the camper and waves to him. When he lifts his arm, I can see that his sleeves are stained red from his elbow down, and my imagination runs wild. The casual way they act as people are being slaughtered all around us is astounding.

Running away from him would only send me back into a position to be caught by one of *them*. Is it worth leaving the man who is promising to keep me safe?

Not likely.

Instead, I remain rooted to my spot until he backs the truck up and opens the back door for me to climb in and lay on the floor until it's safe.

"How do you expect to convince me you aren't the villain in my story when you're always around when bad things happen?" I question doubtfully from the passenger seat once I've climbed up to the front. When he turns toward me with a look that makes me feel even more bare than I already am, I wrap my arms around my torso protectively.

"I'm there to save you, little lamb. Never to hurt you."

"I'm supposed to believe that bullshit?" I jeer, raising my upper lip.

His head swivels to look me in the eyes as he asks, "Have I done anything to prove otherwise?"

My cruel expression falls.

"Well... no." I bite my lip. "But that doesn't mean anything. You could be setting me up for these situations just so you can swoop in and look like the hero. None of this stuff happened to me before you appeared in my life."

Turning onto another road, he moves his jaw from side to side, the tendon in his neck twitching enough to shift his mask. "The last thing I want is to watch you suffer."

"Then, you'll have to explain, because the only time you show up seems to be when I'm suffering."

"It's hard to explain–"

"*Try*," I insist, interrupting whatever excuse he was about to give.

I'm tired of excuses. I'm tired of being lost and confused. I'm tired of sitting on my hands and waiting for things to happen to me.

With a sidelong glance, he releases a heavy sigh. When I can tell he's struggling with where to start, I turn in my seat to fully face him and point to the black bandana still secured tightly around his head.

"Why don't you begin by taking that mask off and letting me see you in broad daylight."

"What's the matter? You can't get a good look at my features when my tongue is buried inside of you?" He snarks back, his tone light and teasing.

My only response is a scowl.

He sighs, reaching behind him to undo the knot and release the bandana. As always, I'm awestruck by his beauty. It doesn't belong in so much ugliness.

"Better?"

Nodding, I stick my nose into the air. "I know your name," I announce confidently.

*Sebastian.* It sounds just as rich and full of life as he seems. I only know it from the man in the forest spitting it at him like a curse word. As soon as he said it out loud, my mystery man recoiled, his eyes flicking over to me like he was checking to see if I caught it.

"My name is meaningless unless you know the full thing."

"How so?" I push.

"Because once you hear it, you could remember it," he rushes out, abruptly stopping himself as soon as the words leave his lips.

He made a mistake telling me. That much is obvious. Something tells me he's not a person who is used to making mistakes.

Awkward silence falls over the vehicle, sitting between us like another passenger. When it's clear he won't be trying to explain any further, I puff up my cheeks and blow out my breath.

"You speak as if we know each other, but I can assure you… we don't."

I would remember eyes like those.

"You have no idea how much you don't know."

Pointing an accusatory finger at his face, I shake my head. "See, like that. You can't expect me to trust you when you say things like that to me without explaining what the hell you mean."

He turns the truck into a parking garage and I'm careened into the door, nearly falling out of my seat and onto the floor. His foot slams onto the brake, and the hoodie he gave me rides up my legs when my arms lift to the dash to catch my fall, exposing my ass before I can pull it back down.

Sebastian reaches his hand out in an attempt to stop me, but he's a fraction of a second too late, and instead of landing on my lap to hold me down the way he intends to do, he ends up groping my bare ass cheek. When I expect him to instantly pull away, he surprises me by keeping it there.

I awkwardly clamor away, scooting back onto my seat and further into my door. He doesn't even apologize or attempt to look embarrassed. Instead, he continues the conversation like nothing happened.

"It's obvious that I'm keeping secrets. I don't try to hide that from you. The answers you want will be revealed with time, as you're ready for them."

I'm captivated by his words, my body frozen beneath his warm touch. My mind tells me to open the car door and run as far away from him as fast as I can. Given the past twenty-four hours, that seems like the most appropriate response to a man who is associated with people who hunt and torture people for fun.

But my heart is telling me to stay. My soul is telling me to listen.

Once I'm righted in my seat and we're driving again, I ask, "who decides when I'm ready?"

"You do. Because despite all of that, I think you know that there's truth to what I'm saying. A part of you—way deep down—knows who I am. You recognize the small pieces I share with you, even though you fight against it. So *please*, Stardust. Please just give me some time to sort out how to tell you everything without scaring you away."

"And what happens in the meantime? More people try to kill me? How am I supposed to accept that you're connected to all of this and still trust you?"

"I don't know," he answers honestly. "But have I ever lied to you?"

*No.* Not that I'm aware of. In fact, he seems to be the only person who tells me the truth anymore.

"Fine. I'll wait. Not because I trust you, though. I'll wait because I think you're right—there's more to this story than I can comprehend right now, and I'm not in a state to take on any more life-altering news."

We pull into a parking spot on the second floor, and he ushers me over to an elevator. As soon as he pushes the top button, I know that he's taken me to his penthouse. I was so turned around and exhausted, I didn't even see it when we pulled in.

"You'll stay here for the night while I go return my father's truck," he explains over his shoulder as we walk out of the elevator doors. I stop in the entryway while he rushes around the room to flip the lights on.

"You're leaving me?" The question comes out more whiny than I intend for it to, but I'm too tired to care. I don't want to be alone. Not after what I just went through.

Sebastian pauses at the bottom of the stairs, turning toward me. "Would you prefer I stay?"

"I'd prefer not to be alone," I vaguely reply, shifting on my feet.

His boots are still tied tightly around my ankles. When I glance behind me and I realize they've left a trail of dirt, I bend over to take them off.

I do want him to stay with me. A side effect of having him there to rescue me any time something goes wrong is that I've come to rely on his presence afterward, when my mind finally catches up and my emotions settle in. It's happened often enough that I've been trained to reach for him in those dark times.

He remains quiet, seemingly considering what I said and figuring out a plan to oblige. "Fine," he breathes after a few moments, walking back toward me when he notices how much I'm struggling to untie his knots.

"I'll stay with you tonight, and then bring the truck back to him tomorrow," he says as he kneels onto his knee the same way he had done in the woods. But instead of allowing his hands to graze my legs like he had done in his moment of weakness, he pulls away.

Once the laces are loose, I step out of the boots and he stands. "Do you *have* to go back?"

He considers me for a moment, tilting his head when he sees something unexpected. "If I don't come back, they'll realize something is astray. I have to keep up appearances. At least until I can get you somewhere they won't find you."

"Fine," I huff, walking past him to climb the stairs.

"Where are you going?" he calls to my back.

Turning slowly, I point in the direction I know his guest room is in. "My room."

With a breathy laugh, he shakes his head. "No. You want me here with you… you're sleeping in my room."

When I don't immediately respond, he closes the distance

between us and scoops me into his arms, then walks us in the opposite direction.

"I need a shower and I'm hungry," I complain, fighting down my nerves at sleeping in his space.

As wrong as it is, I'm glad he's insisting I stay with him. I didn't want to sleep alone tonight.

"There's a shower in my room. I'll make us something while you're in there, and then we'll go to bed."

I'm too exhausted and hungry to argue, so I lay my head against his chest to signal my agreement and he brings me into his bathroom, only setting me down to start the shower. Once it's as hot as it can be, he hangs a fresh towel on the hook beside it and walks out, muttering something about making food.

The moment I step beneath the water, I begin to cry.

47

*The Wolf*

My father is awake and waiting for me when I pull his truck back in beside the camper. My initial thought is that he's angry with me for leaving, and I spent the entire drive here coming up with an alibi for my disappearance.

The smile he greets me with has my steps faltering.

"How was it?" He asks excitedly, and I realize he still thinks I've taken part in the hunt.

I suppose in a way, I did.

"Eye opening," is all I can think to say.

Never in a million years could I have guessed that the Order is an elitist cult that hunts people for pleasure. Is it disturbing? Absolutely.

Is it surprising? Not quite.

I feel like this revelation offers explanation to a lot of weird behavior over the years.

He seems pleased with my response, unable to contain his smile.

"Did you feel that rush the moment you got her hands on her?" Tipping his head back, he moans. "God, I love it."

Flicking my eyes to his malnourished legs, I ask, "did you partake in the activities this year?"

He shakes his head. "I sat this one out, but Garrett brought a little fun back for us old men."

I don't even want to ask what that means, especially when I see him run his tongue across his lips like a hungry dog.

As much as I want to tell him how repulsive I think this all is, I'm better off getting as many answers as I can so I can kill them with just cause.

"Is this the only event where you guys do… that?" I don't know what to call it. Every word that comes to mind will be offensive to him.

"Already craving more?" His lips kick up teasingly, and I have to busy myself with grabbing a cup of coffee to hide my scowl.

"No, there's a couple other opportunities throughout the year. This one doesn't cost anyone, though."

"There's a charge?" I wonder aloud, tamping down my tone to keep him from catching on to my game.

He looks around us, making sure there's no one within hearing distance as he explains, "I shouldn't be telling you any of this, but what the hell? You've obviously had a great time."

I do my best to hide my scowl.

"The Order puts on these… events where people pay handsomely for the opportunity to hunt their own prey, just like this. Fully customizable, though. It's nice little exercise to take a load off and get away from the pressures of everyday life."

"The room at the cottage… Is that for this sort of thing, too?"

My father chuckles. "That was an experiment to see if I could handle it on my own. I could, but things got a little too messy for me. The Order pays people to clean everything up once the fun is over."

"What do they do with the unclaimed prey?"

His smile falls. "There is no unclaimed prey."

All this time, I've considered myself a monster surrounded by other monsters. I had it all wrong. I'm a monster surrounded by demons without remorse. Skin-walkers without souls who attack those they view as weak, and then laugh about it after.

There's hundreds of them spread across the world. To kill all of them myself would be an impossible feat, especially when they catch on to me.

I need a more concentrated approach. One that will cut the head of the snake and leave the rest of its body squirming around.

We don't talk much more about it. He tries to ask me for details about what I did with my own prey, but I've feigned coyness and refused to share. I'm sure I could recount one of the memories I have from killing a Member before and he'd squeal in delight, but that would be feeding too far into this.

Once I've helped him pack up the few things we used and load it all into the truck, we hook up our camper and head out. Convincing him to leave a day early wasn't hard. Staying outdoors isn't easy for a man who has to take twenty pulls a day just to manage his symptoms. By the time I brought it up, he was already seeming like he was done with the trip.

He got what he wanted by tricking me into participating, anyway. Or so he thinks.

I spend the drive rolling over every possible reason for Charles to have gotten Stardust brought into this so he could kill her out here, and how he managed to squeeze through fate's fingers with his memories intact. He's my biggest obstacle, and the first one I'm coming after.

But not until I make sure Stardust is okay.

48

*The Lamb*

WHEN HE DROPS me off back at my house the following afternoon, I'm understandably shaken.

We didn't do anything last night. I showered while he made dinner, we ate sandwiches in silence, and then we climbed beneath his blanket and I fell asleep the moment my head hit the pillow. When I woke up this morning, he had already left to drop off his father's truck. There was a plate full of food sitting on the nightstand and a fresh pair of clothes for me to get into when I woke. Within an hour, he came strolling in wearing the same clothes as last night.

I have no idea what day it is, or if anyone even bothered checking on me while I was gone. Which is a sobering revelation in itself. My phone is gone, along with my purse with all my belongings. Sebastian thinks they've taken my car as well, since it was no longer parked on the street where I left it when we drove by on our way here.

They were covering their tracks, the way killers do when they don't want to be caught.

Once we got back to the house, I ran another hot shower and stood beneath the streaming water until it ran cold. Then, I scrubbed my body until my skin burned. Sebastian waited outside the bathroom the entire time, knocking every few minutes to check on me.

He wanted to stand in the bathroom with me, but I quickly refused. I've already been stripped bare and exposed for all to see. I needed time alone to process.

As soon as I turned the water off, he was swinging the bathroom door open and tightly wrapping a warm towel around my shoulders. Once I was fully dressed in my own clothes and curled up on the couch, I told him I wanted to be left alone.

He argued. A lot. But I held my ground, the way he insists I do, and he finally relented. With a long list of stipulations.

One of them was not leaving this house without him. The last thing I want to do is go into work and pretend that nothing is wrong, but being alone in this huge home is making my skin crawl. I need to be around people. *Normal people.*

But I suppose that can wait until he's with me. I don't have a car to get anywhere, and walking feels too risky when I could be grabbed off the street again at any time.

Another part of his agreement to leave me here alone is that I'm not allowed to report what happened to me in those woods to the authorities.

*"They will know it was you, and they'll come for both of us."*

I told him I didn't care, that there are people losing their lives in those woods for sport. People who could be saved if we got them there in time.

He didn't budge.

*"We want them to believe that the horrific things they're going*

*through have also happened to you. If you go reporting them, they will make sure you don't slip through the cracks again."*

*"How will they know it's me?"*

*"The police will tell them. You cannot trust anyone, Stardust. I'll make sure they pay. I promise."*

I don't know if I can trust him. He never specified if he was an exception to the new rule. All I know is that the past few days of my life feel like a nightmare that I haven't quite woken up from, and I'm terrified of what will happen when I finally do.

Just as I open my laptop to send Rosie a message explaining where I've been and begging for my job back, my front door opens and closes. Everything in me freezes, my eyes locked on the dining room, waiting for my intruder to reveal themselves.

Have they realized that I disappeared from the woods and come to collect me?

My heart drops at the thought.

Sebastian wanted to stay. He wanted me to stay at his penthouse, and I refused. I needed space.

What good is space if it gets me killed?

I look back toward my room, judging the distance and deciding if I can run in there fast enough. Maybe I can climb out the window and call for help.

Just as I'm about to do it—to spring off the couch and run for my life—Sebastian rounds the corner, his eyes cast down to a small box in his hands.

I relax instantly, as I always do in his presence. It's like he's a salve to my racing, panicked thoughts.

"You scared the hell out of me," I scold, sitting back against the couch to catch my breath. "You don't ever use the front door."

He stops in the doorway, lifting his eyes to meet mine. His usually-styled hair is a greasy mess falling on his forehead, and he's still wearing the clothes he left me in hours ago.

"I do, actually. You just don't hear it."

Pushing away the startling thoughts that swarm my head, I focus my mind on the matter at hand.

His sneaking into my home will have to be addressed another time.

"Have you even showered?"

He pulls something out of the box he's holding, then tosses it onto the couch beside me.

"It should be set up now. I created a new ID for you, but I've already logged into all your accounts."

"This is a phone..." I tell him, turning it around in my hands.

Not just a free phone that comes with the plan when you sign up. It's the newest, most expensive model.

When I swipe my finger across the screen, it unlocks to reveal my home screen set up the exact way I had it on my old phone. Sure enough, when I click on one of the social media icons, my profile pulls up.

"Yes, thanks for telling me. I was wondering what all those numbers were for," he snarks back, collapsing onto the chair across from me and closing his eyes.

*How could he have known all these things?* The red flags spring up, piling on top of one another. Whenever I think I've got a grip on how deep his obsession runs, he surprises me by taking it even further.

"Well... what do I owe you?" I absently wonder, mentally planning out how I'm going to pay him back.

Eyes snapping back open, he levels me with a stare that makes me feel like an ant.

"Nothing."

I hold my arm out and push the phone toward him. "I can't accept this then."

"You can, and you will. You need a phone to communicate with people. I'm sure you've already been going crazy here alone all day."

Damn. Am I really this predictable?

With a negative shake, I set the phone onto the coffee table and sit back on the couch.

"I can get a new one myself. This is too much."

He puffs his cheeks and blows out the breath, clearly irritated. I just stare back at him stubbornly. If I accept this phone, where does that land me? I'm getting too entangled with this man already. Where I should be peeling myself away and moving on, I'm falling deeper into this inescapable hole. The same way I had done with Gabe.

Swiping a palm down his face, he sits forward in the chair.

"If you're having trouble accepting the phone, I hate to see how you'll react to the car."

"What car?"

"The one I ordered for you today to replace the one that was taken from you. It will be delivered to my home tomorrow."

"That is insane,"

"You've said it yourself, none of this would have happened to you if it weren't for me. It's only right that I help you."

"This isn't *helping*. This is…"

Excessive. Generous. Insane.

"Look, I got them for *you*. If you don't want to accept them, that's fine. But they won't be going anywhere else."

"Why is the car being delivered to your place?"

He hesitates, screwing his mouth to the side as he considers how to say his next statement. "You should stay with me for a little while."

I'm immediately shaking my head. "I'm not doing this again."

We already argued about it this morning, and I made my stance clear. I'm not uprooting my life to move in with him—a complete stranger.

"Neither am I. If you insist on staying here, that's fine. But I won't be leaving your side. It's not safe for you to be alone."

"I have a *job*. I have a family and friends who will be looking for me."

"Take a leave, then. Tell them you're on vacation. Better yet, don't tell them anything. The men that took you will realize that you weren't killed in those woods. When they make that discovery, they're going to come looking for you. It would be unwise for you to continue as if this never happened."

"What you're asking of me is completely unreasonable."

"Why? Because you don't want to move in with me?" He has the nerve to look hurt.

"Yes, of course *that*. Because I hardly know you and I just got out of a controlling relationship."

"Fine, I'll find another place and rent it to you, if you insist on being so independent. That doesn't change the fact that I'll be by your side at all times."

"What do you mean you'll find *another* place?"

He hesitates again, rolling his lips. "Haven't you put it together yet?"

"Put *what* together, Sebastian?" I use his name as a weapon, spitting it like a curse word.

"This house was bought with the sole intention of renting it out to you."

"That can't be true. There was an ad…"

It's all making sense. Even the realtor was confused about the rent being so low. Low enough for someone who was just hired at the coffee shop the ad was placed outside of to afford.

How long has this obsession been going on?

"You own the property management company," I surmise, and my chest feels like it's going to collapse on itself when he nods.

"Every dime you've paid me has been placed into an investment account in your name. It's nearly quadrupled already."

"How could you do this? *Why* did you do this?"

"I can't fully explain yet. But it will make sense one day."

"I'm not moving in with you," I insist, slamming my feet in the ground.

He's taken every choice away from me. Herded me into a corner until I had no option but to submit to him. To hand myself over just the way he wanted me to.

"Then, I'm staying here," he says firmly, leaning back into the chair to make himself comfortable.

I stew in silence, refusing to argue any longer and work myself up.

All I want to do is walk over and slam my fist into his balls. But when I really, truly think about it, I have to remind myself of all the times he's saved me. I have to wonder where I would be without him.

Soft snores begin to fall from his mouth, calling my attention back to his sprawled out, sleeping form.

He spent the day spending a fortune on replacing the things that were taken from me instead of resting or showering or attending to whatever he does in his *real life*. Because he knew that I would feel trapped and anxious without it. And even though I asked him to leave, he managed to come back to me right when I started to feel lonely.

There's something between us—a bond or a tie, placed by

some sort of holy, otherworldly force. I've avoided it. Snuffed it down and excused it away whenever it reared its head and things began to feel familiar.

But what if this is how *he* copes with it? What if this over-protective, obsessive behavior is happening because he feels it too—that unmistakable pull?

It would make sense.

It's not functional or sane, but it makes sokay.

Quietly, I slip off the couch and drape a blanket over his shoulders before shuffling off to my bed, knowing I'll sleep much better now that he's returned to me.

**49**

*The Wolf*

THE THREE GRAND Masters of the Order have called a dinner for all the upcoming recruits just four days after the annual hunting trip. Unfortunately, I've found myself included in the group of six men preparing to swear in, and thus required to attend.

My alleged participation in their hunt has apparently nailed my initiation.

I'm anxious to leave Stardust alone so soon after the hunt, and Sienna has been unusually distant since she found out what happened when we got home. I wanted to tell her myself, but Stardust beat me to it.

This is the worst argument we've ever had and I can't even blame her for being mad.

It feels like a bad time to be tied up in a closed-door meeting, but I don't have much of a choice. If I'm going to play the role to get inside information, I have to follow their rules.

My grandfather, Hugh Kensington, and Byron Davis sit at the head of the table—the three most ancient, powerful men in this sick cult. Each man has been a part of my life since conception, and yet I hardly know anything about them. Even my grandfather, who heard I was rejecting the Lancaster legacy in the Order at the age of sixteen and immediately revoked every dime I was set to inherit from him.

I've at least tripled that money since then through the success of Lancaster Tech. He'll never admit to being wrong, though.

The old sour face that decorates my parent's home stares at me from across the table with nothing but disappointment and animosity behind his dead eyes. My father may be a selfish prick, but his father is an abusive piece of shit who refuses to die.

Hugh doesn't even seem comfortable sitting beside him, and they're likely the closest pair that the Order has.

The dinner is a complete waste of time. An obvious ploy for them to isolate the recruits from their families and do their best to intimidate and indoctrinate, as if the hunt didn't already serve that purpose.

If we're still here after watching them mutilate, rape, and murder innocent human beings, I can't imagine three weathered old men can scare us off.

As I'm walking to my car, prepared to head straight to the cabin to check on Stardust before I get a hold of Sienna, I see a text I received a half hour ago from a blocked number.

It's an address. One in the underdeveloped, industrial side of Styx, where no one ever goes unless they want to be hassled by the homeless.

The first thing I do when I get into my driver's seat is dial Stardust's number. When she answers on the third ring, I hang up and try Sienna.

It rings and rings.

Hugh walks past my car as I try her for a third time, the call going straight to voicemail now.

"Call me back," is all I manage to grind out, my gaze never leaving Hugh. As if he senses me looking, his head whips over to my car, dark eyes staring right past the tinted glass. And when I'm sure he can't get any creepier, he smirks.

I look down at my phone, the screen still open to Sienna's contact.

He knows something.

My stomach sinks with the realization. This dinner was a distraction for whatever they've done.

They better hope for their sake that Sienna isn't involved.

Once he folds himself into the back of his town car, I slide my gun from my glove box and latch the holster into my pants, then set up my navigation to take me to the address they texted.

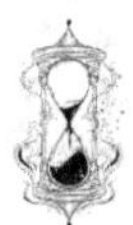

"Fuck, fuck, fuck," I mutter to myself as a large, unmoving lump appears in line with my headlights in the middle of the road. Slamming onto the gas pedal, I propel my car ahead to get a better look.

*It's her.* I know it's her. I can feel it in my fucking bones. The invisible tether between us has broken and shredded, solidifying what I already suspected.

*She's dead, and I've failed,* the intrusive thoughts scream, blocking out the ones that are holding onto hope that it's not her at all.

I pull my car as close as I can, position my headlights onto the lump, and then fling myself out the driver door.

Sprinting across the asphalt to get to her in time, I remind myself that if there's a chance I can save her, it'll be thin. But worth it.

My knees crack against the pavement, hands hovering over the still, bloodied blanket, paralyzed. I have no idea what I'm going to find. What sort of final vision I'm going to be left with. But no one else is here, and I have to know for sure that she's gone. That there's nothing else I can do.

In one quick move, I rip the blanket off and throw it to the side, exposing Sienna's beaten, swollen face first. All the air in my lungs escapes in one huge whoosh, my stomach sinking in on itself as I take in her pale, mangled skin and cloudy eyes. My fingers reach out, gently connecting with the small spot on her neck that isn't bruised or bloodied. Her skin is cold, muscles stiff. When I shift my touch over to her artery, I confirm what I already know.

*She's gone.*

In a detached daze, my eyes slowly roam over the rest of her body—assessing the damage.

Her hair is a matted disarray sprawled around her head, blood and who knows what else caked into the blonde strands. The black shirt I just saw her wearing hours ago has been ripped in half down the middle, her bra a mere scrap of fabric hanging on by a thread around her bruised shoulders. Deep slashes have been carved into her breasts, splitting the tissue apart at least two inches. Her stomach is coated in crusted, brown and crimson blotches with small entrance wounds where they likely stabbed a knife right in, puncturing her organs. Blood still dribbles out of those in a lazy river down her side.

Pivoting my body to the side, I heave up the small amount of contents in my stomach from the dinner that kept me away while they did this.

This is it. This is *fucking it*. They took her again, right beneath my nose. Even when I played their little game so obediently.

They made sure I was caught up in their bullshit recruitment dinner while they were out here mauling her like animals. Ripping her apart at the seams like a rag doll.

When there's nothing left for my stomach to expel and the dry heaving has stopped, I crawl back over to my sister's body and force myself to take account of everything they did to her.

To make a checklist of things I'm going to run through when I hunt and kill each and every one of them.

Her legs lie straight against the pavement, mutilated thighs tucked together like they carefully posed her this way. Perfectly round bruises pepper her hips and wrists—fingerprints left behind from the struggle she made and their attempts to restrain her. My eyes skirt over her bare apex, making quick notes of the telling blood stains spattered all around.

Something has been branded into her left calf. The skin has blistered and bled, nearly masking the familiar serpent I've grown familiar with infecting my father's back.

The sick fuckers even signed off on their kill.

They're testing me. First with Stardust, and now Sienna. They want me to fight back.

Headlights appear down the road, too close for me to hop in my car and hide. I kneel over Sienna's body protectively, my hand firmly wrapped around the holstered gun I tucked into my pants earlier. They approach just as urgently as I did, and when the car veers off to the side and shifts into park, I recognize my father sitting in the driver's seat.

"Sienna!" he wails, falling onto his hands out of the driver's side. "Oh, God, no!"

He stumbles over to where I'm kneeling, collapsing onto his knees at my side to push me aside and drape his body over hers. Sobs wrack through him, her name repeatedly falling from his lips in broken, nearly illegible syllables.

"How did you know she'd be here?" I question, keeping my tone even.

"They called me."

"They *called* you? What the fuck does that mean?" I boom, all control out the window.

"God, I didn't think they'd do it. She was safe! She was safe, she was safe, she was safe," he weeps, crawling across the asphalt to grab the blanket and cover her nearly-naked body back up.

I gape at him, fists clenching at my sides to stop myself from wrapping them around his throat. *He knew.* He knew they were coming for her. Just like before, they leveraged her life to control him, and he said *nothing.*

He *did* nothing.

"What did you do?" I growl.

"I did everything they wanted! I got you to join. I resigned from the board. I did everything right, and they still took her away. Oh, God, they destroyed her! My poor baby girl is gone…" He howls out a soul-shattering cry, burying his face against her blanketed side.

They'll pay for this. All of them. The only way to put an end to this dysfunctional, agonizing cycle is to put an end to the Loyal Order of the Serpent for good.

I'm not just going after the ones who were involved in the crimes against Sienna like I had done before. They were *all* involved. I'm starting from the top and destroying them from within.

"We have to call this in," I tell my father, my voice controlled.

"To the police?" he asks doubtfully, shaking his head. "They'll pin it on us."

"What do you suggest we do? Leave her out here to be

eaten by animals until someone hopefully drives by in the morning?"

Within seconds, my father morphs from a mourning parent into the cold-blooded, emotionless businessman I've always known him to be. His sorrowful expression drops into a bland mask, his reddened eyes the only indication that he was sobbing moments prior.

"We have to dispose of her body," he sniffs, wiping his nose. "It's what they expect us to do."

"You think I give a flying fuck what those sick assholes want us to do?" I seeth, offended that he'd even suggest such a thing with my sister's dead body a few feet away from us.

He turns his shoulders toward me, finally peeling his gaze away from Sienna's pale face. I thought he looked old before. These past ten minutes have aged him beyond belief.

"I think that you're planning revenge against them in that brillant, conniving mind of yours. Just like they expect you will." Tugging leather gloves out of his jacket pockets like he's done this a thousand times, he continues. He has officially detached himself from the situation. Like turning off a switch, he's removed his personal feelings from the scenario.

"They want us rattled. That's why they lead us out here. This is a test for them to see if you'll dodge when they weave. You have to play the game until you have a solid plan in place. Think ahead."

"What about Mom?" I question, hating that he's right. "What about laying Sienna to rest the way she deserves?"

"She'll get her retribution. You'll make sure of it. This is a small concession."

I scoff, turning away from him to give myself a minute to think. He's got one thing right: I plan to get Sienna the justice she deserves.

"So what, then?" I swing back around, surprised to find him leaning over Sienna's body, placing a tender kiss across her forehead. "We hide her body in an unmarked grave and leave her to rot? Let everyone go on a wild chase looking for her, the way they did with me?"

He nods, draping the blanket across her head. "I know a place."

I hate this. Hate that I've had one task in this sad excuse of an existence and I've failed miserably.

*Twice.*

"Why couldn't they just kill me instead?" I wonder aloud, my heart shattering all over again.

"Because they can't control her the way they can control you and me, and they know how much she means to us," he answers gravely, as if he's already considered it. "Grab her legs. We'll load her into my trunk and you can follow me."

While every instinct I have screams against it—while I know it's fucked up being belief—I follow my father's directions and wrap my arms around my sister's legs, hoisting her up and carrying her over to his car. My body moves on autopilot, my mind completely shut off to avoid being clogged with emotions and hesitancy.

"You can't just let them get away with murdering your only daughter," I insist, shoveling dirt over Sienna's body.

The other half of me.

He led me to a field filled with electrical towers a few miles away. We parked on cement and carried her body though the grass as far as he could stand, until we reached an area of soil that was already disturbed.

Large enough to serve as a mass grave. To fit about as many bodies as I saw in that corral a few days ago.

He's ensuring that if they try to twist this on him and call the police on her body, they'll be incriminating themselves in the process.

Clever, waste of a man.

"They have to be expecting a reaction out of you," I continue, heaving another pile into the hole.

Thankfully, I've managed to avoid running into any other bodies.

"I've already been knocked out of my role because of the cancer. They planned this all the way back then," he replies, mostly to himself.

I stop scooping and prop the shovel into the dirt, flexing my blistering hands around it.

"How are you going to make them pay?" I push, because I need to hear him say what I already suspect. That he'll lay down and take it for some ridiculous reason, leaving her justice and all the lives it will take to receive it on my conscience.

"I'm going to sick my son on them to take them down," he replies simply. Predictably. And as I'm forming the most severe words I can muster to tell him what a cowardly piece of shit he is, he goes on to add, "and I'm going to guide you on how to do it."

The rest of the night is spent plotting our revenge and saying our goodbyes to Sienna. Once we're finished, I walk him to his car, then drive myself home.

And when I walk through those elevator doors, I destroy everything in my path.

## 50

*The Lamb*

I'M WAY OUT of my element the instant I walk through the large, double doors of the hall where Sienna's family hosts her funeral. Like the Starfall Ball, it's packed with wealthy, high-class families who seem more interested in catching up on the latest gossip than mourning a young life that's been taken too soon.

They don't have a body. That's the most puzzling part about all of it.

Like she walked out her front door one day and never came back. The police have declared her case a homicide, even though they haven't recovered her remains and there's no true evidence that she isn't alive.

I still hold onto hope that she'll come back. Just like her brother came back after weeks of being gone, I think she deserves more of a chance. It makes no sense that her family doesn't feel the same way.

Still, I pay my respects at the funeral, because there's a

possibility that I'm wrong, and I would hate to live with that regret.

I'm terribly nervous to be here on my own after putting it together that the man Sienna introduced as a family friend was the one to taunt me in the woods. It's possible that everyone here is involved in whatever strange practice that was, and I hardly got to wrap my mind around Sienna being connected to it before hearing the news that she was gone. When I brought it up with her the day before she disappeared, she was just as horrified as me and unless she's an amazing actress, I truly believe she had no clue of what her friends were involved in.

I know Sebastian will be pissed to find that I've left without him, but he's been slipping in and out at random hours of the day, making it impossible to talk to him.

There isn't anything that will stop me from honoring my friend. So, I found a black lace headdress to pull over my face at a thrift store, threw on a cheap black dress, and sent up a prayer to the big guy that this wasn't a trap.

Her mother is easy to spot. She's at the front of the enormous room, surrounded by a group of women clad in various ostentatious forms of black clothing. Tables with framed photos line the walls, and an obscene amount of flower arrangements takes up the back end, with chairs lined up in the middle. People meander around, unsure what to do when there's no body to honor.

When I don't spot anyone I might know, I drag my feet over to the first set of photos, the way everyone else seems to do. Rosie has given me the silent treatment since I had to resign from Old Soul without any notice. I can only hope she'll forgive me someday, when I get the chance to explain everything. Until then, I'm giving her space.

Each picture has two kids in it, both the same size. The frames appear to be organized in chronological order, starting with tiny babies and growing into small children. Where Sienna's hair was nearly white as a child, the boy beside her has a contrasting dark brown. If you ignore that small difference, they're nearly identical. But you can tell, even in the quick shots that were taken, that their personalities are nearly opposite.

Where Sienna poses and smiles dramatically, her brother scowls and broods, crossing his arms or stubbornly refusing to look at the camera. Just as serious as she described him as.

Year after year, they grow older and more distant, but he's always in the background, watching her. It's like their story has been captured in little snapshots.

Once they appear to be around seven or eight, the table ends, and I'm so invested, I rush over to the next one without bothering to look up.

Girl Scout trips, school plays, random sports... Sienna was in all of it. There's one of her smiling in a school uniform, standing beside a suitcase in front of a hotel on a busy New York street. Her brother sits on the ground beside her, his leg kicked out as he rips apart a flower.

She mentioned in passing that she went to boarding school. I wonder what that was like, leaving her parents for most of the year. That could be why her brother was so protective. He wanted to keep her safe.

My eyes keep getting drawn to his unique features. So symmetrical and perfect. I feel drawn to him for some reason, but I can't figure out what it is.

The table ends at the start of them becoming teenagers, and I slowly begin to see why he seems so familiar to me.

But there's no way.

Rushing over to the next table, I find more solo photos of Sienna than there were before. Embarrassing selfies, school events, dances, and parties with friends. None of them had her brother in them. I find myself searching for that face in each one, quickly moving onto the next when I realize it isn't there. Finally, the table ends with a high school graduation photo of the two standing beside each other in their gowns, smiles wide as they show off their diplomas.

My stomach sinks to my feet.

I know that face.

I've seen it before.

Running past a group of people talking in between this table and the next, I practically shove an old woman to the side as I lean in to look at the pictures of her college years. It's more random people attending various events. Sienna smiles in each one, but he's nowhere to be found. He must not have gone to the same school. Did she say he skipped college? I can't remember.

The table ends without a single picture of him, and I turn to find there's only one table left.

There should be double the amount. She deserved a long, happy life, and this is all she was given. Could *he* be the reason why? The man who seems to fade so easily into the shadows.

I rush over to the last set of photos, desperate to see a different face than the one I'm looking for. I'm praying to whatever god there is to let me be wrong. To have this all be a misunderstanding on my part.

What would it mean if the woman who has weasled her way into my life to become one of my closest friends is related to the man who breaks into my house each night?

*Is it possible that they both preyed on me?*

With a deep breath, I offer a tight smile to a middle-aged woman who is crying as she holds a frame against her chest. There's no one else standing in front of this table, blocking the display.

My gaze swings over and finds him immediately. Smiling again, beside a version of Sienna that looks closest to the one

I came to know. He's wearing a suit, his hand wrapped around the black tie as she hugs his side in a sparkling, silver gown.

I snatch the photo up and examine it—seeing a side of both of them that I never knew. One I never could have guessed could be real.

"If everyone could please have a seat," an older man's voice says through the speakers. "The family would like to say a few words."

There's a shuffle in the room as conversations end and people begin herding into their chairs. I should leave now, while there's enough movement to distract anyone from seeing me walk out. There's one person in particular that I'd like to avoid, and he's currently standing at the front of the room, ushering Sienna's mother—his mother—into a chair in the front row. He's in a suit similar to the one in the photo I'm holding, this time with a purple dress shirt. My eyes flick between the two versions of the same man, shocked at the difference. His features appear far more haunted now, as if he's seen things that the photographed version of him could have never dreamt of.

Before I lose my momentum, I place the frame back on the table in a random spot and rush toward the door, my head pointed down at my feet. Right when I'm about to break through the double doors, a funeral home employee slams it shut, stopping me in my tracks. I side step, ready push through the other one, when the same employee steps inside the room, pulling the door shut behind her.

"I just need to go–" I start to say, reaching for the doorknob.

"Sorry, the family asked that everyone stay seated for the memorial service," she coldly interrupts, folding her arms across her chest. When I gape at her, she scowls back, then looks above my head, dismissing me.

What the hell kind of funeral home locks people in a room?

Spinning in my spot, I begin to panic. I'm now trapped in the same room as the man who haunts me to celebrate the life of a woman who did nothing but lie to me.

Who else could have been in on this with them? Is it some kind of sick cult they've formed?

"Hello, everyone," the familiar deep voice greets his crowd in a kind, courteous tone. When I look up at the podium, I'm startled to find him staring directly at me.

Trapping me in his gaze.

"First off, we'd like to thank everyone for coming to honor my sister..." he's speaking to the mass of people standing between us, but his attention remains fixated on me.

His features are even more striking beneath the show lights shining directly on him. Light green eyes are contrasted perfectly by his neatly styled, near-black hair. His beard is clean-shaven, suit pressed.

He looks more like the billionaire that Sienna describes him as and less like the dangerous intruder who has followed me the past couple of months.

And something else keeps nagging in the back of my mind. A kernel of a thought that I can't seem to grasp onto long enough to make sense of it.

I've been here before. Seen these people...

In a life that wasn't mine. Or maybe it was a dream.

God, I don't know.

I find a chair in the back row and stumble over, practically falling into it as my mind races faster than I can keep up.

What was Sienna's last name again?

I look over at a poster honoring her, grateful to find it written in large lettering.

Lancaster.

So, that makes him *Sebastian Lancaster*. His name rings in my ears like a song I can't get unstuck from my head.

"Sienna was the type of person who would offer her support, even when you didn't want it," Sebastian jokes, and the crowd murmurs out one conjoined laugh.

Visions of blurred, blonde hair sweep around my mind. And blood. So much blood.

*Sebastian Lancaster.*

"She had a pure heart, and she could recognize when other people had the same gift."

*Sebastian... Bash...*

He's defending her. He knows that I've put two and two together, and he's trying to explain.

But he doesn't need to. Not anymore.

Because along with the flashes of blonde hair and blood came silky black hair and sleepless night curled up with a dark knight. A man who saved me from myself and believed in me when no one else tried.

*My mystery man.* Not much of a mystery, afterall.

Tears silently stream down my face as I listen to his speech, his eyes continually landing on me every few seconds, as if he's not sure whether I'm going to get up and sprint away or attack him right in the middle of his sister's funeral for what they've done.

But I could never punish him for loving me so fiercely.

He found me again. We lost each other in the chaos that everyone else created in our lives, and he still managed to get to me.

*How?*

Every interaction we've had comes rushing back to me. The vague letters, the odd way he'd speak about a past I never knew, the figs. He was trying—desperately trying—to get me to remember without forcing it.

And in the meantime, my love was stuck living a life parallel to the one we found each other in, alone with his memories.

His speech continues and he recounts a life with my friend that I never knew existed. A bond stronger than anything else.

The emotions flood in, sending tears streaming down my face in hot, uncontrollable streams. I cry the entire time, and he watches me with a contemplative expression until his speech ends and everyone claps. When he steps away from the podium to allow someone else to say a few words, he heads directly to the back of the room, ignoring all the people offering quiet condolences.

Straight for me.

"Stardust…" his deep voice practically moans in despair.

My gaze flicks up to assess him, and I can finally see what a toll this has taken on him.

"How?" I whisper. One word with a million questions behind it.

How did we get here? How did Sienna find me? Was he a part of her befriending me?

So many questions begging to be asked, but his guarded expression tells me this isn't the place to do it.

"Come with me," he says, grabbing my hand and tugging me out of my seat.

He pushes through the double doors I just tried to exit from, hand wrapped tightly around mine as if he's afraid I'll run off. We round a corner and walk to the end of a long hall, where he pulls out a key and unlocks the door.

"This is a private room. No one can interrupt us here," he explains once we're inside.

It's a simple, tiny space for close family to place their belongings or take a break. A long, leather sofa sits against one side and a row of cabinets takes up the other.

I turn to him, gabbing his hands back into mine. "I remember you," I tell him breathlessly. My voice is a mere gasp of air.

Because *finally...* I remember him. I remember *all of it.* Every second we spent together, nestled into our own dysfunctional corner of the world, away from everyone else.

I remember everything he said and did—how unhinged and devoted and obsessed and disappointed he was. Every emotion and memory flows through me, curling around my spirit and snuggling in, as if they've been waiting for this moment to resurface.

I remember the woman I was—how I allowed all these people to trample over me and my boundaries. How it cost me my life—*twice.* His words from before echo through my mind, the desperate pleas he made that day he found me, beaten and bloodied beside Gabe on my dining room floor. The day I took my final breath.

Gabe killed me. He *killed me,* and I've spent these last few weeks in a constant state of guilt over what Bash did to him. It wasn't in cold blood. It was revenge.

Bash stares back at me, his face a blank canvas, devoid of emotion. But I can see the relief swirling beneath the surface, hoping like hell that it's true. He's lived alone with these memories, waiting for me to catch up. And for how long? How long has my love had to suffer in this reality without me knowing who he even was?

His throat bobs as he swallows, shifting his weight before me.

"You remember?" he repeats slowly, and I nod.

"All of it."

"Prove it."

I sputter out a sob, hurtling myself into his arms. And despite the hesitation in those unique green eyes, he catches me. Strong, capable arms wrap around me and they feel so different than they have in these last few months, yet unbelievably familiar at the same time.

*Mine.*

He was mine before all of this came to a head. And he ensured he was mine through the rest of it.

He grabs my shoulders and pushes me back a bit, his gaze roaming over my face like he's seeing me for the first time in ions.

"You asked me not to leave you in New York," I recall. "You told me something was going to happen, and it did. I thought you were batshit crazy, Bash. I ignored you, and it cost me everything."

I'm crying uncontrollably now, my words barely comprehensible. The tears are spilling from my eyes, spilling over in hot trails running down my cheeks and neck.

"I would do anything to go back and tell you everything. Fuck, if I could go back in time, I'd change everything. I'd stop our paths from ever crossing."

Shaking my head, I raise my hand to his lips to stop him from going on. That all seems inconceivable at this point. This man was meant to be in my life. This experience has only proven that fact.

"Tell me now. What happened?"

His fingers wrap around my wrist, guiding my hand against his lips as he trails kisses down my wrist and arm.

"I honestly don't fucking know," he admits breathlessly between kisses. When he pulls away again, he admits, "This has been complete hell."

"I can't even imagine."

"I'm sure you have questions…"

My hands run down his chest. "Nothing that's worth worrying about now."

"Good. I don't want to talk," he admits, kissing a tail down my neck.

"I need you, Bash," I rush through labored breaths, ripping my hat out of my hair before my hands move to my side to unzip my dress. He does the same with his pants, pushing them down just enough to allow his erection to spring free.

"You have me, Stardust."

*Stardust.* God, how many times have I heard that name without realizing the significance behind it? I'll never take it for granted again.

Once the dress is undone, he pushes it off my shoulders and it falls to the floor in a heap. My head rolls back as he returns his mouth to my neck, his arms wrapping around my back to hoist me up before he slams me against the wall.

He's pushing inside of me within the next breath, a low groan rumbling through him as he fills me. I weave my fingers through his hair and work my hips against him as he pumps into me. The room fills with our quickening breaths as we move together.

This is more than two bodies melding together. It's a sacred reunion.

His mouth captures mine and reclaims it, tongue swirling around as his body grinds against me the perfect angle to have my orgasm building within minutes.

I dig my fingers into his back and bite into his neck, sending my quiet cries of pleasure directly into his ear as the wave crashes over me and I'm flying in the air. Within seconds, I feel him twitch inside of me before I'm filled with his heat.

"Fuck, baby," he whispers against my forehead. "You're *mine.*"

With that growled declaration, he slams into me one last time before we both go still with him still planted firmly inside of me.

"I'm sorry it took me so long to get to you," I mutter quietly, kissing his cheek as I roll my hips around his cock.

I can't get enough of him.

He smiles sadly, rubbing his thumb across my bottom lip as he swears, "I would have waited a lifetime for you, sweet little lamb."

**51**

*The Wolf*

SIENNA HASN'T COME to me yet.

I've anxiously awaited the moment for her to appear out of thin air, the same way she had done before. To visit me in spirit, so I can confirm the facts I already know.

In all honesty, I'd just like to see her again. I need to apologize for failing her and beg for forgiveness.

She doesn't come, though.

It only took a few days last time. One minute, I was mourning her, and the next she was sitting beside me, irritating the fuck out of me.

My first thought is that we messed something up. When my father and I buried her in that unmarked grave, we disrupted the balance, trapping her soul somewhere. I even went back to that spot against my father's advice. I looked for her everywhere, just in case she was tethered there somehow. The sinking disappointment as I drove home without any answers hasn't left.

My mother still put on a funeral service for her once the police confirmed what we already knew. That there was no possibility she could be alive. They're still searching for her body, and if we're lucky, they won't ever find it.

Of course, we know the truth—me, my father, and every single man in the Loyal Order of the Serpent. Now, it's a matter of each side figuring out *how much* the other knows before the war begins.

Their days are limited. I've followed my father's instruction and played the game, pretending to be the devastated, confused brother while he transfers his knowledge to me and we come up with a plan.

One of the biggest hurdles has been learning to trust him. Last time I went through this, he chose the Order. I'm not sure what happened differently for him in this new timeline, but he seems to be abandoning the brotherhood he was once willing to kill to protect. Sharing secrets that I would have no way of knowing without an inside source. Even if I still joined their sadistic cult, I'd likely never be trusted with the information my father has been exposed to.

Everything from daily schedules to escape protocols to secret homes and hideouts. With the things my father knows, I can finally make a plan that sets me multiple steps ahead of them, all while they think I'm absolutely clueless to what they've done.

As soon as I get the green light, I'm slaughtering them.

I only hoped Sienna could be around to witness it. She always enjoyed watching them bleed.

I can't stand dodging awkward condolences from employees and people I've never met, so I've taken to working from Stardust's spare bedroom. I've closed myself off from everyone once the realization came that I can't trust anyone. Not fully.

Eliza has pushed for me to take time off and heal, but she

has no idea how deep this runs. If I allow myself any more time away, Lancaster Tech will be taken over by the Order. They already tried when I was in the hospital through the oddly vague deal that Hugh submitted. It was a warning from him. A promise of what was to come if I didn't obey his wishes.

When I absolutely have to go into the office, I bring Stardust with me.

She hasn't left my side since our reunion at Sienna's funeral, outside of the quick meetings I squeeze in with my father to go over logistics and pertinent information that can't be shared over the phone. I think we both realize how easily people can be ripped away, and neither of us is willing to give up the future we missed out on before. I couldn't be happier or more obsessed with her.

I knew the moment she walked into Sienna's funeral that things would change between us. By the time I had taken the podium to give my speech, it was obvious that something was wrong. I had assumed it was because she finally realized that I was the elusive brother Sienna always spoke about, but no one ever saw. There was no time to warn her beforehand. Not when there are monsters lurking around every corner and it's unsafe for her to be alone. The first thing she would do when she discovered her two worlds were colliding is run. I couldn't afford to risk it.

So, when I saw her broken expression from across the room, I assumed it was her shock over the betrayal from her friend. Never could I have dreamed that she would come back to me—fully and completely.

"The people who hunted me in the woods… is that who killed her?" She asks from beside me in her bed that night.

I turn to face her, tucking one arm beneath the pillow as the other reaches across the blanket to touch her bare skin.

My hand grabs hers up from her stomach and clutches it tightly.

"Yes."

"Are those the same ones who did it before?"

"They are," I confirm delicately, rubbing circles on her palm.

"What are you going to do about it?"

"What do you mean?"

Turning to mirror my position, she shrugs. "Last time, you told me you killed people…"

"And?"

"Were you going after Sienna's killers?"

Smart girl. I never admitted that my victims were tied to Sienna's death back then. I was just trying to scare her when I told her all that. To get her to realize the seriousness of the situation and stay with me so I could keep her safe.

In hindsight, that wasn't the best approach.

"I was," I vaguely admit, pulling away to run my hand along my chin. I'm trying to find a way to explain that I'll be doing the same thing, only this time, I'm targeting the men at the top. The ones who made the call to kill her. But how much can I say without scaring her off?

"Things are different now," is what I land on.

"So, you aren't even going after them?" She rears her head back, eyes squinting.

"You sound disappointed when you say it like that…"

"You can't just let her killers roam free."

"I don't intend to."

With a hesitant smirk, she twists back on the bed, facing the ceiling again as she tells me, "I want to help then."

"You want to help me kill people?" I ask incredulously.

She nods, picking at her nails. "Yes."

"Absolutely not," I rush out, stamping down the idea

before it can even grow legs. There's no way I can put her in that position and bleed my darkness into her like that.

Slamming her hands onto the bed, she turns back to me, mouth open in indignant surprise. "You can't tell me no."

"I definitely can. And I am."

Her face falls into a mulish pout, lips pursed and brows furrowed. "Then what are you going to do? Rush in there with guns blazing and hope you hit as many people as possible?"

I chuckle at that vision, earning a scowl from her.

"I've got someone on the inside," I vaguely explain, unsure how much I want her to really know.

Too much knowledge could incriminate her.

"That's all you're going to give me?" She gripes irritatedly.

"For now, yes." I know she'll pull it out of me if she truly wants it, but I won't hand it over voluntarily. Not when we're talking about life and death.

"What about me? They attacked me, too," she whines. "I deserve a chance at revenge."

"They'll pay dearly for that. Trust me."

"You really think you're not going to let me help you?" I don't like the way she words the question, as if she plans to do it whether I like it or not.

"I know I won't," I clarify sternly.

She huffs out a petulant breath, turning her back to. I don't care if she's mad so long as her soul remains pure and her conscious clean.

When enough time has passed that I think she's fallen asleep, she surprises me by muttering, "regardless of how I feel about you, I refuse to live trapped beneath you for the rest of my life. You can't control me like he tried to do."

I consider that for a moment, begrudgingly realizing that she's right. I have no authority over her to dictate what she can or can not handle. Who am I to deny her a shot at redemption when I'm taking mine without tolerating any pushback?

"Fine. I'll show you what it's about tomorrow. Then, you can decide for yourself."

Her shoulders relax at that, but she doesn't respond. Even my relenting words sounded like I was offering permission, but she has to realize how difficult it is for me to share this after doing it alone for so long. It's clearly an area we both need to work at, but I'm willing to do it for her.

Within a few minutes, her breathing evens out and soft snores begin to fall from her mouth. I'm so worked up about hunting Sienna's killers, I don't fall asleep for hours.

## 52

*The Lamb*

THERE'S A LOCKED door inside my garage.

I've noticed it before, whenever I pull my car in or out, always in too much of a rush to get to wherever I was going to bother with it. Based on the way it's built out into the back yard, I assumed it was just a simple storage shed. Probably still packed with random things from the home's owners over the years. Given that I hardly moved in with anything, I never had a use for the extra space.

That's where he leads me.

Once he has the door unlocked, he swings it open to reveal a space that I can only assume was used for killing and processing hunted animals—a butchering room. When he flips a switch beside me to illuminate the space with harsh, fluorescent lights, I realize that's *ex*actly what this is for.

Perhaps this was once the home of a hunter.

A worn and scratched, metal table beside a single leather

chair takes up the center, while various black tool boxes and pegboards line the small walls. Hanging from the board is a myriad of weaponry—from knives to machetes to guns—anything you could think of to kill with.

Mostly knives, though.

It's cramped, despite its size.

He leaves the door open, but steps into the space behind me. I can feel his breaths against my back as he watches my head swivel around, absorbing the reality of what has been right beneath my nose this entire time.

"You asked for the truth. This is it."

I spin around to face him. "And what, exactly, am I looking at here?"

My question comes out in a whisper.

"This is where I killed them."

I'm not used to this. I don't think I ever will be.

He admitted to his crimes in our past life together—I remember that now. But I dismissed them as an inflation of the truth. A way for him to chase me off when he thought things were getting *too real.* Surely, I wouldn't have wanted to stay with him when he was admitting he was a serial killer, right? I thought it was all lies.

That's exactly what he is. Same as the rest of them. And just like then, I can't seem to dig up that little seed of self-preservation that would make me want to run. To get away from this feral, vengeful man before he can use one of these weapons on me.

My eyes reluctantly leave his to take another slow catalog of the room. *Torture devices.* That's what I'm surrounded by. Not tools or weapons for hunting. This is what he used to find justice.

This was his courtroom.

"And now? How is it still completely stocked? Did you

come back and set it up when you…appeared here." Regard-less of who he was in our previous life together, none of that happened this time. Not in the same way.

So then, why would he have a need for all of this?

He reaches out and grabs a knife with a smooth matte black, stainless steel hilt. Twisting and turning it in his palm so we can both admire the way the light catches its shiny blade, he begins to answer. "I didn't have to add much back then, honestly. This room was built by my father after they bought the cabin. I never bothered looking in it after the first time he and my mother paraded us around to show off all their new upgrades. But when everything went down, and I knew I needed a safe space to get answers, this is what immediately came to mind."

Setting the blade back into its cradle on the wall, I watch with rapt attention as he reaches over and grabs its much larger twin. He tests the sharpness, flicking the pad of his thumbs against the edge. "You can imagine how surprised I was to find that he had everything I needed. I think that's the first time I realized he had dark secrets, too."

"He killed people in here?"

Given the past couple of weeks, that doesn't surprise me at all, honestly.

Bash looks back at me, eyes sunken and haunted. "I've recently confirmed it, yes."

I suck in a breath, more disturbed by that than the presence of the killer before me. "Do you think he did this to Sienna?"

Broad, wide shoulders lift in a casual shrug. "I have no idea of his true involvement in what happened to her. I just know that he's slaughtered many others, and he's going to pay for it."

"I want to help."

"Absolutely not," he repeats the same answer as before.

"She was my friend, Bash. The only one I had."

"And? That's hardly an excuse to go on a murdering spree."

Crossing my arms, I jut my chin out stubbornly. "I'm helping, whether you like it or not."

"I won't allow you to do anything that would put your life in danger."

"*Allow me?* I hate to break it to you, but you aren't in charge of me. Besides, I'm not asking for your permission." I've suffocated under a man's thumb for long enough.

In a flash, his hands are wrapping around my shoulders, twisting us around until my ass is planted firmly onto the table. The cold metal bites against my exposed thighs.

"See that? How easily you can be blindsided? *Manhandled?*" he seethes, brows pinched together in a deep glower. When he sees my nostrils flare at the accusation, his expression softens.

"I'm *not* some weak little thing for you to throw around. For *anyone* to throw around. I'll train. I'll get stronger and faster. But I won't be told no."

Swiping his hand down his face, he groans. "I didn't mean to say you're weak. I'm sorry, Stardust. You're the strongest person I know. It's just... When you're in the room, nothing else exists. My entire world spins on your axis. I can't concentrate on anything if you're there."

"That's not my problem."

Something in him shifts at those stubborn words. In a split second, his face morphs from the sympathetic, sweet version of him that I've come to know, to the cold-blooded killer who once painted these walls with blood.

And I've just transformed into his prey.

"Everyone underestimates you, don't they little lamb?" He

paces in a semi-circle around me, those bright eyes never leaving my face as his fingers flip the blade around his knuckles effortlessly. "They think you're some cheap toy to play with and discard when they get bored. To break apart and throw away."

My eyes fall to my lap, focusing hard on my own intertwined fingers to stop the sudden rush of tears from spilling over at the accuracy of his words.

*A broken toy, worthless and obsolete.*

That's all they see me as. It's all they've *ever* seen me as. Even Halen, who jumped at the opportunity to control me like her little puppet.

That's why his immediate dismissal of me helping him cut so deeply.

"But they're wrong, aren't they?" He lowers his voice, stopping between my legs to brace one hand beside me on the edge of the table while the other uses the tip of the knife to gently nudge my chin back up. Then, he leans forward. So close, our foreheads brush. "You're not their little plaything— you never were. You refuse to break for them."

Shaking my head, I weakly lift my gaze to meet his hard stare.

"Yes," he growls, the blunt edge of his blade pushing harder against my skin. "Don't deny it."

"You're wrong. They've broken me multiple times," I find the bravery to insist, my voice cracking with the admission.

They've broken me, and I can't seem to find the will to piece myself back together again.

"No, they haven't. They've tried like hell. They've betrayed you. They've even killed you. But they haven't broken you, and that, my beautiful little Stardust, is exactly what is so enticing about you."

He shifts, lifting his other hand to skirt his finger across my collar bone, dragging up my neck in a slow, tantalizing trail of heat and lust, before it rounds my chin and slips between my lips. Just as his fingertip moves past my teeth and grazes my tongue, he slowly pulls it back out, sucking it between his own lips with a groan. The knife in his other hand remains evenly in place through the whole thing, never puncturing skin or causing pain.

Just threatening.

I don't know how he's able to so flawlessly make me go from the verge of tears to the verge of an orgasm in a matter of seconds. He's gotten just as good at playing with me as the rest of them.

"Even I forget sometimes. I try to shield and protect you, but you don't need that, do you? I see it. And you know what the best part about *them* not seeing it until now is? That I get to witness their horrified reactions as you show them exactly. Who. You. Are."

I gasp as he shifts again, faster than I can react, and his free hand slips into the spot the knife was just in and then wraps around the back of my neck, tugging me closer to him until our mouths meet—teeth clashing and lips smashing. I hear the metal blade clang against the cement floor as his tongue invades my mouth and begins moving against mine.

And I submit to the overwhelming desire that's building in my core. I don't push or flail or fight against this dangerous man, the way I probably should. Instead, I take what I want. My arms wrap around his neck, gripping him tight as he releases my neck to scoop me into his arms. My legs encase him possessively, fusing us together as our mouths greedily feast on one another.

His erection grinds against my center through our clothes, and my body reacts, meeting his rhythm. In another shift, he slams me back onto the table, pushing me down until I'm lying before him, legs spread wide. Strong fingers grab at the seams of my leggings and pull, ripping them apart in one swift motion. Swiping my panties aside, he runs his finger down my slit, testing my readiness.

"Always so fucking wet for me," he muses in a low, pleased growl.

I can hardly breathe with him like this. So possessive and in control.

He pushes my thighs apart until they are flat against the table, then begins circling me like a predator would before it strikes. Once he reaches the head of the table, he runs his finger along my collarbone, reaching across the room to grab something from the hooks on the wall.

It's a knife. A much larger one than he had before with a smooth, steel handle. He examines it silently above my head before continuing his pacing. The cold blade hits my sternum as he passes my right side, then drags down my torso with every step he takes back to my legs.

It should scare me. Seeing him in this mode—the primal animal. So in control, yet ready to be set off at any given moment. It shouldn't have me writhing against the table with the need for his touch, especially in such a vulnerable position. One move, and he could have me dead.

But I know he won't. I trust him. Which is exactly what he's trying to prove. He wants me to know that he can handle this—me being in here, seeing him in this state— after speaking so adamantly against it. And as a man of few words, this is him silently asking if I can handle it in return.

"Do you know what I've done in this room?"

The smartass in me wants to say nothing, technically. But I know that's not what he means, so I nod once and bite my tongue.

The blade comes down to my pelvis, where he twists his wrist and slices my panties into two without any effort.

"I've skinned people alive here. I've sliced them open and

watched their blood seep out in rivers onto the floor. All while they were still alive."

Pushing the vision of what he's describing out of my mind, I shake my head. "You had a good reason. They were bad people."

The knife leaves my skin, and when I lift my head to check what he's doing, I realize he's begun flipping it around through his fingers again, thinking—a nervous trait, I'm realizing.

"No, baby. I did it because I liked it. Because I enjoyed ripping the life force from their bodies."

"You aren't going to scare me."

"This doesn't scare you?" He asks, running the blade back across my skin, starting at my hip bone and ending right above my slit. When I shake my head, my breathing erratic, he flips it over in his hand. Wrapping his gloved fingers protectively around the sharpened edge, he sticks the hilt between my pussy lips.

"How about now? Scared yet?"

I do my best to remain still, holding my breath so he can't tell how fast it's coming out. "No," I tell him in a deceptively even tone.

The hilt runs down my slit, the cold metal moving past my clit before it stops right at my entrance.

"You must be terrified now."

"I trust you," I tell him truthfully.

Clicking his tongue, he shakes his head. "Such a dirty girl," he admonishes, as if I'm forcing him to do this.

He begins moving the knife in small, tantalizing circles around my entrance, his pace quickening as my hips buck forward. The other hand comes down on my groin, pushing my ass back against the table and holding me there. When I can no longer hide my short, quickening breaths, I give in to it, allowing myself to chase this unconventional high.

Bash notices, the corners of his eyes tightening as he fights off his own arousal. The smoothe hilt slips further inside of me as he pushes it forward, then pulls it back out the slightest bit. I release a garbled moan, which is the only encouragement he needs to continue.

Over and over, he fills me with his knife, stopping just in time to prevent the blade from slicing me in two. It's an erotic exercise of trust and self-control, and I only last a few moments before my body begins to shake and the orgasm I've been trying to chase takes hold of me.

Bash pulls the knife out one more time before he disappears for a fraction of a second. His hands wrap around my hips as he yanks me toward him, until my ass sits at the edge of the table. My thighs are shoved into my stomach as he slams his cock inside of me.

I see stars.

The force of my winding orgasm kicks up and doubles as he thrusts inside of me. He grabs my legs up in each hand and hooks them over his shoulders, leaning forward to give himself deeper access.

In a small moment of vulnerability, he turns his head and kisses the inside of my knee, reaching his hand around to rub circles against my clit. I throw my head back against the table, the sensation of my second orgasm so powerful, all I can do is scream his name into the ether and pray to whatever dark God sent him here that I'll survive him.

"Mm… that's right, baby. Scream for me." He thrusts into me even harder, pace quickening as his own ecstacy builds.

And I do. I scream as pure euphoria takes hold and rips through me. He continues his rhythm as I squirm and pulse beneath him, unable to control my body. Just as I reach the crest and my descent begins, Bash groans and I'm filled with a pool of his hot arousal.

He leans forward between my legs, covering me with his

body as his lips pepper a trail of kisses along my jawline and he pumps the last of his orgasm into me. Once he's completely emptied, he lays his head across my chest and my hand comes up to twist my fingers through his soft hair.

"I can't lose you," he murmurs once everything is still.

He's back to his usual, compassionate self as the predator has been effectively proven ineffective and chased away. His fingers thoughtfully draw delicate circles against my chest, and I have to remind myself that this was the same hand that just held a blade against the same spot moments prior.

"But I also can't control you. If you've got the craving for revenge, I would be a hypocrite to deny you."

I can't help the smile that takes over my entire face. "You're going to let me help?"

Lifting his head, he snarks, "I thought I don't *let* you do anything."

"I want to do this, Bash. We both need this in order to move on with our lives."

His teasing smile falters, a dark thought crossing his mind before he catches it and forces his face into a neutral expression. "I'll teach you what I can, but you have to listen to my instructions and let me guide you."

"I'll be the best student," I assure him confidently.

His brow kicks up at whatever dirty fantasy crosses his mind, and then he peels himself off of me. "Let's go get cleaned up so we can get started."

"Yes, boss," I tease through a smile as he leans over to pull his pants back up.

Unfortunately, my clothes are flung around the room in scraps, so I'm forced to awkwardly cover myself with my hands as I scoot off the table. When I look back to him, Bash is already staring down at me with a dark shadow cast over his face.

"I'm not sure how I'll survive this with you," he admits, licking his lips.

"As long as you don't rip my clothes apart, we should be okay." Even as the taunting statement leaves my mouth, I know it's not true.

This experience has already bonded us, and we've hardly survived it. Once we begin slaying our enemies together, there will be no turning back.

**53**

*The Wolf*


MY FATHER LEANS over a blueprint of my grandparent's home, his finger tracing a hallway that runs behind his bedroom and leads into a hidden office that I've never seen before.

Sienna and I used to play all over that home, chasing each other down the long corridors and weaving into random guest rooms while our parents visited. I thought I was familiar with every square inch of the sprawling mansion, but these blueprints prove that I've only been exposed to a fraction of it.

He called me this morning to inform me that it was time to set our plan into motion. After weeks of pouring over every random piece of information he had, I was starting to believe he was just blowing smoke up my ass. Sienna's death has taken a heavy toll on him and my mother, even more so than when it happened *before*. He craves revenge just as badly as I do, and even though I plan to kill him for his own sick mistakes by the end of this, I'm glad to have him as a resource this time around.

We've gone through the motions with the police, but haven't accused anyone of the crimes against Sienna the way we had done before. There is no body this time. No court hearings or bribes. No corrupt judges. I've completely bypassed that process by purposely being vague when they question me, only going along with it for my mother's sake.

Instead, I'm taking the case on myself, delivering punishments to every single person involved in her brutal murder with my own two hands.

Our first target is my grandfather—the useless, sadistic piece of shit who put the call out for Sienna to be attacked, and then ensured I was distracted as it happened so I couldn't interfere.

I hacked into their phones and found the messages planning it all, including the location of the burner phones that sent each of us her exact location that night. They were sent from right beside where her body was found, probably as soon as she was dumped there. When I showed them to my father, he was the one to decide he would be first.

"He'll know you're there before you even get to the door," my father explains in a detached, cold voice. "When he sees you on the camera, he's going to try to slip into this hallway and into his office. His staff doesn't even know about it, so they'll try to tell you he isn't home." He points to the spot marking a doorway into his bedroom. "He'll probably have this door locked and barricaded, but you can also get into the hallway from this room."

Jabbing his finger into one of the guest rooms on the main floor, he glides it across the paper, mapping out a path.

"There's a set of stairs at the end of the hall that will lead right into the office. There's a faux bookcase to disguise it, but you'll just have to enter this code into the keypad hidden behind the 'L' encyclopedia, and it'll open right up."

He hands me a sticky note with four numbers scribbled on it, then looks back at the blueprint.

"He won't expect you to come from there. Once you get to him, he'll try to distract you as he moves over to a desk or a bookcase and grabs a weapon. Don't fall for it. Your best bet is to attack the moment you get in there."

I nod my head, planning out how to incapacitate him before he can reach anything. I've already made that mistake before, with the man standing before me, and it cost me my life.

"Take the staircase behind his desk, and it will lead you straight into the garage. I'll have a car waiting for you to load him into. After that, I don't care what you do with him."

"You don't want to be there when I kill him?" I question, surprised that he doesn't want to be the one to deliver the fatal blow.

There's no chance in Hell that I'll be giving that away when it comes to killing him. Not after what he's done.

He levels me with a stare, blinking slowly. "I trust that you'll ensure he receives an adequate punishment."

Such an odd thing to bond over. I'm sure that when he used to imagine all the great times we'd have slaughtering together, it was alongside his brainless brothers and plunging knives into innocent people for sport. Not breaking into his childhood home and murdering his own father. I suppose the darkness I've been succumbing to has been passed down through generations. Where I thought I was putting an end to toxic cycles, it turns out I'm just evolving them into new, even worse ones.

Some might even say that I belong in the ground right beside them. I'll accept that fate if it comes. But not until I can stop the Order from bleeding any further into society.

That evening, I set Stardust up in my penthouse with extra security outside the elevator doors, and then headed out to do exactly what my father and I discussed.

He was easier to capture than we thought, and within the hour, I was driving his limp body down the expressway to the cottage, where I plan to show Stardust exactly what she's signing up for.

54

*The Lamb*

THE KNIFE in my hand hovers six inches over his chest, unmoving. I count his slow, shallow breaths, promising myself I'll make the plunge after five... then ten... then twenty.

"I can't do it," I finally admit, swinging my gaze over to Bash, who has been watching patiently as I attempted—and failed miserably—to build up the courage to take this old man's life.

He's done all this work, priming our victim into this perfect, unconscious state for me to step in and deliver the fatal blow.

And I can't even do it.

"That's okay," he soothes, pushing off the toolbox he's been leaning against to stand across from me at the metal table, our victim lying lifelessly between us. His hand slowly wraps around the blade of the knife I'm still holding out and he pulls it out of my death grip.

"What's wrong with me?" I ask brokenly, disgusted with myself.

I'm a coward. I've always been one.

So weak and easily swayed. Ripe and ready for anyone to come around and mold me into whatever they want me to be. So easily manipulated. I'd walk through fire if someone I loved asked me to do it. This is the first thing I've done for myself, because I want retribution for my friend, and I've already failed so miserably.

"Nothing is wrong with you…"

Of course, that's his response. He never wanted me to be a part of this in the first place.

"You said I couldn't handle this, and you were right. I'm a complete failure," I tell him pitifully.

"You think that your inability to kill is a failure?"

"I think my inability to complete a task makes me pathetic."

Shaking his head, he sets the knife down beside the man's head and straightens his stance, gesturing toward the unconscious body between us.

"This isn't a *task*. It's a *murder*. And your hesitation to take a life is not a weakness." Pausing, he rounds the table and stands beside me, grabbing my hands into his, dwarfing them. "Your humanity is not a flaw, Stardust. It's what makes you so different from every other person in this sick world. It's why you're so alluring to me… to men like this."

"I just want to be able to help. To do *something* other than distract you."

"You aren't trying to learn some simple new skill like riding a bike or drawing. You're not going to be able to jump in head first and expect not to drown a little the first few times."

"Did you struggle?" I find it hard to believe if he did.

"No. Because I was driven by blind rage and had absolutely nothing to lose."

When I roll my eyes and turn my face away, he squeezes my palms and pulls me back. "Let me finish," he says in a stern command.

"It was easy *then*, but it hasn't come as easily to me this time around."

"Because I'm distracting you," I surmise, interrupting. But he shakes his head.

"No, and stop trying to think for me," he says, the dark warning clear in his voice. "It's difficult because with you here, I can see beyond all of this. I want a future... one that doesn't include time in jail, or being haunted by all the lives I've taken, or a life *without* you. So, yes, I'm protective of you, and it might be a little distracting, but that's not the most challenging part. The hardest part is ensuring I do everything carefully and correctly. It's getting retribution for my sister and ensuring they can't do this shit to anyone else. But it's also making it possible that one day, we can move on from it all without looking back."

"You think that can happen?"

"Of course, I do. What do you expect, little Stardust? That this will be our end?" He huffs out a humorless laugh. "This is nowhere close to our end."

Breathing out a small sigh of relief, my eyes drop to the man beside us. "What do we do about him?"

"I'll handle it. You can go inside."

But I'm already shaking my head. "No. I need to be here to at least witness it."

"Are you sure?" His brows pinch together in worry, and I try to push away the shock that he isn't insisting that I obey him or throwing out any condescending comments about me not being able to handle it. He's allowing me to make the decision, despite how much it bothers him.

Do I think I can handle this? I have no idea.

Still, I square my shoulders, stubbornly ignoring the little voices in my head that tell me I'm insignificant.

"Yes."

With a single nod, he turns away and grabs the knife back up. "You were going for the chest before," he begins, pointing with the tip of the blade. "That's not a bad place to start, but you have to watch out for all these ribs." As he explains, he scrapes the blade along the spot I was aiming at before.

Flipping the blade on its side, so it runs parallel with the ribs, he mocks the motion of stabbing the space between them. "He's knocked out, so you've got the advantage of time to get your strike right. If you come in like this, you could easily hit the lungs or heart. Instant death."

Next, he moves the blade up to the man's neck, aiming the blade for the middle. "I prefer to hit here. It's a simple stab, then drag. You'll hit the carotid artery. It's messy, but it will incapacitate him, and it's almost instant."

He gazes down at the man's face, his expression morphing into the killer I've seen him become a handful of times. "Of course, depending on how much you want your victim to suffer, you may not want to offer something so merciful."

"What did he do?" I ask, realizing I never even bothered to get any background information on the person whose life I was about to take a few minutes ago.

Bash tears his eyes away from the table, and when they finally meet mine, his pupils are so dilated, the green has nearly disappeared. "This is Albert Lancaster."

"Lancaster? As in…?"

Bash nods, understanding the unspoken question. "My grandfather. One of the three Grand Masters of the Order. He's also one of the men who kept me distracted that night so the rest of them could strike."

"On his own granddaughter?" I gasp.

"There's no honor among thieves," he mumbles.

Something about the bitterness of his tone tells me that Albert had more to do with what happened than that. This was obviously a personal kill for him. One that hit close to home.

And he was willing to give it to me anyway.

I consider the face lying before me, taking it in for the first time. He's handsome, just like Bash. But there's a sinister twist in his features that isn't present in Bash's. He has the type of face that anyone would fear.

Which made him the perfect person for the job. Who would go against an Order from a man like him? Even if it was to kill his own family.

"I don't understand any of this, Bash," I confess. "If he's her grandfather, how could he do any of this to her? There's got to be some familial bond that prevents it. Didn't he love her?"

As soon as the question leaves my lips, I realize how silly it was. Gabe claimed to love me for years, and he attempted the same thing. Not in the brutal way that Sienna was murdered, but it was murder just the same. Sometimes, it's the people we think we can trust who end up fucking us over the worst.

"He made a choice to punish me and my father. Today, he'll die for it."

"Was he one of your victims before?"

I seem to forget that he's already lived through this hell. Already taken lives.

How odd was it for him to see them walking around, alive and well, after he woke up again?

"No, I never made it to him."

His patience is wearing thin. I can sense it in his clipped tone and the way his arm muscles, toned and corded, are tensed and stiffened. He wants to deliver this blow so badly, but he won't do it before I'm ready.

As fucked up and backwards as it sounds, this small act of restraint—this blatant show of respect—is far more than anything else who has claimed to love me has ever offered.

"I'm ready," I tell him, swallowing through the lump that's formed in my throat.

My hesitation has slightly faded, now that I know who he is and what he's done to my friend. But I doubt I'll ever truly be ready.

In complete fascination, I watch the man I've come to love with every fiber of my being as he lifts his arms, both hands wrapped around the hilt of his knife, and then crashes down into the man—Albert's—neck with a squelching sound.

It's loud. And wet. And bloody.

My ears are ringing, and it takes me too long to realize that the screeching noise echoing off the walls of the small room is coming from my mouth.

That the liquid covering my shoes is my vomit.

And that the arms wrapping around mine are Bash's.

55

*The Wolf*

"I CAN'T LIVE HERE," Stardust declares early the next morning.

I've been sitting in the chair set off in the corner, quietly working on data while I waited for her to wake.

Last night was rough. Once I got her calmed down and back into the house, I had to dispose of my grandfather's body and clean up the mess we made. She had fallen asleep in my arms on the couch, so I carried her off to bed and went back into the kill room to work.

But she woke up and came to find me a couple hours later, and all the emotions she felt when I put the knife in his neck came barreling in again when she saw his body neatly wrapped in plastic and my bloodstained hands placing the last piece of tape across the seam.

"Okay," is all I say.

I stand from my chair and set the laptop on it, then go to sit beside her on the bed.

"I can't cook and shower and sleep and pretend there wasn't just a dead body in my garage," she explains with tears glistening in her eyes. Before they can fall, she blinks them away.

I was afraid of this. I knew that killing would be too much for her. She's far too empathetic to rationalize taking someone's life, especially when she's been in their position multiple times now. It's her biggest strength. One of the things that has attracted me to her, simply because I don't possess that quality.

I'm driven by rage. She's driven by compassion.

She insisted on it, though. Promised me up and down that she could handle it, and I'm not capable of telling her no. So, I did all the work and prepped the body for her. I made sure he wasn't awake and bombarding her with his pleas to spare him. Although, given that it was my grandfather, I highly doubt his pride would allow for him to beg. He'd probably just coldly stare at her when she made the fatal blow, and that's arguably worse.

Of course, I had to show her where to drive the knife. I think if I had to do it over again, I'd just have her drug him and be done. But I enjoy the blood. I like to watch them suffer, and killing Gabe was disappointingly anticlimactic because he got to drift away without any pain.

"We can stay at my place in the city," I offer hesitantly, opting to leave out the fact that she spent months doing exactly what she's describing when we went through this *before* and I was killing right under her nose.

It's always been a sore subject with her—moving into my space—but I truly don't give a fuck where we are. As long as she's with me.

Nodding her head, she perks up. "I think that's a great idea," she pipes the compliment as if she didn't lead me right to it.

My expression falls. "I can handle these kills on my own."

Her response is an immediate scowl. "Don't," she warns.

"I can't put you through something that is clearly too much."

She sits up, and the shift puts her face directly in mine as she insists, "It was my first time, Bash. I *want* to do this. Stop trying to tell me what I can handle."

"I don't want it to break you," I admit in a lowered voice, my gaze falling to her lips. "What is the point of getting you back if the first thing I do is destroy your life?"

"She was my friend," she reminds again. "Sienna was one of the only people who bothered to acknowledge my pain and help me through it. She didn't deserve to die."

"I know–"

"And furthermore," she goes on, holding her finger up to stop me from interrupting her rant. "These men targeted me, too. They stole me up from the middle of the street, stripped me down to nothing, and treated me like an animal. I have every reason to want revenge for that."

My stomach sinks. We haven't had a chance to talk about what they did to her in the woods, or how she's been coping with it since. They killed Sienna for it days later, and things have been a whirlwind since then. I guess I assumed that because she appeared fine, she was.

It all makes sense now. And she's right. How can I claim to have more justification in killing them as retribution for what they did to Sienna, when she's been personally attacked by them? I can't.

"Then, we'll work on it," I promise, my voice cracking with sincerity. "I'll get past my own reservations about you killing, and we'll figure out how to make this work for you. Starting with packing your bags and bringing you home."

"Home?" She questions with that sarcastic little pitch that makes me want to slam her into the bed and punish her.

"Yes, Stardust. What's mine is yours."

"No, that only applies to married couples." Shaking her head, she scrunches her nose, the way she always does when my fortune is mentioned.

"Have I not told you? We're getting married."

Lifting her left hand, she makes a show of glaring at the empty ring finger, pulling a rare laugh out of me. "I don't remember being asked."

"Do you truly think I'd give you the choice?" I tease, although I'm still half serious. She could say no a hundred times, and I'd continue asking until she changed her mind.

Her smile falters as a shadow passes her face with whatever intrusive thought that just invaded her mind.

"I'm afraid to plan ahead," she admits, dropping her head to watch her hands fidget with the blanket.

"Why?"

"Because we already lost each other once. It could happen again, and all we'll be left with are the empty promises we made to each other."

"This promise isn't empty. You *will* be mine, Jovie Benvenuti. As soon as this is over, I'm taking you to make it official. Your ring is tucked away in my office at home."

She allows herself to smile, tucking her chin further into her chest as she plays with her ring finger and shyly mumbles, "Jovie Lancaster."

I could melt into a puddle on the floor at the sound of her name beside mine. "I prefer Stardust, but that sounds nice too."

"Fine. Let's kill these assholes so we can get married."

I've never loved her more.

## 56

*The Wolf*

OUR NEXT VICTIMS are my choice, and someone my father is adamantly against.

"They're inconsequential to the overall plan," he lectures over and over.

But Charles remembers our past lives together, and is therefore a threat to *my* plan. Plus, he and Logan threatened Stardust. That can't go unpunished. We can't have open ends if we're going to be successful in this. Charles could be in Hugh's ear already, outing me as the Serpent Slayer.

My grandfather's death was publicly declared a heart attack. Thanks to my father's pull with the media, no one questioned it. Not even my uncles, who could have easily driven over and demanded to see the body. Once Stardust and I were finished with him, I brought him back to his home, where my father met me and made his calls. I have no idea who he brought in to take the corpse away and prepare it for a funeral, but he assured me they would be discreet and there would be no records of the knife wounds to his neck.

The whole experience reminded me that he's not at all the man I thought I knew. Where I've always viewed him as a boring investment banker with a hard-on for some strange men's club, he's been slaughtering people and covering up their deaths for longer than I've been alive. He's done this sort of thing before, and has the process down to a calculated tee. Where I would have simply dumped the body off to be found by the Order, he's playing a longer game, creating illusions and weakening them before they even realize he's switched sides.

Charles and Logan won't be as easy to excuse away as my grandfather's death was. They'll be the first tipping point for the Order. We'll have to move fast once they're gone to prevent them from catching up and attacking us. My father claims he has a plan for that, too. One he'll reveal to me when it's time.

Despite his reservations, he still helps me with coming up with a plan. He and Charles have been friends for decades, so he has a good idea of what his usual patterns are.

Although, not much has changed since the last time I made preparations to kill him. He's a creature of habit. Every day begins and ends the same, and each week carries the same schedule. I don't waste any time with them. Four days after dropping my grandfather's body off at his home, I'm dragging their limp bodies out of my trunk and into the kill room.

I've pulled the table out and replaced it with two chairs facing opposite directions. I want them to know they're dying together in the hell they created for themselves. I want to watch the fear and devastation cross Charles' face as I murder his son right beside him. I want Logan to hear Stardust's taunting voice from all directions, just as he tried to do to her in the woods.

Only once I have them both tightly secured to the chairs, I bring her in.

"These are the men from the woods," she exclaims excitedly, circling their unconscious bodies with her hands behind her back.

She's settled into this role far easier than I could have ever hoped. I thought it would break her when I killed my grandfather and she collapsed to the ground. I was wrong. It only makes sense that the light inside of her would overpower the hate she carries and prevent her from continuing.

I thought I had ruined her.

That despite every other horrible, traumatic thing that has happened to her, it was me revealing my true self that finally set her off.

But she recovered quickly. And that light I had assumed would prevent her from continuing? It only pushed her further.

She wants to do this because she's loved and lost and hurt. She's tired of being a victim of circumstance. A mere passenger in the crazy shitshow that life has handed her. There's a hunger inside of her that even I don't possess, and it's the driving force behind her need for revenge.

There is one thing Sienna did that I can never thank her enough for, and that's offering a shoulder of support for my girl when no one else would. When I was too much of a coward to step out of the shadows and remind her that she's better than every piece of shit she's allowed to disappoint her for her entire life. When her family couldn't get their noses out of each other's asses to see her crumbing right before them.

Sienna was a friend to her, just like she claimed to be.

And one of my biggest regrets will be doubting her intentions when she saw how much I cared about this woman, and took it upon herself to ensure she was supported and loved. If I could only say one last thing to her, I would express my gratitude for keeping her going when every other sign pointed at quitting.

"I thought you might be excited for these ones," I tell Stardust, dragging my feet over to the row of knives I've laid out.

Perhaps if she has enough of an emotional tie to the victims, she'll have less of a difficult time taking their lives.

"What are we going to do to them?" she wonders hesitantly, stopping in front of Logan to lean forward and examine him closer.

"Whatever you want," I answer. "They should be waking up soon."

Doubt crosses her face, and I pause.

"What if I freak out again?" She mutters into her chest, fidgeting with a syringe I prepared in case we need to kill them quickly.

"Then I'll help you through it," I promise. "And if you decide you can't handle it, I'll bring you inside and take care of them myself."

Her eyes swing back to their slumped forms, then she surprises me with a sinister smirk. "I think I can handle it."

I return her smile, fighting the urge to hoist her up onto one of these toolboxes and take her before they wake. "I love when you show your teeth."

Charles moans, then shifts in his seat. It doesn't take him long to realize he's restrained, and he begins shaking his arms around in panic, fighting against the rope I have wrapped around them.

"Ready to play?" I ask Stardust, offering her one last chance to back out before she sees a side of me that she might not like.

Nodding her head, she bites her lip. "Let's do it."

I step in around the chairs and position myself before Charles, staring down at him with my most menacing glare.

"Hello, old friend."

**57**

*The Lamb*

THE SWITCH TURNS ON, and he's a completely different person.

A beast of prey.

I can't help the bolt of excitement that courses through me at the sight of his predatory side. It calls to me on a deep, soul level, coaxing out the darkness within me.

He stares down at the old man from the woods like he's absolutely worthless, twisting the knife between his fingers, the same way he had done with me when I was his victim in this room.

"Ah, so you do remember," the man says hoarsely, fighting against his restraints again.

"How could I forget a hate that runs so deep within my very being?" Bash rumbles, tilting his head.

The man's words from the woods ring back in my ears.

*"What are you going to do? Tie me to a chair and slice me open? Douse me in gasoline and throw a match at me?"* He had asked.

That's what Bash did to him *before*. And he remembers.

Is that why he's been chosen as our next victim?

"They know who you are," the man rushes out. "They're already planning to destroy you for good this time."

The words are said just as the other one regains consciousness behind him. He groans and shakes, fighting the rope the same way his father had done.

"Just in time." Bash smiles, keeping his eyes fixated on the older one like he doesn't want to miss one second of his reaction.

He scowls up at him, grave understanding slowly falling across his features.

"What the hell?" The younger one yells in a panicked tone. "What is this?"

"Logan?" The old man calls out, struggling to turn in his seat. But Bash has tied him tight enough to ensure that he can't. He's allowed him to be close enough to hear every torturous, sick thing that's done to his son without being able to do a thing about it.

My eyes raise to the brilliant man who stands before me as my chest fills with admiration.

"Let him go," the old man demands, sweat pouring down his temples.

Bash raises a brow at him.

"Let him go, and you can do whatever you want to me," he amends in a less hostile tone.

"Where's the fun in that?" Bash asks, stepping around to face the other one—Logan. He was Sienna's friend. The one I think she was hooking up with.

"Bash?" Logan questions hoarsely, face twisted in confusion.

"I can't lose him again," the old man cries. "I'll cooperate however you want me to. Just let him go."

"Why should I offer you such a generous mercy?" Bash

grinds out, quickly slicing his knife against Logan's arm, causing him to release a scream that bounces off the walls and rings in my ears. The old one squirms at the sound, and Bash smiles. "I had to lose her all over again. Why shouldn't you have to relive your own personal hell right alongside me?"

My stomach turns as I watch the blood drop from Logan's wound onto the plastic-covered floor in thick, crimson globs.

"You took the girl from the hunt. The Order demanded a life. They wanted balance," the older one yells.

"They wanted to punish me for taking back what was rightfully mine," Bash bellows. "What *you* tried to take."

"I had to see how much she knew of the Order," the man calls back defensively.

"You were trying to punish me for killing you," Bash quips, stepping back into his view. "You specifically targeted her because you wanted to take her from me. But you didn't anticipate for her to be such a hard kill."

Logan begins to nod out, his head lolling to the side as a line of spit falls from his mouth.

"She's lucky you were there," the man grates out as something evil crosses his face. "I would have skinned her alive."

My eyes snap to him, and I'm stepping in front of his pathetic, strapped form before I can think of something clever to say.

"Well, good thing I was," Bash coos. "Because now, she gets a chance to do the same to you."

He offers me the knife he's been holding, the other man's blood still dripping wet off the smoothe metal. I take it hesitantly, keeping my eyes locked onto Bash, who offers an encouraging nod that appears to say, *have fun with it.*

"Are you such a fucking coward, you can't kill me yourself?" the old man spits to Bash in a weak attempt to rile him up.

He sees the calm that's taken over me, and it's startled him. I'm not throwing the knife into him, blindly stabbing like the crazed, scorned woman he expects me to be.

He'd rather deal with the devil he knows. The one he thinks he can distract long enough to get out of his restraints. I've been watching his fingers reach for the knots around his wrists, desperate to untie them.

He's got hope—that fickle thing I refuse to have.

"I trust that you're in good hands," Bash throws over his shoulder as he makes his way back to Logan, quickly snatching another knife up on his way.

There's a loud smack, and then a groan as he comes back into consciousness.

"For all the drugs I've watched you take over the years, you sure are a lightweight," Bash teases, slapping him across the face a second time. So hard, I'll be surprised if there isn't already a bruise forming on his cheek.

"Go ahead, girl," the old man whispers, nose scrunched in mock disgust. "See how close you can get before I grab the side of your head and slam your skull into this cement floor."

My eyes flick to Bash, who is watching me carefully. He's expecting me to fail, just like I did before. He handed me the knife to prove myself, but he's staying close by in case I can't take it, just like he predicted.

The difference between then and now is that I have a personal stake in this. These men were prepared to rip me to shreds in those woods, the same way every other unfortunate soul I was forced to spend hours waiting in the dark with was tortured.

Still, there's a filter in my brain that prevents me from throwing my arm back and jamming the knife into the man's neck, in the same spot Bash pointed out on his grandfather.

"Were you fucking both of them?" The man questions bitterly, wincing when Bash does something to cause the other man to scream again. "They *are* twins. It could be like fucking the same person, if you think about it."

My upper lip rises at the vision he's painted, disgust rolling through my belly. The knife feels heavy in my hand.

"She was so fucking tight," he whispers, rolling his eyes to the back of his head in mock ecstasy. "I got the first turn with her, you know."

My eyes widen at his admission, flicking up to Bash, who has stopped whatever he was doing to torture Logan to send a murderous glare into the back of the old man's head. He works his jaw back and forth and flips the knife in his hand, contemplating.

He gave me this kill. He knows it, the man knows it. But he knows exactly what to say to crawl beneath Bash's skin and pull a reaction from him. To make a mistake that will grant the man an advantage.

Bash remains rooted to his spot, exercising a level of restraint I never knew he had.

"You should have heard the way she screamed when we carved into her," the man goes on dramatically.

Angry heat blooms across my chest. Bash told me how he found her after we left her funeral. He explained the gruesome scene he arrived to in a broken, detached voice. I could hardly listen to the details. To imagine my friend like that… to know the things she went through. It nearly broke me. That was when I made the decision to help him carry out their punishments and end the tyrannical reign this elitist cult seems to have.

"She was always such a firecracker. It was nice to watch the will to live fade from her eyes as we all railed into her and she realized no one was coming to save her."

Bash bites his lip, his pupils so large, the greens of his eyes have nearly disappeared, just like they had done when he killed his grandfather. Logan hangs his head and groans in pain. I'm not sure if it's from what Bash has already done to him, or if it's difficult for him to hear what his own father did to his friend.

That small filter begins to fade away, allowing the darkness to creep in and take over.

"They're going to do the same to you," the man promises me, and my heart leaps as darkness squeezes it, turning it black and cold. "They're going to rip you apart from the inside out. They'll shove knives inside your pussy and carve it up to prove a point: that you don't fuck with the Loyal Order of the Serpent and walk away un–"

His speech is cut off by the squelching sound of my knife dug deep into his throat. Directly in the spot Bash showed me.

I don't stop there, though.

My hand pulls back and shoves the blade back into his flesh. It scrapes against his collarbone, and I feel every inch of the collision of metal and marrow vibrating into my hand. I repeat the same motion, taking care to hit a different spot every time.

His body wiggles and shakes with each strike, jumping up and down with my force like a rag doll. The metallic scent of his blood has filled all of my senses, fueling me.

It reminds me of the night I killed Gabe. An entire lifetime ago, yet it feels like mere months have passed.

Over and over, the wet sounds echo off the metal toolboxes surrounding us as I mutilate his body, the same way he did to my friend. The same way he tried to do to me. And Bash watches in stony silence, his body still as a statue.

I'm so fucking sick of men thinking they can just take and take and *take* until there's nothing left. Then, when there's no more than a jaded corpse, they move on to their next victim, as if the last one never existed.

Gabe did it to me before he did it to my mom. This man did it to Sienna before he tried to do it to me.

Round and round they go, spreading their disease while we're left picking up the pieces.

No more.

*NO MORE.*

Hot tears stream down my face in escaping rivers of pent-up emotion. Blood splatters my face, my hair, my clothes. Until I'm covered with it, just like my insides have been covered with the darkness that pushed me to do this.

When he's nothing more than a minced up sack of flesh, I drop the knife and fall to my knees as it clatters against the cement beside me. I try to push the darkness back from my mind, but it's too strong. It fights against me, hungry for more.

But I can't. I can't do this anymore. I've succumbed to the pain and now I'm drowning in it. I'm consumed by it.

Within seconds, Bash's arms envelope me, pulling me up into his hard chest. And the darkness inside of me fills the room until everything turns black.

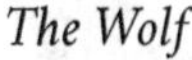

## 58

*The Wolf*

IT'S my father's idea for me to be at the office when Logan and Charles are found dead in Charles' home the following day. Stardust and I got a little too messy last night, which made staging them difficult. After laying into me for twenty minutes straight, my father called his guy in and they managed to make it believable enough to continue with our plan.

In true honesty, I don't give a fuck if their bodies are found in the middle of the street with my name branded into them, the same way Sienna was left. The Order will know it's us as soon as they receive the news. They know what happened in those woods—how the two men came after Stardust. They know she's still alive, too.

Hearing the things they did to Sienna only gave me the push I needed to see this through. I've had a taste of their blood, and now I want more. The only thing keeping me from going absolutely feral is the promise of a future with my little lamb when this is all over and the demons are slayed. Signing my name to these kills would incriminate me beyond repair.

I've snuck her into my office through the fire escape, ensuring no one is around to witness her with me. The Order will be watching us under a microscope now. They'll likely send someone straight to the cottage to retrieve her when Charles and Logan are discovered. But my father and I thought ahead. While he was arranging the bodies, Stardust and I scrubbed the kill room clean of everything, erasing every trace of our victims and hauling every tool or weapon out of the space, leaving nothing behind but a few old paint cans. We loaded them into my truck to be discarded into a storage unit on our way into the office.

Stardust hasn't slept in that house in over a week. Her neighbors could confirm.

When they try to send the police to our door, there will be no evidence of the crimes we committed.

"So, this is what it's like to be a fancy CEO," she teases, spinning around in my chair.

"There's a lot more spreadsheets involved," I joke, adjusting my tie.

I've been nervously looking out the window for the past hour, watching for anything that seems out of the ordinary.

"Maybe one day I can work here again."

Swinging my shoulders around to face her, I shake my head. "You won't have to work for anything ever again, little lamb."

She rolls her eyes irritatedly, reminding me of Sienna. "Not this marriage talk again. I still don't have a ring."

"You do have a ring, I just haven't given it to you," I bicker, irritated that I've forgotten to propose already.

The courtship hasn't even begun and I'm already a shit husband.

"What if I *want* to work?" She asks, her voice raising just enough to tell me that's exactly what she wants. After Gabe, she'll never rely on a man again.

"Then, you'll be given a corner office and a salary that exceeds your value."

With a bashful smirk, she sticks her tongue out at me. "Come relax," she drawls, closing the distance between us to grab my hand up and tug me over to the chair.

I don't resist when she pushes against my chest, and I collapse into the chair she was just spinning in.

Her fingers make quick work of unbuttoning my pants and sliding my boxers down until my erection springs free.

Before she can lean forward and take me, I wrap my hands around the hem of her shift and lift it over her head, exposing her perky, plump breasts. She sighs as I cup them in my palms, gently squeezing.

Once I'm finished playing, she leans forward into my cock. Running her tongue up the bottom of my length, she stops at my tip and rubs it back and forth against the flattened surface, sending shockwaves through my balls that almost have me finishing before I even make it into her mouth. She smiles at how reactive I am, then grabs the base of my cock with one hand and shoves the whole thing down her throat. When her lips meet her hand, she sticks her tongue out and laps at the base of it, then pulls back and repeats the process.

My fingers wrap around the back of her neck as my hips lift from the chair, sending my cock even deeper into her throat. I feel her gag before she shifts on her knees, then allows me to continue fucking her mouth. I reach with my other hand and pull her bra down, kneading her breast and massaging her nipple between my fingers.

I'm finishing in an embarrassingly short amount of time

Just as I begin to spill into her mouth, there's a knock on

the door that causes her to try and jolt upright. I fight it, holding her head in place until my balls are fully emptied, mumbling a garbled, "just one minute," to whoever has broken us away from this moment.

Stardust adjusts accordingly, leaning forward on her knees to suck out every drop. When I release my hold, she sits back on her toes and breathes out a sigh. Our gazes meet, and I watch in complete ecstasy as she uses her index finger to wipe away the cum dripping from her lips, then sticks it into her mouth and sucks it dry.

There's another knock, and I tear my eyes away from her beautiful sight to scowl at the door. "We're not finished. Go under my desk until I can get rid of whoever the fuck is bothering us," I whisper the command, pointing toward my desk.

She nods, then goes to fix her bra. "Don't you dare put those tits away."

I can tell she wants to argue, but I've already moved toward the door and fastened my pants, leaving her no time. Tilting my head toward my desk in another silent command, I watch as she crawls across the floor, ass halfway hanging out of her dress. My cock hardens again, and I have to adjust myself before putting my hand on the knob. I don't open the door until she's completely out of sight.

"What took you so long?" Eliza grumbles impatiently, putting her hands on her hips. Her iPad sits awkwardly in her hand as she tries to hold the stance.

"I was on a personal call. What do you want?"

"You don't have personal calls. You don't even have a personal life," she counters, lifting the iPad up to show me what appears to be a contract.

"What's this?" I ask, ignoring her insult.

"The contract for Triad. They sent it this morning and the

board wants to go over it tomorrow. We should look through it so I can get your notes together."

I'm completely blanking on who the hell she's talking about. "Triad is…?"

Eliza rolls her eyes, impatiently explaining, "The harness supplier who submitted their proposal when you were… away. The board looked at it and wanted to move forward."

"Who signed the contract?"

Her eyes drop to the screen, finger scrolling until she gets to the bottom of the document. "It's signed by a…. Charles Simon." Her voice breaks at the name, and she holds the device up to look at it closer.

*Fuck.*

Grabbing the iPad from her arms, I look at the document myself. Sure enough, Charles' signature is there, in black and white.

"Who allowed this contract to be pushed to the board?" My tone is more harsh than I intend for it to be, but Eliza isn't phased the way anyone else might be.

She seems to recover from whatever spell has taken over, her face twisting into a stubborn, angry scowl. "If you remember, *sir*, you were lying in a random-ass hospital bed and nowhere to be found and your business had to keep running. The usual process was disrupted without you here."

"I have policies in place to prevent that exact thing. I'd expect that my board would have offered me enough respect to at least follow through with them."

"I don't know what happens in those meetings, Bash. I just know that there's a contract we're supposed to be going over, and I need your notes."

She begins to shoulder her way through the door, but I step in her path to stop her. "I'll put them together myself. I have no intention of working with Triad."

She rears back at my aggressive reaction, but where I

expect her to argue and berate me, she appears to exhale a long, relieved breath.

"We need to talk about something else," she admits, dropping the iPad to her side as she steps back, silently accepting that I won't be letting her into my office.

"It can wait," I insist.

"I'm really not sure that it can…"

I pause at her hushed tone, my hand stilling against the door that I was about to close in her face. For the first time, she doesn't look like my hardass assistant. She looks like a concerned mother. I can't figure out what could have possibly caused the sudden shift.

"Can it wait until this afternoon?" I ask, a little more gently.

Her eyes drop to the floor as she tugs her bottom lip into her mouth, then shifts on her feet. "Fine."

"Put it in my schedule so we aren't interrupted," I tell her, then close the door, eager to get back to my girl.

## 59

*The Wolf*

ELIZA SCHEDULES our meeting that evening, at the time she's usually walking out the door and rushing into the busy streets to get home.

That's my first indication that there's something wrong. The second is the box sitting atop her desk with all of her belongings inside of it. Whatever she plans to say today, she has no intention of returning once it's out.

Stardust has snuck out the back door to wait in the car and give us privacy. I wasn't thrilled with the idea, but she could tell that this is important to Eliza, so she insisted on giving us space.

"This won't take a lot of your time," she greets, helping herself into the office and into one of the chairs across from mine. Slapping a piece of paper onto the desk, she says, "First, I'd like to formally submit my resignation…"

"You don't have to do that, Eliza."

She nods, stopping me from saying anything else.

"It's been an honor to work with you these past few years. I'm so grateful for the experience and the opportunity to watch you grow into the man you are today. I've always said I see you as another one of my children, and I wholeheartedly mean it."

"What is this about?" I press, swallowing past the lump of emotion in my throat.

"I was placed into this role by the Federal Bureau of Investigations," she begins in a grave tone, holding my gaze. My brows kick up into my hairline with that, my mouth going dry.

"We've got several task forces involved in the investigation against the Loyal Order of the Serpent and the various crimes they've committed."

"What?" I breathe, collapsing against the corner of my desk. "But I'm not in the Order…"

"I'm aware. They, however, have not accepted your decision, have they?"

"I'm a legacy." As if that's enough explanation for the things they've done.

"Yes, well… There's a lot of pieces moving at once and several agents positioned in various roles surrounding members and legacies."

"So, all this time, you were lying?" She planted herself in my life, fooling me into thinking we were like family, just so she could get to the Order?

She sighs, crossing her arms across her chest as tears well in her eyes. "Like I said, I've been blessed to have been assigned to this role with you, Sebastian. I knew you had nothing to do with those sick bastards from the beginning. I'm glad I was right."

Swallowing, I shrug. "So, what now? You just up and leave?"

She nods. "I've arranged for someone to take over my role

at Lancaster Tech next week. A regular civilian. We've gathered more than enough information to carry out the case, but you've been cleared. I can't give you much more than that."

*How could I have been cleared when I was set to join as a legacy?* It makes no sense.

"When you disappeared…" she begins, pausing to clear her throat. "I searched high and low for you. Your parents were… uncooperative to say the least. They didn't even have any information to give the police when they were asked for your schedule or patterns. Anything to point them in the right direction."

Dropping my head, I look down at my feet. She's only confirming what I already suspected. I've always kept my personal life a secret from them. Although, they never pretended to care either way.

"Sienna called every day without fail, demanding answers," she supplies, a little more brightly.

Pushing my lips to the side, I fight past the emotions welling up behind my eyes at the mention of my sister. She deserved better than me as a brother.

"I knew where you were," she goes on in a sad voice. "I tracked you down in that hospital within the first few days. I had an obligation to the bureau to report your whereabouts, but I just… couldn't do it. Not when you had those sick bastards on your back."

"So, you let me sit there alone?"

"It was the safest place you could be—right where they left you. They wanted you out of the way for something. We knew it had to do with Lancaster Tech. I confirmed it when several documents were attempted to be pushed to the board, all of them supposedly signed by you. And all of them with other businesses of the Order."

"I had no idea…" There had to be a reason for me being in

that hospital when the timeline shifted—I knew that. But I could have never imagined it ran so deep.

I feel like I've completely lost my grip on this situation.

How many things has she kept from me? How much has flown right beneath my nose?

"If the bureau found out where you were, they were going to place you into witness protection. I knew you had a bigger role in this than providing the Order with one more company to launder money and resources through."

"So, you lied," I surmise.

"I made a judgment call that led us to answers we never would have gotten if I hadn't. It also resulted in removal from my post."

There's a long pause where our emotions catch up to us. Years of working together, and she was only here to get to the Order. The two people who ever cared about me—gone from my life in the blink of an eye.

She swipes at a stray tear, and I clear my throat uncomfortably.

"What now?" I ask her, my voice breaking.

"I'll be on desk duty until we finish the case. I shouldn't even be telling you all of this right now. I was instructed to walk off as soon as I found a replacement."

"What happens to the existing members? Will they be punished?"

Will the FBI be barreling into their clubhouse as they discover that I've killed one of their own?

"I'm not privy to that information."

She looks straight into my eyes, seeing right through me. I can tell there's something important that she wants to say, but appears to abandon it at the last minute, and settles on something else instead.

"I know they've taken Sienna from you–"

"They've taken *everything* from me," I correct, clamping my jaw when I realize what she's said.

They know that the Order is behind Sienna's death. Could they know that I've buried her in an unmarked grave, too?

She flattens her mouth. "You can't let them bring you down with them. I'm begging you, Sebastian, don't do anything stupid. Trust that there are powers working to bring them down."

Standing from her chair, she holds her arms out to ask for a hug. With a deep breath, I step forward and pull her into my chest, already mourning the loss of the only mother figure I've really had.

"I'll miss you," I admit.

"I know," she mumbles into my chest, pulling back to offer a teasing smile. "I'll be around. You can't get rid of me that easily. Now, get downstairs to that girl you've had locked in here all day."

With a knowing grin, she turns away and starts for the door. At the last second, she grabs the door frame, teetering in the doorway of my office.

"I'm proud of you, son," she whispers. "You're a brilliant man, and I know you're going to do great things for this world."

Before the tears can fall from her eyes, she knocks on the door frame three times, then swings into the empty main area. With a hole punched into my chest, I watch her stroll toward her office for the last time.

**60**

*The Lamb*

ONE THING that's conveniently left out of a caterpillar's metamorphosis is the part where they turn to goo before becoming the beautiful butterfly everyone loves so dearly. The ugly transformation, when everything they once were is completely erased to make room for the new, better version of them.

It takes a great deal of patience and understanding from those around as you sort through the worst parts and make room for the good ones. If you're lucky, they'll still be standing there, cheering you on by the time you earn your wings.

Unfortunately, I was never granted that luxury from my family. They've been resistant against every change I've attempted to make, until being around them became so distracting to my experience, I had to step away.

I wish my sister had been there with me through my metamorphosis. I wish I could have relied on her to help me through the traumatic experiences I've gone through this past year.

But holding a grudge against her is only taking energy from my own reserves. That's why I accept her invitation to dinner at our favorite restaurant one random weeknight.

"You've changed," she comments from across the table once we've finished our meals in awkward silence, her chin resting across her hands.

"I had to," I tell her, sipping my water for lack of something better to do.

This is it. It's time to face our issues head on. To open the box and let it all out. That's what this whole dinner is about.

She drops her gaze to her empty plate. "I'm sorry I didn't believe you. I haven't been able to figure out how to tell you how badly I feel about that."

Shrugging, I roll my eyes. "They ensured I would be impossible to believe."

"How have you done it, Jovie?" she wonders, tilting her head like she's seeing me for the first time. "How have you remained sane through all the bullshit?"

I laugh at that, pinning her with a look that says I've done the absolute opposite, and she begins giggling with me. "I had good friends to get me through."

"They must be keepers. I know you can't say the same about our old friends."

"*Our* old friends?" I question curiously.

Wincing, she leans back in her chair. "Once Kennedy successfully pointed out what an insufferable bitch I was being to you, it wasn't long before I noticed the patterns they fell into as well. Gabe really was a manipulative, abusive prick, wasn't he?"

Nodding, I roll my eyes. She hasn't even heard the worst of it.

"I had money saved up to leave. I was going to just disappear one day and never look back. Call you and Kennedy every week with updates and live on the road until I found somewhere that felt like home."

I've never admitted my plan to anyone, too afraid that they'd break my trust and tell Gabe before I could leave. It feels good to finally let it out.

Halen's eyes widen as big as saucers. "You did!? What happened?"

"Mom moved in. Started having an affair with him. He found the account. Two weeks later, he tried to kill me." I recall the events in a dull, detached tone.

Halen sighs, shaking her head. "Mom is a piece of work."

"That's an understatement."

"She's another one Kennedy has opened my eyes to."

I don't want to waste any time talking about the woman who has betrayed me beyond repair, so I shift the subject.

"How is Kennedy? I miss her," I admit through a sad smile.

"She's been your biggest advocate. It's killed her that we haven't been talking, but I know that's my fault, too."

"We were all just trying to survive an impossible situation," I excuse, my stone-cold heart softening the slightest bit at the grateful expression that falls over her face.

She's made mistakes and owned up to them. That's the most I could ask of her.

"How is the house coming along?" she wonders, sipping from her straw.

My face sobers at the thought of what Bash and I have done in that house since the last time she saw it. "I'm not living there anymore."

"You moved?" she exclaims, a little too loud.

Nodding, I bite my lip. "Yes, I live in New York with my boyfriend."

Assigning Bash with a rudimentary title like *boyfriend*

feels so insulting, but I'm not sure how else to refer to him. Soul mate? Stalker? Fiance?

He did mention a ring before…

If only it were that simple. If only mine and Bash's first time living together wasn't because being apart is a threat to both of our lives. Even now, he's hanging out at a cafe across the street to give us the space we need. I have to remind myself that one day soon, all of this will be a distant memory.

Halen's mouth hangs ajar, eyes wide in surprise. "New York? Boyfriend?"

I shrug, biting back my smitten smile.

"I'm glad you're happy," she tells me with watery eyes. "I want the best for you, always."

"I know, Hales. I feel the same about you."

We chat for another hour, all the hurt and resentment long gone. There are no talks of mental health or God or controlling boyfriends. No cults or FBI agents or killer boyfriends. We're just two sisters catching up in our favorite restaurant. And I couldn't have hoped for anything better.

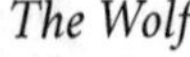

**61**

*The Wolf*

THE ORDER IS HAVING an emergency closed-door meeting to discuss the deaths of Logan and Charles. As a long standing, trusted member, my father has been invited.

I told him not to go. That I don't trust their intentions when they have obviously realized that I'm behind the Simon's deaths. He's insisting, though, claiming that they fully believe I've been working on my own and that he's still controlled by them.

Still, he left me with every note and document we've been pouring over for the past few weeks, along with a detailed manifest of every single member in the Order and their last known addresses.

"If you're right and they're setting a trap, promise me that you'll hand this over to your assistant in the FBI, so she can put an end to this once and for all," he had told me, sliding the stack of documents across his desk.

He wasn't shocked when I told him about Eliza.

*"There's always been something off with her,"* he claimed with an irritated scowl, shaking his head. And I suppose that's true. He's never trusted her, even when I made it clear she was someone who meant a lot to me.

His health has taken a steep decline since Sienna's death. I'm not sure what is different this time around, but he's absolutely tortured over the loss of her, the same way I had hoped he would be when we went through this before. It's given us something to bond over for the first time in my life, and while it doesn't excuse away his crimes with the Order and the sick things he's done in his lifetime, it makes the thought of killing him a little harder to bear.

Stardust and I are to wait in my home while they meet at the huge, ancient church they've renovated into their clubhouse a few miles away.

"I just don't see this ending well," I tell him one last time as he limps off toward my elevator doors, but he brushes me off.

"These men are my brothers. If I'm to die by their hand, then so be it."

With a worried expression that negates his whole statement, he pulls me into his side for an awkward, wobbly hug that nearly sends him careening over his cane and into the floor. Stardust dives to catch his cane before it falls to the ground, handing it over to him with a meek, sheepish smile.

She's unsure about him, given the way things ended *before*. So long as he's providing us with valuable information, she's tolerated his presence in our lives. It's only for a short time anyway, until we can finish this and get the happily ever after that we deserve.

"Your mother should be getting on her plane," he reminds me distractedly.

He planned a trip for them to Mexico before the emergency meeting was called, insisting she still go. He wanted to get her out of dodge after Charles and Logan's deaths were discovered.

At least, that's what he told me.

"Let me know when your flight leaves," I tell him, shoving my hands into my pockets.

Something like sadness crosses his face before he wipes it away, scratching his cheek.

"Be safe and don't do anything stupid while I'm gone. God loves you, kid. Don't blow it," he mutters in an uncharacteristically heartfelt goodbye.

I'm too stunned to reply, so instead I watch him walk away in a silence that he appears to appreciate. With one last wave, the elevator doors close and he disappears for good.

**62**

*The Lamb*

THERE'S BEEN an explosion at the clubhouse for the Loyal Order of the Serpent, decimating every square inch of the old church and two buildings set on either side. They're suspecting it was a suicide bomber.

New York is in a state of panic. People are confused and terrified for their lives. The police are trying to keep the crowds controlled and having it constantly roll on the news is only making the terror worse.

Bash nearly ripped the TV off the wall when the breaking news report flashed across the screen. He called his father's phone at least a hundred times, only to be ignored. His mother has only just landed in Mexico, her phone bombarded with the heart-wrenching news.

"He did this," Bash insists, pacing before me through the space in front of the couch. "He was acting odd before he left. He knew he was saying goodbye."

"How can you be sure? Someone else could have set him

up to go there so they could kill him. They haven't released the body counts yet."

It's not the most comforting alternative, but it makes him relax a little. Either way, Bash has lost his father. It's something that wouldn't have bothered him a month or two ago, but now it's probably devastating. As much of a monster as he was, he made sure his last breaths counted.

"Eliza will have access to the counts before the news stations," he mumbles to himself, tapping away at his phone to send her a message.

Within minutes, her response comes through.

"She says there's at least a hundred bodies but more are being sorted through."

One hundred bodies. One hundred souls, gone forever.

The guilt at those numbers is chased away by the dark realization that every single one of those men deserved it. They've tortured far more than that amount of people in their lifetimes. So long as there are no innocents involved, I'd call this a win for us. For all of society.

"He wouldn't have done it if he didn't think it was the right thing," I rationalize weakly.

"He wanted to keep my hands clean," Bash says, running his hands through his hair for the millionth time. "He wanted me to ride off into the sunset like some fucking movie."

"Why don't we, then? We've earned this Bash. Why don't you see this as the win that it is?"

"Because, Jovie. *I* wanted to be the last thing those bastards saw before they died. *I* wanted to make sure they felt every ounce of pain they've put my family through. I needed it, and he couldn't even let me have it."

"He was protecting you."

Inhaling a deep breath, he shoots me a look like he wants me to shut up, so I push my lips into a thin line and turn back to the TV.

"What did he say about giving something to Eliza?" I question, quickly realizing that his father has made this process entirely easy on Bash.

"It's a list of all active and inactive members," he explains distractedly, typing something into his phone.

A map, leading them directly to every other cockroach that attempts to escape unscathed.

"Bash, this is amazing. He gave you that because he knew it would end the Order for good. Didn't you say this was the main charter?"

I stand from the couch, running toward his office to grab the list. Bash follows close behind.

"Yes, this is where the leadership is based," he answers to my back.

I flip through the pages that were left behind, stopping on a folder with the Serpent crest stamped onto the front of it.

Hundreds of names and addresses are listed. Every single one of these men have taken part in this sick cult's rituals. They've hurt and stolen and raped and destroyed. And now, they're all going to pay.

"He sacrificed himself to take out the main hub," I muse, fingering through the list. Even businesses are listed, along with their crimes.

"He knew that taking this from them would get him killed. I bet that's why the meeting was called in the first place. They were going to punish him, but he struck first."

It's all making sense now. He spared us. After a lifetime of sin and crime, he turned around and saved his son from meeting the same fate.

Bash looks over my shoulder at each page, the disappointment from earlier fading away.

"Let's tell Eliza we have them," I urge.

"What if they figure out what we've done? Murder is illegal, Stardust. They can't just turn a blind eye to it."

"They can if we negotiate it," I quip, slamming the folder shut.

He hesitates for a while longer, until I break his stubborn resolve down enough to text Eliza and tell her we've got something she may be interested in seeing.

And then, we wait.

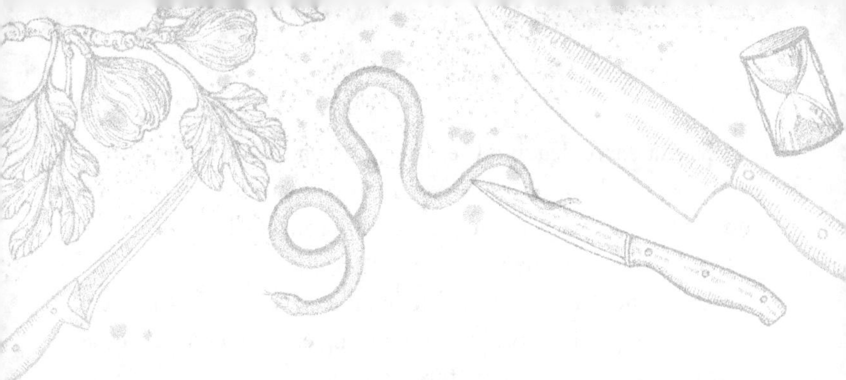

# EPILOGUE

*The Lamb*
  *Three months later*

IT'S odd how quickly you can return to normal after being thrown into fight or flight so many times. How the recovery time seems to shrink with every traumatic event.

I've been existing in a constant state of fight or flight for a year now. Longer, if you consider the effect my relationship with Gabe had on my mental health or that I've had to relive the past few months of my life.

I'm finally comfortable and safe enough to say I'm done with purely surviving. I'm existing on a completely different plane—one I never realized was possible. One where I can enjoy my days and appreciate what I have while it's still here.

This may have been the point of the shift: To ascend.

Bash has struggled with doing the same.

Once we negotiated a blanket immunity deal with Eliza and her team in the FBI, we gave them the list and set them loose. His father managed to hit every high-ranking member in his massacre, leaving them scrambling like little ants after you step on their anthill. Every man who attempted to crawl out of hiding and take on a leadership role has been exterminated by the FBI. The rest are in hiding.

Bash and I have never felt happier. We're able to freely move through the world without being encumbered with the fear that one of us is being targeted.

We're enjoying the weather in Seattle, where he's expanded a new branch of Lancaster Tech with me acting beside him at the head of the merge. New York is beautiful and Styx will always be considered my home, but we both needed a break. A chance to get back onto our feet in a city neither of us has been murdered in.

The first three months were spent in mourning. With all our enemies slayed, we were left alone with our thoughts screaming inside our heads, which led to processing a lot of things that were put on the backburner.

Like the loss of Sienna and the hole that was left in our lives. Or the fact that I was hunted in the woods by the men Sebastian and his family celebrated holidays with. And that I stabbed a man to death.

Each thing has been laid out and examined from every angle until they didn't have us in a chokehold anymore. We're slowly on our way to actually living somewhat *normal* lives.

We've gone over what happened to us countless times, comparing experiences and mapping timeliness. None of it makes sense. From the times we died to when we each woke up in that hospital, we've got memories of two completely different versions of our lives, yet we've only got the proof to back up one of them—this one. Whether it be a timeline shift or an ascension or something completely different, I'm happy to have been given a second chance to come back and do things right.

Halen and Kennedy have already made it out to visit us three times. During their last stint, they were looking into renting a home down the street. As much as Bash resents them for their roles this past year, I would love to have family close to us again. Especially since my mother is missing and his mother has retired away to the Caribbean, too hurt to live in the city where her family was ripped away. She and Bash talk on the phone weekly, and we have plans to visit her next month.

As the last surviving Lancasters to inherit their legacy, Bash and Sylvia have more money than they know what to do with. But they have plans in the works for a charity that provides refuge to families and victims of cults.

Not long after I had to leave my job at Old Soul, Ginny was discharged from Sunnybrook with a good bill of health. They've resumed running the cafe together, the way they always intended to do, and Ginny is on her own road to recovery. Rosie has even begun to thaw her frosty attitude toward me.

Things are okay, and that's the best I can hope for. It was all I craved when I was withering away under Gabe's control and being hunted in the woods. Like when you have a stuffy nose and can't breath, so you promise whatever higher power that if they just give you a moment of relief, you'd never take breathing through your nose for granted again.

*I'm okay.*

I'M MARRYING my soulmate this evening.

It feels so surreal to even say. The path we took her was long and winding, but we managed to fight against fate and death and time to be together. As far as I'm concerned, we should have made our love official the moment we stepped off the plane in Seattle. She's been wearing the ring I gave her —a gold, diamond-studded heart, modeled after Sienna's locket—since the night we signed our immunity documents with Eliza.

Stardust has placed the locket into a jewelry box, only bringing it out for special occasions.

Today, it's strapped around her neck, the golden heart dancing along the hemline of her crimson dress.

The color of blood spilled.

The color of figs left behind.

The color of passion and love shared in the most unlikely circumstances.

I wouldn't want to start over with anyone else.

The officiant has been speaking to us and the small crowd of witnesses sitting in the court benches for five minutes now, but I can't hear a word he's saying through the whooshing in my ears as excitement takes hold of me.

*Finally.* Finally, she's mine. Finally, we have a shot at this chaotic, devastating, exhilarating thing called life.

I've struggled the most with my need for revenge. Sienna's death is still an open wound I can't seem to heal. Not having her around in spirit has messed with me worse than when I did, and I thought I was going insane. My father sacrificed himself to save me, but I wasn't ready to be stripped of the chance to take the lives of the men who wronged me and the people I love. And like an itch I can't scratch, the need for blood still lingers.

I'm a killer, afterall. It runs through my veins and has been passed down to me for generations.

Stardust struggles with the same instinct. The tricky part comes with figuring out how to tame it.

"I do," she promises through a wide, toothy smile, and I'm reminded again that she's all I need.

That smile can keep me going for years. That tongue can bring me right to my knees. That body can make me move mountains.

"I do," I blindly parrot, allowing myself to smile back.

"Good. Now, shut the fuck up and kiss her already," a familiar feminine voice calls over the officiant's low droning.

It comes from somewhere behind me, and my blood freezes in my veins when I realize I couldn't have imagined it.

When no one else reacts to the intrusion, I allow myself to turn my head, reluctant to get my hopes up.

But all of my restraint goes crashing to the ground when the translucent, milky vision of my sister appears in my line of sight. She smiles widely, offering a cheesy thumbs up.

The officiant finishes the ceremony, and Stardust leaps into my arms, covering my mouth with a kiss.

When we turn back to walk out of the court house as husband and wife, Sienna is still there.

# A B O U T   J E N

Jen Stevens was born and raised in Michigan, where she enjoys the weather of all four seasons in a single day. After obtaining her Bachelor's degree, she quickly realized the corporate world wasn't for her and instead took on the daunting role as her children's snack maid. Reading has been an obsession for a long as she could remember, while writing has always been an escape. Jen could quote The Office word-for-word and proudly refers to herself as a romance junkie. She could live off anything made of sugar and has recently obtained the title of Lady. Most of all, she loves connecting with readers!

Check out Jen's website and socials for the most up to date publishing information: www.jenstevenswrites.com
or scan below

Socials: @authorjenstevens

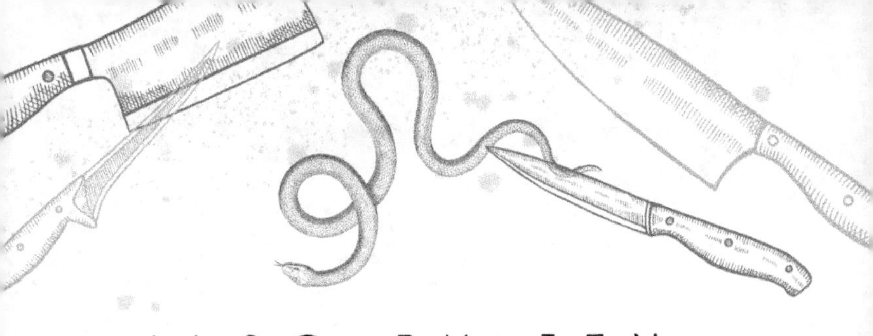

# ALSO BY JEN

<u>Dark Romance:</u>
Ugly Truths (Grimville Reapers Book One)
Untold Truths (Grimville Reapers Book Two)
Prey Drive (Parallel Prey Duet Book 1)
Fallen Prey (Parallel Prey Duet Book 2)


<u>Contemporary Romance:</u>
Advice from a Sunflower


<u>Urban Fantasy Romance:</u>
Calling Quarters (Beacon Grove Book One)
Counting Quarters (Beacon Grove Book Two)
<u>Catching Quarters</u> (Beacon Grove Book Three)


Switching Graves (Ravenshurst University Book One)
Splitting Secrets (Ravenshurst University Book Two)